Murder Central

Copyright © 2023 writing as Ashlie McAnally

All rights reserved. No part of this publication may be reproduced, stored, or transmitted in any form or by any means, electronic, mechanical, photocopying, recording, scanning, or otherwise, without written permission from the publisher. It is illegal to copy this book, post it to a website, or distribute it by any other means without permission.

This is a work of fiction. Names, characters, places, and incidents are the author's imagination or used fictitiously. Any resemblance to actual persons, living or dead, businesses, companies, events, or locales is entirely coincidental.

ISBN: 978-1-0683368-0-5

Cover Design: kulbirgharra.com
Editor: Kirsten Rees | Book Editor & Author Coach

Connect with the author:
Instagram: ashlie.mcanally_author
Facebook: Ashlie McAnally author
Twitter: A5hlie_Mc
Tik Tok: ashlie.mcanally_author
Email: ashlie.mcanally.author@gmail.com

Acknowledgements

This book has been a couple of years in the making and I'm so proud to finally see it in print. For years I wanted to write a novel, but couldn't quite pin down any ideas. It was suggested I write a memoir from my time in court after covering everything from funny to high profile cases over a nine year period - but that wasn't for me.

After moving jobs and working in the centre of Glasgow, passing the location where this crime takes place on a daily basis, the idea was born! A fictional book gave me the space to be creative, develop characters, add plot twists and experiment with writing.

Getting to this stage would not have been possible without a lot of wonderful people. I've had unwavering support from my husband, my parents and all of my family and friends. I'm overwhelmed by the level of interest from people before many even knew what the book was about!

My editor Kirsten Rees has taught me more than I ever imagined and has been very patient while I embarked on the steep learning curve that is novel writing.

Thank you to Heather Suttie for the ongoing support and advice. And, for hosting the event with journalist and presenter Susannah Constantine, who gave me the courage to take the leap and put my idea into writing.

And to my beta readers and fact check sources! My close friend Kayleigh McKinlay was with me at this event. I'm grateful to her for being my first source of feedback and who has championed my writing from the outset.

A huge thank you to Savannah Morrison, Siobhan McCluskey, Lauren Crooks, Kay Sword, Leila Kirkconnell, Leslie Johnson, Gillian Balharry, Jessica Wilcock, Helen Forbes, Gill Warnock, David McGuigan, Barbara Edmond, Mhairi Alexander and Kathleen O'Donnell.

Contents

Part I - The incident	1
Part II - The catalyst	37
Part III - The aftermath	87

Part I - The incident

CHAPTER 1

"Are you ready?"

He gripped the door handle. "Aye, yes. Yes, I'm fine."

"Don't fuck it up. Or it won't end well."

The grip tightened. "No, it's sorted. I'll get it done. He's finished. Fuck him, he deserves it."

"Just remember the plan."

The tyres of the black Peugeot skidded to a halt, causing an ear-piercing screech, echoing through the cold, concrete building.

***

Helen McKenzie stepped into the car park holding hands with her twin girls just as two masked men got out of their car, blocking in a white Audi. She heard a car door slam and an almighty scream. It wasn't an obvious cry out or even human sounding; it was more like a howl from a wounded animal.

Bang. Bang. Bang. Bang.

Precise and determined, like the tiny lead bullets knew exactly what they had to do.

Helen gripped the tiny hands of her daughters as several people bolted towards them. Terrified, she immediately yanked her children down and pulled them all behind the closest car. Helen's shoulder-length hair dislodged from behind her ear, obstructing her vision as she clutched her girls. The hem of their jackets, the collar sticking out at the nape of their neck, anywhere she could wrap her desperate fingers around to hold them out of sight.

Tucked away, holding her breath, she watched some people stumble over themselves as they ran back into the train station. Desperate to flee, a couple of people fell to the ground beside them

1

as they tried to escape.

Then, as the final gunshot rang through the car park, the sound of panic was severed by silence.

Helen did not know who was firing the shots, who was being shot at, or when it would stop.

"What's happening mummy?"

"Sshh, sweetheart. We need to be really quiet," she said into her little girl's ear. Looking down, she saw the fear in her children's eyes and wanted nothing more than to be anywhere else. Helen peeled her hand away from her little girl's mouth and kissed her forehead.

Has the shooting stopped? Will they shoot me because I'm witnessing this? Surely they won't harm my girls?

She pulled her girls close to her chest, a hand over each of their blonde heads. Helen prayed this would not be the last time she held them. She felt like her heartbeat would deafen them.

Helen heard more doors slam and a car drive off. Screams echoed as though fear had once again been unmuted. Peeking from behind her hiding spot, Helen saw onlookers rooted to the spot, aghast at the carnage.

The black Peugeot backfired as it sped down the ramps towards the exit. The tyres squealed as they struggled to grip the wet ground with each sharp turn. There was no time for careful manoeuvring. Helen heard metal scraping along a wall. The getaway car, she presumed, made contact with the walls of the narrow lanes as it hurtled towards the exit.

She jumped on hearing a colossal crash and believed she felt the building shake as wheels screeched. Helen got back to her feet and smoothed her hair. Both girls continued to cling to her legs. The sounds of the tyres lessened as the car sped off.

Catching her breath and clutching her girls' hands she desperately wanted to comfort them. Helen dropped to her knees, fighting tears, desperate not to show her fear. Cupping her girls' chins with each hand, she studied their little faces. She had never seen such fear in their eyes. "It's okay, girls, we're okay. Mum is here, and everything is okay."

PART I

They nodded back at her looking unsure.

Helen settled into a comfortable position leaning against a wall that shielded the girls from the crime scene in front of them and continued to hold them close as sirens wailed faintly in the distance but grew louder. Helen knew she was safe but couldn't bear even to look anywhere near where it happened. Her priority was making sure the girls were okay.

An older woman approached. "Would they like some chocolate?" She had tears in her eyes. "I hear it helps with shock." Helen nodded gratefully.

MURDER CENTRAL

CHAPTER 2

Daniel Tonner sat in the driver's side of the Audi, his arm on the door frame, drumming his fingers, eyes fixed on the rear view mirror watching the entrance to the stairwell. His associate Josh Slaven was due back to the car any second. A bead of sweat trickled down his left temple. Daniel realised he was holding his breath. "Stop being so paranoid," he said to himself.

His head snapped to the side as he heard tyres screech and saw a car drive up the ramp from the level below blocking his car in. Without a second thought, the paranoia he tried to dismiss took over and he lurched out the car. As he ran to the door of the stairs Slaven passed him.

"Cops! Run!" Daniel shouted as he hurtled himself down the first set of stairs beyond the door, tumbling to the ground on the landing at the bottom. As he scrambled to his feet he heard the unmistakable sound of gunshots. Daniel stared up at the door he'd just come from, his eyes wide. Nausea swept over him. He leaned against the wall to stop himself from falling. Daniel heaved as vomit shot up his throat.

He wiped his mouth with his sleeve, one hand still on the wall beside him to steady himself. For a few seconds Daniel stood with his back flat against the wall, like a gecko, his hands on either side. The coldness of the concrete cooling his sweaty back. His chest heaved, his breath heavy as thoughts raced through his mind.

Daniel closed his eyes tight, replaying the events leading to this.

Did the cops follow us? Were they behind us the whole time? Did they shoot Josh?

He began to pace up and down the landing of the car park, clasping his hands behind his neck. He knew Josh Slaven was known to police, wanted by enemies and feared by many. Unlike him, Slaven had gotten his hands dirty on more than one occasion and appeared to take pleasure in the pain of others.

Daniel thought back to the moment when their boss told

PART I

him that he was working with Slaven that day, he was desperate to impress. So often Daniel had been told how much he pissed Slaven off with his sloppy attitude. Today was supposed to be different. "Fuuuck sake," he shouted, his voice echoing.

Suddenly, his chest tightened and a pain shot down his left arm. *Am I having a heart-attack?* He slid down the wall, clutching his chest. *What is the boss going to say?* The pain intensified, he pulled his arm across his chest hugging it into him. *What am I going to do?*

Daniel felt as though his throat was closing up. He croaked as he fought to get air in. His mind replayed the moment Slaven got in the stolen car an hour earlier.

"If this goes tits up today, I'll take care of it, okay?" Slaven had told him. When Daniel asked him what that meant, the gangster replied "There's nae messing if this guy hasn't got the cash."

The feeling of unease washed over him, just as it had in that moment. The car had been parked next to the staircase on level five of the car park, as was strictly instructed. Slaven had told him what to do. Slaven was always careful and he hadn't said anything about being followed. The pain in Daniel's arm and tightness in his chest were interrupting his thoughts. Like being cuddled by a boa constrictor.

"If I don't die now, the boss will kill me anyway," Daniel muttered. More sweat trickled down his back. He was aware his breathing was laboured.

At least air is getting in.

Back in the present he could hear sirens and noise from the floor he escaped from. As the phone in his pocket vibrated, taking a deep breath to summon the energy he reached in with the pain-free side of his body. It was the boss calling. A surge of pain shot through his chest and arm and he felt he would pass out. Moments later a message flashed up from another associate.

Call the boss. Now.

A fresh wave of vomit made its way up his throat.

***

Barely a minute passed after the incident, when a convoy of police cars arrived in front of them and officers began to pour out.

With a child hugging each leg, Helen turned to see the Audi still in situ with the driver's door lying open. It was riddled with bullets and surrounded by discarded cartridges. A man sat in the passenger seat; his lifeless body slumped across the gear stick, leaning onto the empty driver's side, in a pool of his blood with four very visible gunshot injuries.

Helen swallowed hard as police officers walked towards her, fighting off the tears. Officers led Helen to a room in the Central train station, normally reserved for staff, with Ella and Jennifer, her wispy-haired eight-year-olds. Everything was a bit of a blur. They had only gone into the city centre to collect some clothes from Next and get the girls a toy. Now, she was going to talk to the police about a murder.

Two women police officers were trying to comfort the twins. Jennifer was still in tears, and Ella said nothing, clutching her mum's side.

"I didn't even really see anything. I just heard a car screeching, doors slamming, shouting, and then... gunshots."

A fresh wave of panic rose through Helen's stomach, but she caught herself before tears were given the chance to escape. She took a deep breath.

"I panicked and pulled the girls onto the ground. There was shooting and screaming. Why was there shooting? Did someone die? Oh my God, who died?"

Someone's relative had just been shot dead in a car park. The very thought of losing anyone was too much. Helen couldn't stop the tears.

PART I

CHAPTER 3

Steven Coyle pressed his head against the hotel's window when he heard a car backfire and rev on the road below. He assumed it was another boy racer with a heavy foot.

After all, this was in the centre of Glasgow – that was to be expected from time to time.

He grabbed his phone from the charger, noting it was 4.52 pm when he dropped it in the pocket of his Barbour jacket. His table was booked for 6 pm at the Italian restaurant La Lanterna on Hope Street, a few minutes away. Steven liked visiting that restaurant whenever he visited from Manchester.

Steven planned to have a pint or two in Wetherspoons after running the errand he had to do, but he wasn't sure if it was courage he craved or if he could trust himself to stop at just a couple of drinks. Nerves were taking over, but he still wanted a relatively clear head. It was the first time meeting after a year. He wanted to make a good impression.

Patting the pockets of his denim to check for his wallet, he then applied a quick spray of aftershave.

Steven made a final check of his gelled hair before he left his room at the Radisson Blu. Feeling hopeful and slightly optimistic, he left a bedside lamp on as he closed the door behind him. He wanted to make sure everything was in decent shape should he not be the only person returning later.

Stepping into the lift, he couldn't help but check himself again in the mirrored wall. The glass box glided down the three levels, and he walked out onto the bustling street. Steven had a feeling of unease as he pulled his phone out and punched numbers into the keypad to make the call.

Errand completed.

Just as he took his seat in the pub with his first cold pint of lager, Steven glanced at his phone, 5.12 pm. With the task completed, he had a bit of time to kill before his dinner date.

7

His thoughts were interrupted by sirens and blue lights. Immediately, he looked out the window and down the street. A police van and, a few minutes later, three police cars and an ambulance turned into the car park. Nervous, he checked his phone yet again a few minutes later. This was going to be a night to remember.

***

"Any available call signs to attend NCP at Oswald Street immediately regarding a firearms incident? Suspects have fled the scene. ARVs have been authorised to carry out a search of the area."

PC William Field held his breath as his colleague Michelle got in the car juggling her Co-op sandwich and can of juice. They were already on patrol in the Gorbals, parked on Crown Street. William gestured toward the radio. She nodded back at him. "This is not a routine control room call," he muttered, forcing the car into gear and pulling off. "It is going to be a long night".

"What the…Here we go." She groaned and hit her fist on the dashboard, saying, "Foot down, William."

He nodded.

"Mike Foxtrot 243, on our way. Over."

They sped towards the NCP car park on the other side of the River Clyde. His heart rate spiked. William felt the surge of adrenaline.

PART I

CHAPTER 4

Slamming the driver's door with one hand, William put his police hat on with the other. He and his colleague acknowledged the other officers at the crime scene as they began to walk around the car park. A police firearms armed response vehicle was already there, with specialist officers securing the area. Other constables who had responded to the call out dotted the car park floor, comforting clusters of terrified people.

William's attention was drawn to a brown-haired woman with her arms around two young children as they were being ushered away from a police van by two officers. Seeing one of the little blonde girls crying tugged at his heartstrings.

How awful for innocent children to be caught up in this, he thought.

Stepping under the blue and white tape, he walked closer to the damaged Audi. Across the gear stick on the centre console, was a bloodied body.

The passenger windows and windscreen of the Audi had four jagged holes where the bullets perforated the glass at lightning-fast speed, puncturing the man's head and chest. The headrest and the back window were spattered with the victim's blood. A pool of syrupy liquid gathered underneath the dead man's head.

Did he slump over when he was shot, or had he tried to duck to avoid the flying bullets? Who was driving? Who did this?

So many questions rattled round William's head.

Michelle ran the car registration through the police national computer. Relaying to William the information given over her radio, she said, "Okay, so it is registered to a Jane Campbell, who reported it stolen two days earlier from Govan."

"Car reported missing from Asda car park, owner called on Tuesday. Seemed like it was opportunistic at the time. Mrs Campbell returned to the car park after her shift to find it missing." Michelle took the details of the owner to speak to her later.

9

MURDER CENTRAL

William watched his colleague walk past him and down the ramp from the car park on to platform 15 of Glasgow Central Station, retracing the steps of those who had retreated in horror. As she left his sight, William saw others from his shift arrive.

He turned to follow Michelle but Sergeant Arthur Black called over to him. William wasn't sure how to react when his boss told him, "Josh Slaven has been shot dead". He was a feared gangland figure after all.

As William spoke to the senior officer he felt his phone vibrate in his pocket. Making his way to take witness statements he quickly sent a couple of messages then turned his attention back to work.

Rummaging in his body armour for his notepad the hairs on the back of his neck stood up. There was tension in the air and indistinguishable chatter amid the chaos around him. He wiped a bead of sweat with the back of his hand as it trickled down his face.

William's mouth was dry, and his legs shook as he took a step towards a witness. One at a time, William wrung his hands. He had read somewhere this was meant to ease stress.

Another sweat droplet tried to trickle down his head; he caught it again with a sleeve and then adjusted his hat to absorb the water oozing from him.

Approaching a distressed-looking man, William's stomach dropped. *What has happened?*

He cleared his throat several times until he found his voice to ask him what he saw.

"Yes, they just…shot him." The man kept running his hands through his now messy hair.

"Did you see any altercation or hear anything before that?" William asked, scribbling in his notepad.

Shaking his head, the man looked down. "No, when I got to the top of the ramp and walked into the car park, I just saw two men with guns standing in front of that car." He gestured towards the Audi a few yards from where they stood. "Then they shot him three or four times! The two of them, eh, well then they got in the…. the…the car that was parked waiting and sped off. I, eh, well, that's

10

all I saw." His voice shook. He paused as William took notes.

"Did you see anyone else?"

"Like, who?"

"Anyone else with the victim," the officer explained. "Anyone getting out of the driver seat?"

Looking confused, the man replied, "I don't remember seeing anyone else, just the men with the guns."

William scribbled more details in his notebook. "What makes you say it was men, what were they wearing?"

"Oh, I don't know, actually." He put a hand on his forehead. "Just the height and stature, I thought it was men. They were dressed in tracksuits, I think, with balaclavas on. Black trainers or shoes – I assume it was men."

The shocked witness, whose face had drained of all remaining colour, gave his contact details and William allowed him to go on his way.

Several others were still giving statements, many visibly upset and shaken. They had been escorted away from the scene to try and minimise their distress as more police arrived and the car park was taped off.

"William, anything useful?" Michelle asked him, breaking his trance as he stared at the car park entrance from the platform.

"Eyewitness accounts from witnesses. Cold-blooded murder." William looked at his colleague. "Josh Slaven was shot dead"

Her eyes widened, meeting his gaze. "Fuck, really? Definitely him? I didn't see his face."

"Yeah, definitely him. Sergeant Black already confirmed." He nodded to the man ordering forensic officers around. "Nobody saw the gunmen's faces. Officers are now out looking for the stolen getaway vehicle, believed to be a Peugeot. Was only a matter of time before someone took him out."

"Yeah." William nodded. "He was a bad bastard. And some sad bastard is going to end up doing time."

"Shame. More of a public service," said his colleague with sincerity.

CHAPTER 5

The Peugeot sped up until they pushed 105mph as the car hurled along the dusky motorway.

"Tell him it's done," the driver yelled.

The passenger fumbled with a pay-as-you-go phone thrust into his hand and frantically typed.

Done. Over and out.

He hit send and locked the screen.

Nothing else was said during the thirty-minute journey. They parked up on a street corner where a streetlight was out.

"Get rid fast and call Chick," the driver barked, tapping the steering wheel furiously.

Following his instructions, the passenger door was thrown open. In the dim moonlight, no one would have spotted the character in dark clothes get out of the parked car with his balaclava still on and hood up. Within seconds, he had tossed the package over the bridge into the fast-moving water below. In silence, he climbed back into the car and called the number that had checked in on them minutes before the fatal hit. It had all been set up to be seamless – in theory.

"Aye. It's done, and guns are gone. Yeah, yeah, we'll find another spot." His hands shook so much he could barely tap the screen to end the call.

After a few minutes, the car stopped again. The three men climbed out, one took the petrol from the boot and threw it over the car and the driver lit a match and tossed it through one of the windows with the keys. They all watched as the fire took hold.

It was beautiful and there was something quite mesmerising about the flames dancing as dusk fell. As captivating as it was, they weren't hanging around. They couldn't afford the risk. "Let's go, boys!" the driver shouted, leading the way.

Seconds later, they disappeared.

***

PART I

A farmer, driving home from work, saw the orange glow ahead on the country road. He detoured along the street to investigate, finding a car completely engulfed in flames. Fearing someone could be in trouble, he immediately dialled 999.

"What service do you require?" the operator asked.

"Fire service, please. There's a car on fire on High Kype Road in Strathaven."

"Is there anyone nearby that you can see?" the female call handler asked.

"I can't see anything but a car in flames, but there's bushes nearby. I'm worried it spreads.

"An appliance is on the way, sir."

The farmer ended the call and reversed further back up the dark country road, watching the interior warp and melt until nothing was left but the shell of the Peugeot.

In the distance, he saw the blue flashing light of the fire engine. As it approached, he made off home, praying nobody was injured.

CHAPTER 6

News spread fast in Glasgow, and it wasn't long before it reached local news outlets in the city and beyond.

April McCann read the comments on social media, speculating about what happened, but it was clear a man had been shot in the city centre NCP car park.

This has the hallmarks of a gangland shooting, but these things don't often happen so publicly.

She prayed nobody had been caught in the crossfire.

This story could be stopped in its tracks if arrests are made quickly, April thought. *If it is gangland, there could be repercussions, soon.*

At age twenty-seven and four years into her journalism career, this could be her biggest story yet. She could only hope.

Despite the repeated warnings not to work on risky stories on her own, she didn't always have time to wait for photographers to respond before getting started. As a freelance reporter, the more information she got quickly, the better position she would be in.

April grabbed her bag, jacket, and car keys and headed out of the tenement flat in Dennistoun she shared with her partner. As she got into her car she finished typing a text message.

Off to this shooting, if you're about?

April texted a handful of photographers she often worked with and trusted. She slammed her car door as she sent the same message to her police contacts, on the off chance they could help fill in the missing information. "This could be a long night", the journalist said to herself as she turned the key in the ignition. When April reached Broomielaw, only a few streets away from the NCP car park, parallel to the River Clyde, she could already see the reflection of blue lights surrounding the area. An ambulance blocked Oswald Street, which lay perpendicular to the river, preventing people from coming and going from the scene.

She drove past the Riverside Casino before turning right into Brown Street and back along Argyle Street to get a parking space as

PART I

close as possible, eventually parking on Robertson Street. More and more streets had become one way over the years, but April still had a few favourites she relied on for spaces.

Known as Glasgow's financial district, the streets were lined with tall office buildings in a grid-like format that hid the adjacent streets from view.

Police tape stretched the breadth of the roadway between the car park and a derelict building across the road, blocking her path. Nosey pedestrians gathered at the corner of Oswald Street. This was either a complete non-event that had seen some poor bugger attacked or a serious crime that was worth reporting. That was the beauty of journalism. Sometimes, it didn't lead to much – on other days, the adrenaline kept April going to see the story through.

Standing for a moment, taking stock of the situation she thought about how life can change. Less than a decade earlier she was studying journalism at Strathclyde University which is little over a mile away from where she was standing. Now she was in the real world investigating a potential murder. She had always been fascinated with crime and justice.

Her phone pinged with a text message from a police contact.

Slaven shot in the head. Found in stolen car. Gunmen away.

Shit, she thought. *Maybe a coffee and adrenaline are needed on this occasion.*

April opened a blank email on her phone to make notes. She said the words aloud as she punched the letters on the screen.

"Rumours of a shooting were right enough – but Josh Slaven? He was a feared gangland enforcer who was usually on the firing end of a weapon. Known for getting his hands dirty unlike others in the criminal world, Slaven often flexed his muscles – metaphorically and literally. Known for torturing enemies just short of death; injured enough to spill what information he wanted from them and an agreement not to tell the authorities but alive enough to suffer silently and never consider repeating the betrayal. This time someone had taken a chance and taken him out. Who would be brave enough?"

15

Just then her phone vibrated with a text from a police contact. **Rumour has it, Barry Harris involved. That's the intel.**

April raised her eyebrows. She recognised his name from a story she'd written about when he was convicted of traffic offences and how he was part of McColl's gang. He was one of the lesser known ones.

As she paused for thought, the first call of the night came through from the editor of the Daily Mail newspaper while her phone was still in her hand.

"Hi, April. I hear you're on the ground at this shooting. We've heard Josh Slaven has been murdered?"

"Yes, that's the chat. I'm just here so will see what I can get from police. I have just been told young Barry Harris of McColl's lot might be involved? Do with that info what you can."

"Right, thanks April. I'll get someone on to that. I'm calling you because we're pulling together background, assuming there's no arrests yet. What's your knowledge of this guy?"

April laughed. *Where to start?* Having covered courts for a few years, she was well-versed in the makeup of gangs in Glasgow. The fallout from before her time as a journalist was still ongoing. She suspected the recent incident proved this.

"So Slaven is part of the Clarke gang, not by name but by affiliation, of course. Crime boss Thomas Clarke took him on when he was a teenager after Slaven attacked Jack Finn, the nephew of rival gangland boss Mick McColl." She paused as there was silence on the other end of the call.

The editor cleared his throat. "Carry on, April. I'm just taking notes. This is quicker than a cuts check!"

"You'll probably remember Finn was attacked while he was stopped at traffic lights on a quiet residential road in Govanhill and left needing extensive hospital treatment and surgery to reconstruct his face. It was never proven that Slaven was behind the maiming, but everyone in the relevant circles - and even the wider area – knew it was him. Even the police had been informed, but there was no evidence, so they said."

"Aye, that's right," the Daily Mail editor said, "Clarke is from Springburn, and McColl is Govan? Their feud has been going on for decades!"

April heard pages turning on the other side of the phone as he took notes. "That's right. When Finn dared to enter into a lucrative and not entirely above board business with a man from the local area, a meeting over a coffee at McDonald's was as far as he got before Slaven was ordered to put an end to the partnership. A week later, he was attacked." She stopped to let the editor catch up.

"Since then, there had been tit-for-tat attacks between the two gangs. Actually… remember Mick McColl's cousin's wife died after a mistaken identity. The hitman took her out by mistake, when plans changed, and her husband was the one who had taken their three children to a friend's party instead of her. That was awful. Grief rippled through the entire community and only escalated the hatred between the two sides."

April heard the hustle and bustle of the newsroom behind him.

"It's mad," she said. "Now, after a decade of employment, if you can call it that, Josh Slaven has met an abrupt and brutal end. A high-risk lifestyle and now he's dead. I bet the spotlight is on McColl and his guys now."

"Thanks, April. If the cops want to hold off from arresting too many, we'll get a few days out of this."

She laughed, but she knew he wasn't joking.

CHAPTER 7

April got as close as she could and approached one of the officers guarding the police tape at Oswald Street. She was aware she didn't fit the stereotypical ashen-faced, middle-aged male journalists often depicted on TV. Her long dark hair was swept up into a ponytail, and her fresh, makeup-free face often made her appear younger. April had a spring in her step and a thirst for information.

"Sorry, can't help you, we have no idea what happened," the officer said as she pressed for details.

"But there's been a shooting..." April probed. It was more of a statement of the obvious than a question hoping he'd believe she already had insider details.

Shaking his head, staring directly ahead, he muttered, "Can't say."

"I want to stamp out any rumours and will use this as background. There's information circulating on social media—"

"Sorry. Can't say." He ignored her smiling face and walked off, speaking into his radio.

This wasn't a new attitude by the police at crime scenes. It was often difficult to get any rumours confirmed – or denied, which was just as important.

April retraced her steps to where she had parked her car. She stopped briefly, then walked further and made her way to another cordoned area.

She stood at the top of the street outside the Radisson Blu, looking across to the Motel One hotel on the opposite corner where tape blocked off the street down to where she had been standing with the unhelpful policeman. Looking around, she thought it best to go somewhere busier and made her way to Glasgow Central Station in search of a witness or someone with an opinion. April was hopeful someone in there would be willing to say something significant about the incident, and it was more sheltered than outside in the cold.

PART I

April went up the escalator to where the ticket gates allowed passengers to go onto the platforms, including 15, which led directly to the car park. The station was still busy with people who – judging by their demeanour – were witnesses to something. The station was thick with police officers and, as expected, police tape blocking off areas to the public near the crime scene causing some delays and cancellations which added to the mayhem.

Behind April a woman in a business suit, court shoes and carrying a handbag spoke loudly on the phone. April took a couple of steps to the side to make sure she heard what was said.

"The train's been cancelled due to some… incident." The woman looked around her, and lowered her voice before she added, "There's been a shooting I'm told! I know, I can't believe it. I don't know…I'll try. Okay, I'll call you back."

The troubled-looking woman ended the call and looked around for something. It wasn't clear what, but she appeared lost.

April saw an opportunity.

"Excuse me, I'm so sorry to bother you. I can see you look concerned. I'm a journalist investigating the incident that took place in the car park this evening. I'm terribly sorry. Are you able to help me with any information, please?"

It took a second for the lady to register what was being asked of her. "Hen, I don't want to be in the newspaper…"

"You really don't need to be. I'm just looking to gather information that I can check out and verify. We don't need to use your name." April smiled at her, hoping it would be convincing.

"Really? People won't know I've told you anything?

Shaking her head emphatically, April said, "No, I assure you, they won't."

"Okay, pet, well, I mean, I don't really know anything." She took a breath. "But… I was due to get the train from platform 15 over five minutes ago, but they've suspended all of the services from there because, apparently, something happened. I've no idea what … but my friend Julie left work earlier, and she got on the train at 4.30 pm. So if it happened at that time, then she wouldn't have made it

MURDER CENTRAL

on the train, and she would have let me know. Then I heard someone got stabbed or shot in a car. There was children there!" She gasped, finally taking a breath as she threw her hands on top of her head.

"Are you okay eh…?"

"Pauline," she said, puffing her cheeks out.

"Are you okay, Pauline?" April touched her shoulder lightly.

"Yes, I'm fine, but if someone was shot or stabbed, that can't be good. They're probably dead. And to do it then, it's so busy!" she said, eyes wide with alarm.

April handed her a business card in case she heard anything else and advised the woman of alternative transport to get home to Paisley.

Her phone pinged again from the same contact.

Attention on McColl. Gunmen fled but suspected to be revenge attack. Slaven in passenger seat of Audi but no driver present.

Why was Slaven in the passenger seat? Who was driving? How did they get away?

It didn't take long before more comments filled social media pages with unconfirmed rumours that a hit had been taken out on Slaven. Everything from the gun being his and turned on him to a full car's worth of people attacking him, leaving him for dead, as well as the suggestion it was an inside job.

Peppered throughout the dozens of messages was a concoction of heartfelt messages as well as vile slurs and hate-filled comments about the gangland figure thought to be responsible for dozens of knife attacks and disfiguring men across the west of Scotland.

Shaking her head, the journalist sighed. "He thought he was untouchable, but someone had found him and finished him," she said to herself.

April came off social media and composed a quick email to all the regular newsdesks to let them know she was at the scene, and it was understood to be a shooting, as the rumours suggested. She ended it saying she would send more when she had it.

She made her way through the train station, littered with police

20

PART I

speaking to people. Some were in tears being comforted. Others fidgeted while speaking animatedly to officers. There was a heavy, sinister atmosphere hanging over everyone.

Over the next few hours, April asked anyone who would stop and talk if they had any knowledge of the incident, if they saw or heard anything. She thanked everyone for their time and politely asked them to call her if they remembered anything.

Word of a shooting had gotten out, and it appeared people were aware it took place in the NCP car park.

"It was just near the pay machines at the entrance to the train station just as a bottleneck of passengers spilled into the area", one person told April.

As she walked towards the exit closest to Gordon Street, her phone rang.

"This is obviously thought to be the work of McColl, fucker hated him. No idea who Slaven was with. Won't know much more tonight, but ID is confirmed." It was her police contact who was calling from an unknown number.

April listened so intently that she didn't see the man in a police uniform despite a high-viz vest until she ran directly into him. Her phone fell to the ground, bringing her back to reality.

The tall police officer stared down at her as she bent to pick up her mobile and check that nothing had fallen from her bag.

"Sorry, too engrossed; I wasn't paying attention." She felt her face flush.

He laughed, and his body relaxed, untucking his arms from his body armour, and turning to face April. He looked quite young but with a hint of greying in his beard and sideburns.

"In a rush?" He smiled. "Seems like you're in a hurry to get somewhere."

It was unusual to speak to such a friendly police officer. He was good-looking too.

"You could say that." She blushed further at her carelessness and tried to compose herself. "What's going on here?" she asked casually, not wanting to give away her true reason for asking nor passing up the opportunity to get some information from the handsome police officer.

"Ah, can't say too much. You don't want to be hanging around here, though." Almost instantly, his stance returned to the on-duty officer. "There's been a serious incident, and eh, you should be careful walking around on your own," he said with another smile and what she thought was a sparkle in his eye.

April stood up straight, pulled a card from the left pocket of her Mac overcoat, and handed it to him. "Actually, officer, I am aware there's been a crime committed. I'm a freelance journalist trying to establish the facts. All about accuracy, you see," she said in a tone that suggested she was mocking her professionalism.

Oh God, does this sound like I am flirting? she thought. *If it makes him hand over some much-needed information, it might be worth a shot.*

He studied the card and she wondered if this would shut down their conversation immediately.

The officer turned round to his colleague who had shouted over to him, then raised his hand to acknowledge he heard his call before meeting April's eyes. He stared at her as though debating something serious internally.

A few moments later, he snapped out of his trance, meeting her gaze. "I wish I could be more helpful. I really do. You've got a job to do, and so do I, but I can't say any more at this stage."

She sighed, disappointed that this was how it was, but knew there was no point in arguing. "Okay, thanks anyway, PC…?"

"Shaw, PC Shaw. Nice to meet you, April." He flashed another grin at her.

He turned and walked to where his colleague was a few paces away, speaking to a busker standing with a guitar outside the Blue Lagoon chip shop.

Having lost valuable time, April raced back to her car to swiftly cobble together a piece based on information she had and announce the death of feared gangland figure Slaven. Maybe publicising this would bring others out and help lead to the gunman. No one had

PART I

been arrested yet. The case wasn't yet live. Using all the information she had gathered and details from her contacts, April sent her article to all eagerly awaiting news desks, hoping she'd make their deadlines, then called it a day.

CHAPTER 8

After arriving at the scene, William and his colleague Michelle questioned several traumatised eyewitnesses. Some were workers heading home for the day, others holidaymakers who had returned from a relaxing break, parents with small children and teenagers. One group of young people out with their friends were shocked by the terrifying shooting and the aftermath of seeing a dead body in the abandoned car.

Accounts varied from those who were unfortunate enough to see the balaclava-covered gunmen shoot Slaven at point blank range before getting into a car and speeding off, while others saw someone fleeing the Audi seconds before the victim got into the car and was shot dead. They described a man falling out of the driver side of the car wearing a dark coloured hoodie and running to the stairs.

"He screamed at the man as they passed one another but the man got in the car anyway and then he was shot", William noted from someone who saw the horror unfold. A few people saw the victim get into the white Audi car before realising his fate. Some people saw the moments after the bloody attack and felt the sinister atmosphere as the emergency services raced to the scene only to pronounce the twenty-eight-year-old dead.

William saw the horror in the eyes of people who would remember what they saw for the rest of their lives.

His shift finally ended three hours later than usual, but he couldn't walk away any sooner. So many distressed and scared people struggling to come to terms with the horror they stumbled across earlier that evening. And that was before all the paperwork they had to fill in before clocking off.

"How can someone get away from the car so quickly? Surely they can't outrun gunshots?" Michelle asked, as she fixed the stray hairs poking out of her otherwise neat bun.

"Fuck knows, luck?"

"Come on, William, nobody can run that fast."

PART I

"True, we'll find them. The gaffer has guys checking CCTV of Broomielaw and around that area." He was deep in thought about how to solve the mystery.

"Great." She nodded enthusiastically. "Forensics will be all over this. I'll see how the eyewitness statements stack up. That woman with the two kids looked traumatised. I hope they're okay."

She looked at William, who looked back at her with concern. The queasy feeling in the pit of his stomach told him this was connected to his plan.

CHAPTER 9

By the time she got home with an over-tired Jennifer and Ella, who had barely said two words since speaking to the police, Helen felt like she'd been hit by a truck.

The police said they would try and speak to the girls in the days to come to see how they were coping and maybe discuss counselling options, but they didn't want to overwhelm them right after the incident. Helen drove home in such a daze she didn't notice biting her nails until pain shot through her finger and blood oozed out. She forced herself to keep her eyes on the road and focused on getting her girls home to their house in Bridge of Weir.

Since her husband's death Helen relied more heavily on her mum for support and help with the kids. She called Janet to come and stay with them that night. Helen walked in the front door to the sound of the kettle boiling and instantly felt her shoulders drop.

Ella had stayed quiet and very pale since the incident. Jennifer, however, was still tearful, but her tiredness almost overwhelmed her, and despite fighting sleep to cling to her mum, she could not keep her eyes open.

Helen cuddled both girls on the couch, watching as they dozed off. Their fear momentarily slipped away from them as they dreamt, hopefully of something other than guns and getaway cars.

As they sat in silence with the television on low in the background, terrified to move for fear she would wake her precious girls, Helen felt her emotions getting the better of her. Her eyes stung as she fought tears, and the lump in her throat gradually rose. A single tear escaped, trickling down her cheek. Then another and another.

Janet allowed her daughter to slip away to another room, instead taking up position with her granddaughters on the sofa, carefully and quietly so as not to waken them.

As Helen stepped into the kitchen she caved to the sobs she had held in for so long, trying not to show fear in front of her daughters but inside dying to scream.

PART I

The floodgates opened, and tears tumbled until she couldn't see or breathe. She cried and cried until she, too, felt exhausted and drained. The realisation of what happened that day reached the surface and bubbled over.

A mere twenty yards from the car they took refuge behind, a man was shot dead. Helen knew there was crime in Glasgow. She always imagined that it happened in dark alleys or intimidating streets where gangsters met for the intended purpose of causing harm. She didn't expect it in a public car park at rush hour. Her children were there and innocent bystanders could have been caught in the volley of bullets.

Helen let the tears flow until her eyes were raw and her throat sore. She splashed her face in the kitchen sink, letting the cool water calm her. She took a bottle from the fridge and poured herself a large glass of wine. Without stopping for breath she drained the glass and smoothed the front of her clothes.

Helen took a deep breath to get back into mum-mode, quietly walking back into the living room. She picked up Jennifer and took her up to her bed. Behind her, Janet carried Ella. They laid both girls on their mum's king-sized bed, and Helen climbed in beside them. She needed to be close to them, too.

***

You didn't have to make it so fucking public.

The message was sent before he could change his mind. Three dots appeared on his screen and moments later a reply.

You wanted it done, it is. He's finished and the getaway car is gone. We made it happen. You're fucking welcome.

What about the guns?

Gone, don't worry.

What are you going to do when they start sniffing about?

It's under control, everyone knows the script.

CHAPTER 10

After hiding in the stairwell and wandering round the city centre, avoiding the boss Daniel accepted he had to face the consequences. He stared at the phone screen. Slowly, he took his gloves off and unlocked the screen to reply to the message from his associate that he had received hours earlier.

I think shots were fired at car with Slaven. I ran but no fukin clue what happened. Dunno what to do.

He had ignored calls from Clarke. He knew he should phone him back but the adrenaline was still pulsating through his veins and the pains in his arms and chest hadn't eased. Daniel also knew he wouldn't make any sense and would undoubtedly say the wrong thing. Before Daniel had the chance to think about anything and what he would do, his phone rang in his hand. He thought about ignoring it again but knew the consequences would already be bad enough.

"Get here now." Clarke's voice was low, and Daniel could feel the tension.

After everything, there would be plenty of questions for him.

He shoved his phone back in his pocket, pulled his hood up and tighter round his face. He got on a bus that would take him to the Northeast of the city. During the short journey, his mind wandered.

Daniel had assured his partner-in-crime, quite literally, that he was capable of the job.

He had collected the Audi from the area of derelict ground at the Barras in Glasgow, as he was told. The registration plates were meant to be changed to disguise the car for the hit, but for some unknown reason, that hadn't happened. "I did what they wanted", he muttered under his breath. He rubbed his hands together then sat on them as he stared out the windows.

I followed the instructions to park in the quiet corner of the dingy car park at Glasgow Central Station.

He had envisaged himself as something of a Scottish James

PART I

Bond and liked the idea of being hidden in plain sight. Working with Slaven had given him an edge, he thought. He just had to convince Slaven that he was worthy of respect. Never did he think the night would take a turn and that they would become targets. He replayed their plan in his head.

The cameras never worked in the car park, we would never have been caught. I stopped at the stairwell door like I was told.

Keeping those plates on the car had been very risky. While this oversight made the whole thing more difficult and increased the risk factor, Daniel wasn't one to question those who made the decisions. He valued his kneecaps.

But the plan went up in smoke when the Peugeot blocked him in the corner of the car park.

The bus jostled, bringing Daniel back to reality. He looked across the bus to see a man around the same age as him with a little boy. It made him sad about his own life. He had no career, the work him and Slaven did wasn't a vocation.

Daniel was sort of a tax man – at least that was how he described it to his own wee boy – taking from people what they owed. Sometimes it was money, often their dignity when they were beaten so badly they were reduced to a crying wreck or worse – frequently defecating through pure, unadulterated fear.

What had just happened to Slaven?

By the time he got to Clarke's house, others involved with the kingpin were already there: Phil, Stef, and Chaz. None of them were known for manners or pleasantries.

"This is fucking McColl's lot. You didn't see them?" Phil's words sent spittle at Daniel as he walked through the front door.

"I bet it was Chick McNeil, he *hates* Slaven. He'd take any chance to finish him off." Stef muttered through gritted teeth.

All four men huddled in the small living room of the semi-detached house in Springburn.

"Naw!" Daniel protested with desperation. "Didn't see a thing. I panicked when the car blocked us in, so I ran. I thought Slaven would run, too!" He threw his arms in the air in disbelief.

"Well, he's dead," Phil declared very matter-of-fact.

He stood over Daniel, who was perched on the edge of an armchair. "He's fucking dead. And that car is still there."

On realising the magnitude of what happened, Daniel looked round the room at each of the other men. Chaz slumped onto the three-seater sofa nodding, looking forlorn while Stef shook his head then rested it in his hands.

"Why did you leave him?" Phil probed further, not allowing for silence, and to let Daniel know he wouldn't get a break anytime soon.

"And what was I meant to do? Stay and get shot, too? I thought he would run, stupid bastard. Why didn't he run?" He paused for a second, then a fresh wave of fear hit him square in the gut. "Where is Clarke?"

Without looking at him, Phil gestured upwards with his head, meaning their leader was in the house and hadn't unleashed his wrath on Daniel yet.

"Anyway, why were the plates on the car not changed?" he asked Phil. "Now a dodgy motor is there, and my fucking prints are probably on it somewhere. You had one fucking job, mate."

Waving a dismissing hand at Daniel, he barked back, "You should get rid of those clothes just in case you're recognised, or there's anything on you at all. Just bin them or burn, or something."

Daniel heard a muffled sound upstairs when Thomas Clarke's mobile rang and was quickly answered, but Daniel couldn't make out what was said.

Silence again, then Clarke thumped down the stairs.

They all stood when he entered the room, partly out of habit but mostly out of fear and respect.

"This better be the last fucking time they come near us." He spoke quietly but with as much impact as if he'd shouted at them through a megaphone.

Daniel wanted nothing more than to run again, only this time much further away. It was a matter of time before the police came sniffing around them, given Slaven's connection.

PART I

"Talk to nobody, do nothing," Phil snarled. "Dan, where's your burner?"

"Turned it off, obviously," Daniel said, pointing animatedly to the pocket of his tracksuit trousers.

"Give it here," his associate demanded, holding his hand out.

Daniel reached into his pocket, but it was snatched from his hand before he could do anything. Phil took the sim out, threw it on top of a candle, and lit it.

"Where's *your* phone?" Phil barked.

"Bedside cabinet," Daniel said, locking eyes with Phil. "I am not that fuckin' stupid."

Phil's mobile rang. Daniel noticed he hurriedly cancelled the call.

"Good. Now, the rest of you do the same." Phil removed the sim from his pay-as-you-go "work phone" and tossed the tiny little metal card onto the candle's flames. The others protested, but Clarke agreed.

"Aye. We'll replace them, but best be safe."

Clarke's phone rang again. The room fell silent.

"Laura, hen. I'm sorry. Where are you? Aye, Daniel was there... No, he had no idea." There was a pause while the crying, distressed woman on the other end wailed and ranted.

"I know...I know – he should have told you. I'm sorry, hen. What do you need? Maureen was going to come over, but—"

He was cut off again while Slaven's heartbroken wife continued to sob and shout.

"Right, okay, okay. What about—"

Looking crestfallen and furious at the same time, Clarke launched the phone across the room, knocking over a plant pot and taking a picture frame off of the wall.

"How the fuck did this happen? Who knew they were there?" he snarled, looking at each of his men.

Although it wasn't the best timing, Daniel asked, "Boss, the job. What about it?"

He and Josh Slaven were expected to stop in at another car park

31

at Charing Cross, then make a few house calls to a string of anxious men who owed money to Clarke.

"A temporary reprieve, for now," Clarke said quietly. "Police will be sniffing about. It's too risky. Right, all of you disappear. Talk to nobody and *do* nothing."

Daniel watched as the others left, Stef and Chaz on their motorbikes, followed by Phil, who said nothing before driving off.

Maybe he should just have stayed in the car. He was certain to have a fate worse than death shortly.

PART I

CHAPTER 11

Phil could barely think straight when he jumped in his car and sped away from Clarke's house. He had no phone after burning his sim. He raced to the closest convenience store to buy another pay-as-you-go.

Back in his car, sitting under a streetlight, trying not to draw too much attention to himself, Phil dug into his jacket pocket and pulled out a scrunched-up piece of paper. His breathing was heavy, and he aggressively punched the numbers into the cheap phone.

It rang out.

Phil tried again, and it rang out.

He rang a third time but waited for the voicemail.

"It's me. New number. I need to speak to you. Text me the second you get this, and let's meet."

Phil turned the radio off as he slowly pulled up in front of his house and crept inside, and upstairs. He undressed as quietly as he could in the hallway and climbed into bed beside his wife. Tucking his phone underneath his pillow Phil lay facing the ceiling, unable to relax.

At 3 am, Phil got a text.

Strathy, you'll find me. 30 mins.

Not that he was able to sleep, but he was fully awake when the message came through. Strathclyde Country Park in Motherwell wasn't too far, and the roads would be quiet at that time.

Beside him, Lisa stirred and came to as he got out of bed.

"What are you doing?" she croaked, rubbing her eyes.

"Nothing, nothing, just can't sleep. I'm going to clear my head, babes," he whispered back, leaning his muscular frame over to kiss her.

What she didn't know and all that.

He pulled on black jogging bottoms, a dark hoodie, and a beanie hat covering his brown hair, then left the house.

With that, Phil made his way out of his street. While he

remembered, he grabbed the new brick-like phone from the passenger seat and turned it off. He hoped he remembered to keep his personal phone on silent, or Lisa would go off her head. After the night's events, he was bound to have messages streaming in all night.

The thought of anything happening to Lisa or his kids was unbearable. He hated that they might be in any danger.

His hard-man exterior momentarily lapsing, he slammed his hand on the steering wheel. But something kept him involved in this dark world: the money, the street cred…the fear. A combination of things, but in moments like this, he often wished he had gotten a nine-to-five job like most other people his age. He wasn't clever, but even the most stupid people he knew had jobs that got them by.

On the face of it, and as far as the tax man was concerned, he worked at a local car wash. A job that paid for lavish trips to Tenerife and Santa Ponsa, where the family looked like any other. They had two children, a boy and a girl. His social media influencer wife Lisa loved to share their "perfect family" pictures on her Instagram page.

Phil was tall, lean from his manual job washing cars all day, and tattooed —a full sleeve was on his right arm and several across his shoulders and back. He gave off an air of authority saying and doing very little until he was pushed. Then a hulk-like creature was unleashed.

His wife, Lisa, was blonde and curvaceous with too much lip filler. She was a stay-at-home mum who occasionally picked up bar shifts in their local pub. And earned money from modelling clothes and promoting makeup online. They were on the face of it, a working-class family. Phil worked hard to provide, Lisa would tell everyone. They put on a good show.

Many suspected the car washing was a cover for something else; some even knew, but nobody dared challenge them.

Maybe it is time for a career change, Phil thought. *If Clarke would let me.*

He could not do anything before they got to the bottom of what happened to Slaven and if his plan for Daniel could go undetected. Or it would be his funeral they would be planning next.

On top of everything, Josh Slaven was his friend.

Phil pulled into the park and drove round until he saw head-lights in the darkness. He slowly pulled up beside the Ford Focus, lining up his driver's side beside the other driver, and lowered his window.

"You said you were going to sort him out. How the fuck did this happen? It was the perfect opportunity," Phil barked at the man in the other car.

He smacked the steering wheel with the heel of his hand. The one person he wanted to deal with had left unscathed. If Clarke found out, it would be his head taking a bullet. Or worse, Lisa's.

"Look mate, I'm sorry, I tried. I didn't expect it to go this way either."

Phil snorted. The response sounded like a schoolboy justifying poor performance to a teacher.

"I handed you him on a plate. He's going to take me down with him next time. You do know that," Phil shot back. "He needs to be sorted. There won't be any more jobs till after Slaven's funeral. The cops are all over us just now. It'd have been fucking two for one with Slaven in the motor. Both of them would've been bang to rights."

"I thought he wasn't the issue, Phil?"

Phil shrugged. "Nah, he's not but collateral damage, y'know, more legit too." He quickly changed the subject. "So have you sussed which one of McColl's lot have done this? It's too far, mate. I know he wasn't a saint, but he has young kids."

"Mate, you know I can't talk about that. Everything is being done. Believe me." The man looked concerned.

Phil stared intently at him, convinced his associate was delib-erately avoiding eye contact.

For a moment, all that could be heard was the low rumbling of the car engines as the men sat parallel to one another with their driver's window down in a poorly lit car park at Strathclyde Park, wallowing in silence.

By day, the area swarmed with children, dog walkers, and laugh-ter wafted across the lake from the theme park. But in the dead of

MURDER CENTRAL

night, the only other noise was the rustling of birds in trees, the flapping of wings, and the odd quack of a duck in the water.

By then, Phil was staring ahead as though in a trance for thirty seconds or so, then became aware of a voice speaking to him "Mate…mate!", the words interrupted his thoughts.

Composing himself and keeping calm before saying anything back. He looked back at the man in the other car "Yes. *Mate*. Nobody wants this plan rumbled. I'll be in touch. We'll try again."

***

Watching Phil's car drive away, he looked in the mirror on the visor. He didn't recognise the man staring back at him.

"How did I get into this mess?" William asked himself out loud.

The sight of his police badge sticking out from underneath his jacket on the passenger side sent a shiver down his spine. He wasn't used to playing with fire.

Part II - The catalyst

CHAPTER 12

Phil first decided to take action after a midweek encounter with Daniel tipped him over the edge. He sat nursing a pint at Shevlanes pub in Springburn. He'd been staring into the abyss for ten minutes when his two associates walked in. The rush of cold air when the door opened snapped him out of his trance, and he nodded at Stef and Chaz. Just as they sat at the table holding two drinks, Daniel charged into the boozer. Phil felt his jaw stiffen.

"Danny, you haven't paid your tab from the other day, pal." Phil heard the barman tell him.

Stef pulled a twenty pound note out of his pocket, sighing heavily. He thrust the note onto the bar, making eye contact with Daniel.

"Cheers, Stef. Thanks mate," he said, looking smug as the barman moved to get his drink, shouting after him, "I'll get my uncle Tam to square you up."

Daniel took his drink to the table, slurping loudly.

Phil took a deep breath, playing with his empty crisps packet like he was practising origami. Forcing a smile, Phil slid his drink closer to him to prevent Daniel knocking it over. He wiped his hands together as anger flashed through him. The younger man's presence and carelessness was forcing his heart rate to creep up.

Phil turned round in time to see a punter trip and bump Daniel from behind, causing his drink to spill as he took a sip. Without taking a second to appraise the situation, Daniel jumped to his feet, pushing his stool back and turning round so fast he almost gave himself whiplash.

"Sorry, sorry," the man said, holding his hands up, laughing at his stupidity.

Daniel's face didn't soften. His eyes widened, and his fists clenched.

"Watch what you're doing, or you will be sorry," he snarled, jutting his chest forward as though moving to fight.

Stef and Chaz pulled him back to his seat, telling him to calm down.

"Do you know who my uncle is?" Daniel shouted after the man, who scurried off to the toilet. "Do you know Thomas Clarke?"

Phil's chest tightened as he stared at Daniel. *Why does he have to be such a clown? He's going to get us in serious bother.*

With his mind made up, Phil took a different route home that evening so he might bump into his old friend William. He'd pretend he had just happened across the police officer he hoped would be on one of his dog walks, he had so often seen him on.

But when he clocked William, something in Phil made him hang back. Instead he watched the officer and his dog for a few minutes. *This has to be done properly,* he thought. He couldn't accost him in the street. He'd get William's attention first, then he would strike.

Phil kept a safe distance, watching as the Cockapoo bounced, barked, and pulled at the lead eager to get home.

A surprise sneeze crept up on Phil, which he was able to stifle, but the noise he did make got the little dog's attention. It stopped in its tracks, looking around, forcing Phil to step behind a hedge, hoping he wouldn't be seen. He could not have William getting spooked at this stage.

After a few moments, the dog was persuaded to keep walking and disappeared into a nearby house with his owner.

Phil waited in the street for a few moments longer, deciding on the best way to approach.

A package to the house, he thought. *Get into his house and into his head, then make contact.*

PART II

CHAPTER 13

William lifted the bottle of Chianti from the coffee table and poured himself a large glass. He topped up his wife's when she returned from the kitchen and plonked herself beside him. As he put his arm round her, pulling her close, they settled in to watch Netflix. Sarah jumped as someone rattled the letterbox.

Sitting up straight with a panicked expression, she glanced at her watch. "Who is that? Are you expecting someone?"

"No, babe. Not a clue." The off-duty police officer got to his feet.

He pulled back the blinds and peered out to the front door. Then, he looked at his watch before going to the door.

An older man wearing a baseball cap and a navy tracksuit looked him up and down then stepped forward. Quietly he asked, "Mr Field?" William's brows narrowed as he looked around the street then silently nodded. The older man thrust a box into his hand.

William looked at the package bearing his name then looked around the empty street again. "I haven't ordered anything. Are you from Amazon?" William glanced into the house behind him then stepped outside the front door, closing the door behind him.

The man flashed a smile at William. "This is a special delivery," then added with emphasis, "officer."

The word reverberated around William's head as the man turned on his heel and walked away.

How does he know I'm a police officer? Who sent him here?

With a dry mouth and feeling light-headed, he ran out to the pavement. The street was quiet save from the faraway purr of a motorbike. Walking back into the house, staring at the box, William had a gut feeling something was amiss but didn't want to worry Sarah. She had enough going on, and undue distress from him wouldn't help.

He bounded up the stairs, calling out, "Back in a minute!"

William tore the packaging open. It was a small, flimsy

39

cardboard box containing a mobile phone and a folded piece of paper with barely visible printed words:

All will become clear, Billy. Got a favour to ask seeing as you owe me.

He hadn't been called Billy, that shortened version of his name, in years. It harked back to his school days. As a police officer, William didn't think of himself as Billy anymore; those days were behind him. There weren't many people who would still call him that, but he could think of someone in particular. A memory he had suppressed flooded his mind.

Growing up in the north-east of the city, William had friends who he didn't associate with socially as an adult. They were from his formative years before life was serious. When drinking cider in the local park and having a kick about at the weekend with a football was all they had to worry about.

The boys' backgrounds were worlds apart, but it didn't matter – who you played football with and drank Frosty Jacks with wasn't a big deal back then. William knew Phil and his friends were rougher round the edges than he was.

Phil and his friends went to All Saints secondary school. William went to Springburn Academy. For all sectarianism was a longstanding issue in Glasgow, it was never something that caused them any problems.

William was quieter than the others. He kept himself to himself – a little out of fear, but also because he was jealous of Phil's reputation and popularity as a teenager. As adults they made different lifestyle choices but William was indebted to Phil.

William's memory was still as vivid as the night it happened. He remembered every detail.

"Billy, fuck off now. Just disappear." Phil grabbed his friend by his shoulders.

Trembling, William stumbled back. "What the fuck just happened?" Their five-aside game had descended into chaos when an opponent punched him in the back. "Mate, we'll all go down for this. I didn't mean to…"

PART II

The exhilaration of fighting back was something he had never experienced before, and it unlocked something in him that erupted like a volcano. He kicked his opponent, swiping his feet from under him, and stamped on his head, leaving the boy motionless on the ground.

"Billy! Get to fuck. He'll be fine. And it was Div who pulled the knife. Don't get caught up in this shit. Seriously, fuck off."

Days later, Phil had spread the rumour that William ran off when the fight started.

At just eighteen years old, Phil was convicted of serious assault and served time.

Seven years later, William decided to join the police. Since then, he'd married Sarah, bought a house, and built a reputation. He had Phil to thank for avoiding a criminal record.

It seemed now was time for Phil to call on his old pal.

MURDER CENTRAL

CHAPTER 14

Leaning against a lamppost, Phil waited outside the gate when William returned home from a back shift the day after the phone arrived. As William turned into his driveway, he recognised the silhouetted figure.

Here we go, William thought, his chest tightening. *This isn't going to end well.*

As much as he had time for Phil, and owed him a lot, William did not want him hanging around his house while his unsuspecting wife slept inside. She had been through enough.

"Officer." Phil stood up straight and made a saluting gesture.

"Alright, Phil", William got out of the car, closing the door behind him. He took a couple of steps towards the end of his driveway. "Aye, what's up?" Speaking at little more than a whisper, Phil said, "I know you got the package. I'm looking for a favour. I need you to get rid of someone for me."

"Phil, I can't just kill someone – I'm a fucking copper." William almost stumbled over his words.

"Not in that way, you prick. I mean, officially. Using the proper channels."

Unsure but curious, William paused. "Right, you're talking about one of your own? One of Clarke's lot?" His eyes widened.

"Aye." Phil rubbed the back of his neck, agitated and looking nervous. "I know you cops are waiting to get someone on something, so let me help, and you'll be doing me a favour."

William didn't know how to respond, looking around to see if any of his neighbours were nearby. He looked to his bedroom window where Sarah would be sleeping.

"Look, I can come back tomorrow when your missus is up if you would prefer an audience?" Phil gestured his head towards the upstairs window.

This was the most on edge he'd seen Phil.

What is he up to?

42

PART II

William looked at his watch: 11 pm and sighed.

He glanced round the empty street for a second time. William put his finger to his mouth and Phil copied his gesture of silence.

Then, he beckoned Phil to follow him up the garden path. He peered over the fence into the back garden, putting a hand up until the coast was confirmed as clear.

Then, he beckoned Phil to follow him into the shed where he had a makeshift bar. Or at least that was the idea; in reality, it was a chair and some electrics powering a light, mini fridge, and stack of mostly unread books.

He hit the light switch and gestured at one of the stools. Phil duly sat as William nervously leaned against the wall with his arms crossed.

William cleared his throat. "So, what is it you want?"

Speaking through gritted teeth, Phil said, "To get rid of Daniel Tonner. I'm telling you he's a wee arsehole, and he's going to get someone killed."

"What has he—"

"Don't ask too many questions. Probably best if you don't know too much." Phil raised a warning hand.

"Sure, okay, but I need to know why you want to get rid of him? I can't do much without that. I will have to cover my tracks. What the fuck do you think I can do that you can't?"

William felt stress rise from the pit of his stomach until it rested in his chest. Beads of sweat trickled down his cold back.

"What is that supposed to mean?" Phil jumped to his feet, his fists clenched.

William put his hands up, then lowered them slowly to calm the angry gangster. Phil met his gaze but slowly sat back down.

"Look, I just…" William said, then stopped. He took a breath and quietly said, "Nothing, other than I am a serving police officer. Anything I do has repercussions."

"Look, pal, you owe me. I don't want to be a dick about this, but I did *time* for you." His voice became steadily louder.

William stepped forward. "I…I didn't ask you to. I didn't mean

43

to hurt that guy. You know I'd never been involved in anything like that before and I trusted you when you told me to run. I didn't think you'd go down when you didn't do anything."

Phil locked eyes with William and narrowed his brows and lowered his voice. "Aye, well, that's the law for you. It was… what do you fucking coppers call it? Art and part? whatever." He waved a hand dismissively. "I was there – they were all injured, we weren't. The only person with any injury was you, and we couldn't tell anyone that, could we? I fucking denied it too. They had nothing concrete on me, but circumstances put me there, and well – I obviously have one of those faces."

Phil laughed. "Look, that was my first rodeo. I've been on a few since, so here we are. If I thought I could do this myself, I would, but the wee shite is always around me."

He sat back down. "Billy, I'm handing you this prick on a plate. Tonner is going to be…running errands, let's say. You'll get him with a shit tonne of money and gear in the motor if you get him at the right place. Goad him into a breach of the peace, and he'll probably resist arrest, too. He's really that much of a fanny. Sound like a plan?"

William rubbed the back of his neck, and a part of him thought this was plausible.

Phil added, "Don't you lot go on intel and all that? Just say you got a tip-off or some shit."

William paced up and down the small shed. Not used to feeling this pressure, he wasn't sure how to deal with it. But this wasn't office politics or how to dodge a night out with his in-laws; he knew he was in deep.

And although Phil knew his old pal was now a policeman and William was still scared of him, many gangland secrets had now been shared. William knew that decision wouldn't have been taken lightly.

"Right." William shifted from foot to foot, then leaned against the shed wall again and rested his head against his left arm. "What do I need to do here then? How do you see this going down?"

William flinched slightly when Phil removed his hand from his pocket holding a phone. "There's a sim already in that phone

PART II

delivered in the box, the number for this one," he held the phone in front of his face, "is stored in it. I'll keep you updated with what's happening, Billy. Don't be a fucking idiot and have it on at the polis station."

William ran his right hand through his thinning hair. The hairline didn't match his youthful face. It was a bugbear for him. Nodding wearily, he took a seat. Phil had him where he wanted him now. William knew his old friend better than to argue.

"Thanks, Billy. Knew I could count on you." Phil smiled as he stood up. "I'll be away now and let you get back to your night."

Silently, both men left the shed and walked back to the street.

"Night bud," Phil said, slapping William on the back.

"Yeah…night, mate."

***

William stepped inside his house, taking a huge sigh.

He sat on the bottom step, took his shoes off, and dropped his head in his hands. Neville, their Cockapoo dog, made his way over to lick his hands, sensing the tension.

The Clarkes were not to be trifled with. If they found out what Phil was up to, they'd both be in trouble. Maybe he could do this without it coming back on him, and they could nail Daniel Tonner. He had to be positive, although every fibre in his body told him otherwise.

What am I going to have to agree to?

CHAPTER 15

Stuffing a bag with his things into his locker at the station, William left the office to drive to Pollok Park after his next shift. He had already made his excuses to Sarah that he had been held up with paperwork. Within a few minutes of parking, after building the courage, William turned on the pay-as-you-go phone.

A few seconds later, the first WhatsApp message dropped.

I'll hand you him complete with gear and cash, if you make sure he goes away.

Then another.

There's 30k in it for you, mate. I know you know this is a good deal and I'll keep on keeping your secret Billy. You get your guys there when I tell you and the wee prick is done for.

He sighed. *Can I really do this?*

William would be the office hero taking Tonner off the streets. The gangster wasn't a high flyer, but he had the potential to improve his status the more his ego grew and he was one of Clarke's lot, so it would be good to nail him.

Can I trust Phil? He was already harbouring a huge secret for William.

Will think on it and check in same time tomorrow.

William punched into the phone and hit send before changing his mind. He waited a few minutes for a response.

Tomorrow. The answer will be yes.

He's not giving me a choice, William thought.

Turning the phone back off, he shoved it back into his jacket pocket, trying to find some way to get rid of the anger starting to build in him. William took several deep breaths and counted to ten – twice. Slowly, William felt his heart rate steady.

Sarah was awake when he got in, lying in bed reading a book. He met her gaze as he walked straight to the en-suite to wash up and take a minute to gather his thoughts before bed.

"Hiya, you okay?" she shouted, sounding worried.

PART II

"Yeah, babe, will be out in a minute," William called back as he sat on the toilet. His mind was still racing.

Did anyone see us? Can this work? Getting away with something once is luck but twice, surely that isn't possible?

William wasn't religious, but asked for a sign from a higher being to help him decide what to do. Phil was not the sort of guy you said no to. William was in his good books, but his old school friend had too much on him to call his bluff with. But William was a serving police officer and an upstanding member of society. He had a family to think about. He couldn't guarantee Sarah would be safe if he refused to do what was asked of him.

It was all too much to think about. They had enough going on already, this was pressure William didn't need.

He brushed his teeth and frantically splashed his face with water as though the feeling of the cold liquid hitting his face would provide instant clarity. It didn't.

He climbed into bed beside Sarah, who had turned her bedside light off and was lying with her back to him. She shimmied toward him, pushing her bottom towards him, encouraging him to cuddle in.

Sarah's auburn hair was in a loose bun that tickled his chin, and her porcelain-coloured skin was soft to the touch. She was his priority.

Mind still racing, his heartbeat thudded in his chest so loudly he feared Sarah would feel it. He reached out and rubbed her arm, a reassuring touch that he prayed wouldn't arouse suspicion.

CHAPTER 16

William couldn't do anything about the bags under his eyes, but he made himself a strong coffee to take in his car on his way to work.

When he arrived, he learned his colleague Michelle had a hospital appointment. Instead, he would work with Davie Donovan, an officer whose usual partner had been called to court to give evidence.

As they patrolled the city, William's mind wandered to the threat from Phil, and he debated for the hundredth time if he should call him as planned or hope it would all disappear.

I am a police officer. I can sort this.

After all, he knew his childhood friend was good for keeping his word. So far, it had gone in William's favour. Maybe it would again.

He bit his nail to the quick, the sharp pain bringing him back to reality. One day, he wanted to be a good dad, but despite five years of trying, he and Sarah had not had a baby. Three pregnancies had ended too soon, and now they were preparing to go through IVF for a second time. The money offered up would take the pressure off and help pay off some debt.

They pulled up at Greggs to pick up lunch and got out of the car at the same time.

"You go ahead, Davie," William blurted out a little too loud and fast. "I've got to call Sarah quickly. I'll be in behind you."

His colleague seemed confused by the sudden outburst but nodded and went to the shop.

William reached into his body armour and turned on the illicit phone he'd tucked away. His hands shook, but he had the overwhelming urge to make the call before he changed his mind. Standing with his back to the driver's door so he could watch who was nearby, he turned the phone on and pulled up the number for his old pal. The phone rang out, and clicked to voicemail.

"Bastard!" William shouted, wondering where that left him as he hung up.

But before he could panic too much, the phone rang in his

PART II

hand. Instantly, he swiped the screen to answer before the second ring.

"Alright mate, hi, I've been thinking…"

There was silence.

"Not the call that we had planned, Billy. I thought we were talking later. What is it?" Phil quizzed aggressively.

William couldn't decide if Phil was agitated or just nervous, but he was on the phone now, so he had to go with it.

"Okay, so this favour. Remind me again what exactly would it involve me doing? I need you to be really specific."

There was another silence at the end for a moment before Phil cleared his throat.

"Right, I want you to get Tonner red-handed. Just as I told you. The wee scumbag is poisonous and needs to be locked up, but I *need* to be kept out of it. If he rats, I am not going down. I will give you all the details you need to get him when he is bang to rights, and the case will be so tight he can't wriggle out. You become top cop, hero, whatever. I get to know Tonner is out the way, and I'm *not* implicated. Find a way to get your lot to his pick up point on Friday. He'll be at that dingy car park at Central Station."

William covered the microphone on his phone while he exhaled. He took some deep breaths to calm his breathing, turning to keep an eye out for Davie. His thoughts frantically raced, almost deafening him.

William looked up in time to see a group of school children walking closer with their lunch, chattering and making noise. He walked in the other direction.

"Right mate, okay. I'll do it. You mentioned £30,000? I, eh, it's not just about the money, but it'd really help us out. It's just that—"

"Billy," Phil cut him off. "I don't need to hear your problems; I just need your word you'll not mess this up because you've got a lot to lose. And so do I if you screw up. Clarke will have my balls on a plate, but he'll do worse to you if anything goes wrong. And Billy, I will *not* protect you again."

Phil's tone was not friendly, and panic was setting in. William

49

had committed now, so this had to work.

"There will be drugs, cocaine and heroin, in the boot of the motor. That won't be Tonner's either but you'll get him on possession charges maybe even supply because there will be a lot. And Billy, make sure you comb the car for weapons. Glove compartment and under the seats. It will all be there."

"Jesus. Okay yeah, don't worry, I'll sort it out. We'll talk later again. Sort timings but I'll take care of him. I'll take care of everything. It won't be a problem. Consider it done."

The line went dead. William suddenly became aware of someone in his path. He looked up to see his colleague holding a baguette in one hand and a can of Coke in the other.

"What was that about?" Davie frowned and waited a moment, then walked past him and round to the passenger side of the car, which was a few paces away.

William froze momentarily, then immediately tried to change the subject.

"Got held up, sorry, I'll just nip into Greggs now." He reached into his pocket for his keys to open the door for his colleague.

Davie pulled the handle to get in, and as he put a foot in the door to sit, he looked across the roof of the car at William. "Whoever needs to be taken care of, I'm in."

William laughed and walked off, trying not to show his true reaction. *Shit,* he thought. *How much did he actually hear? This is the last thing I need.*

When he returned with his lunch in his hand, William held his breath, bracing himself, as he got in the car. He wondered if Davie would probe any further.

They drove without speaking until it was time to go back to their police station. They parked up outside it, still silent. William pulled the handbrake on with one hand, the other resting on the door, ready to leave.

"So, who has to be taken care of, William? Sounded interesting."

William's heart sank, and his stomach knotted. He stared ahead out the front window, lost for words and no idea what he could say.

PART II

All he could think about was getting the money for IVF; he had promised his wife he would get the money. After everything she had been through, he couldn't let her down.

Again, Davie wouldn't let it rest. "William, £30,000 is a lot of money. What is being taken care of?" He asked slowly, pronouncing each word carefully. "The Sergeant might be interested to know, I'm sure."

William turned his body ninety degrees and looked Davie straight in the eyes, searching his face for signs of joking, trying to read the situation. "What do you want? I already told you it doesn't concern you." He tried to sound stern, threatening even, but he knew where this was going.

"Well, £10,000, and I'll keep my mouth shut." Davie had a good poker face.

A laugh escaped from William, partly out of nerves and partly in disbelief. He didn't even know this guy that well, and now he was trying to cash in. Davie must have known it wasn't above board but wanted in on the action.

His colleague smiled back at him, a smile that didn't reach his eyes.

"Look, I've got a few debts to pay off. Tell me what you're doing, cut me in, and we both benefit." Davie shrugged.

William knew what the answer had to be, but he couldn't give in easily. Two days ago, he was a straight-laced cop, and now he was dancing to the tune of blackmailers, pulling favours for criminals, and considering paying someone off with dirty money.

"You have got to be joking! Back off and forget you heard anything. What are you going to tell the gaffer? That I'm getting paid to take care of something? Proves nothing. Piss off and mind your own business."

William opened the door to leave when he felt a tight grip on his left arm. Davie leaned over the centre console with a crazed look.

"Okay, pal." Davie's voice sounded more like a growl. "I've tried being nice. I know you're up to something because I'm not an idiot, and you're a lanky prick, not a small-time gangster. So, help me out,

MURDER CENTRAL

or you're fucked. I'll tell the gaffer in there, and I'll tell *your* gaffer. I'm sure Sarah doesn't need this, does she? Not after everything *she's* been through." He smiled sarcastically again as he sat back.

William felt his face flush as the anger instantly rose through his chest, and the blood rushed to his head. "You bastard!" he shouted, clenching his fists.

His breaths deepened. He knew things would be even worse if he reacted the way he wanted to by putting Davie's head through the window.

They sat in silence for what felt like forever. His thoughts kept coming back to Sarah, the IVF, and about what they had already battled through together. After a few minutes, William's shoulders sagged. The feeling in his chest thinking of it all was so intense he thought he might have a heart attack. William was so angry that he felt his throat tighten, a lump forming. He swallowed hard.

"We'll be getting intel to take down one of Clarke's mob, specific information about where he'll be and when and with enough gear to arrest him. The wee prick is a liability; he'll probably resist arrest, and we'll get him on assault, too. He's ratted out by one of his own who's coughing up cash to stay out of it. Think of it as a public service. He's a wee gobshite who needs to be taken down a peg so badly one of his own wants rid of him. And yes. The cash is for IVF. We've got another round to pay for, so aye, I'm taking the money. Plus, Clarke's mob isn't the sort you say no to."

William put his head in his hands. It was out now; Davie had him over a barrel, and Phil would have, too, if he tried to say no.

A message came through the radio looking for Davie. His colleague was back from court and wanted to speak to him. He got out of the car then leaned down to William's eye level. "Looks like ten thousand is a small price to pay in the long run, buddy."

Davie slammed the door and walked off, leaving William alone with his thoughts.

William's eyes swam with tears as the frustration tried its best to escape.

No going back now.

PART II

CHAPTER 17

Out running that night to clear his head and to stay out of the house, William felt the phone in his pocket ring. It was Phil calling, as planned.

William was being distant from Sarah, and it killed him, but the further she was from this mess, the better. He didn't want to keep secrets, but he also didn't want her to know anything was on his mind. She would only ask questions, and he was too ashamed of the answers.

Phil made it clear during the call that cash would be paid in full when the arrest was made, and he refused to hear any details about how it would be done.

"Plausible deniability with my boss is crucial," Phil told him. "So you'll be paid the cash in full when you arrest his clown but that part is down to you and I know nothing", the words sent a shiver up William's spine. He paced back and forth as he listened to the instructions on the phone.

"Daniel Tonner will be collecting cash from some…people," the gangster said. "But you need to leave them, Billy, turn a blind eye to that. Focus on Tonner.

"Remember, there will be drugs in the boot of the motor. And, make sure you comb the car for weapons. Glove compartment and under the seats. It will all be there."

William listened intently, nodding. He envisaged it as the gangster described what to expect.

"You just need to say it's a tip-off. You cops get them all the time. This has to be believable, and you'll be the good guy who caught him."

Before William could say anything, Phil spoke to him again. "Tonner has a tonne of previous convictions. This should be *easy*."

William thought it best to arrange for the tip-off to happen for real to make it believable – and it would all be sorted. He knew Clarke wouldn't be happy his boy had been caught, but surely, the earlier convictions and a string of charges would be enough to get Tonner off the streets for a couple of years. Phil made it clear to him that he wanted to show Clarke the boy's true colours.

William had no idea what further plans Phil had while the wee rat was behind bars, so his part seemed easy enough. Tonner was a known troublemaker, drug dealer, and an all-round idiot; this should be an easy gig.

***

He didn't see Davie over the following days but tracked down his mobile number from someone else on his shift.

"I've got something to check with him about our shift on Monday," William offered as an excuse for asking. Not that anybody cared. He scanned their faces for any signs of curiosity or worry, then realised he was panicking over nothing.

William decided he needed somebody to make an anonymous call and say that they saw the car driving erratically and going towards the car park. He had a drinking buddy in Manchester he wanted to help out who wasn't too close to home. He only had a week to sort the story; Tonner was "working" the following Friday, and it had to be in place.

As William drove to work the next day, it seemed as good a time as any to cement plans. He hit the button on the steering wheel of his Ford Puma. "Call Stevo."

The phone rang a few times before a raspy voice answered.

"Alright, mate, how's it going?" William cleared his throat, try-ing to sound upbeat and breezy. "Hey Stevo. Good yeah, how are you? How's Manchester treating you?"

There was a muffling sound as the voice on the other end coughed, "Yeah, alright, good to hear from you. What do I owe the pleasure?"

William gripped the steering wheel tight, unsure how the words were going to sound when they came out his mouth but feeling

PART II

like he had no choice but to keep going. "You must be due up for a visit soon? A night in Glasgow is on the cards, grab a few pints and have a catch up."

Before his friend could answer, he hurriedly added, "Listen, mate, I've actually got a really important undercover job I'm working on, can't say too much, y'know how it is, but I have a favour to ask, which would really help us out. Fancy coming up next weekend for a couple of nights? I'll put you up, we'll get that night out?"

He checked his rearview mirror, making sure he was still the only driver on the road, aware his loudspeaker conversation might be overheard.

William hoped it sounded genuine. He wanted to see his friend, but it could also dig him out of a deep hole.

"Eh, does sound good, William. Quite short notice though, what is the favour – how can I help with your top secret work? I mean, I could maybe work it so that I can come up next Saturday. Let me get back to you."

William glanced in the rearview mirror. He could see sweat glistening on his forehead. He didn't want to sound panicked or desperate and could tell his friend was trying to help. But he was so close to getting over the first hurdle that he was struggling to concentrate on the road.

Glancing down to see his speed had crept up to 44 mph on a 30 mph, he instantly took his foot off the accelerator. "Aw, mate, right. I can't say too much. I'll explain more soon, but it's for a job next Friday if you can work it? I'll put you up in the Radisson, nice wee place. You help out on Friday and have a night to yourself, and I'll meet you Saturday when I'm off? You'd be doing me a solid. I'll call you later, but I'd really appreciate it if you can. I'll call Mikey and Tom, too?"

He was pleading; he knew it sounded desperate, but he couldn't stop himself.

After what seemed like forever, he heard Stevo sigh. "I'll see what I can do, should be fine. I'll text you later. Really need to get going to work, but I'll be in touch. Bye, Will."

He ended the call. The first obstacle was almost overcome. Almost.

PART II

CHAPTER 18

William frantically tried calling Davie several times, but the phone rang out. Instead, he arrived at work half an hour early hoping to catch Davie before his shift.

Just as William pulled up to the station, Davie texted.

Busy with Mel, CU b4 shift followed by a thumbs-up emoji.

How 2002, William thought, but knew Davie was not one for using his words at the best of times.

William shook his head at the screen, chewing the inside of his mouth, unsure of what to do with himself until Davie arrived.

His hands trembled as he waited in the staff room, making tea and playing with his phone, trying to look busy when Davie tore into the room like a tornado. No matter where he was going or what he was doing, he looked on edge, spoiling for a fight.

Davie crashed into the room, battering the door closed, slammed his phone onto the table then went to his locker.

William watched the fifty-three-year-old, stocky policeman with a shaved head akin to a gangster himself. He had a permanent scowl and was almost always angry. *Maybe he argued with Mel,* William thought.

If he did, it'd soon be round the station. She was a serving officer who had left her long-suffering husband for Davie, and their drama was often discussed between the different shifts.

William strode over to Davie who was ramming things in his locker. He cleared his throat, speaking in a low voice barely audible.

"Next Friday, just about 5 pm, there will be a call of someone acting suspicious at the Central Station car park. Fuck knows what the details will be yet. Busy time, so plenty of eyewitnesses, the case will be tight."

William turned to check nobody was hovering at the door. He leaned in closer to Davie. "We'll be on shift in the area. If you get the call, you act surprised." He checked the door a final time then and, barely above a whisper, said, "If you hear on the radio, act normal. If he gets lifted, he should get remanded. You'll get your cash when I do."

Davie sprayed his aftershave and fixed his hair, despite it being shaved in-to-the-wood, with a hand as though styling a quiff. He turned to face William. His eyes narrowed as he stared. "Right, well, I want twelve grand, pal."

William's insides crumpled in disbelief and jolted like someone had punched him in the stomach. The pain in his abdomen felt as though he really had been.

The feeling of being on the cusp of a heart attack crept over him again. It would have been preferable at that time, a real reason to let everyone down without consequences. The money was earmarked for IVF and credit card debts from the last round. It was the main reason he agreed to go along with the potentially career-ending plan. William didn't want to think about what could go wrong, only that he was too scared of Phil to say no, of what could happen to Sarah if he didn't agree, and how the cash would help them.

"Are you joking? What are you playing at?" William asked desperately, trying to straighten himself up and not sound like the coward he was speaking to a man a foot smaller.

"Ah, change of circumstances on my end, you know how it is. Got to rob Peter to pay Paul and all that."

William mentally batted away another vision, this time of smacking Davie's head against the metal locker. Despite being taller than his colleague, he was no match for the pocket rocket, and it wouldn't do his career any good. The risk was too high to get this wrong. He had to be assertive, make sure everything went according to plan and move on.

If I pull it off and stay on Phil's good side, maybe I could ask for more money? Thoughts raced round his head. *This isn't the reason I joined the force, but taking bad people off the street is, and this is the ultimate end game. Everything else is a means to an end. Is it not?*

"Fine!" William said as he brushed past Davie.

He wanted to shove him to the side and throw a chair to release some of the fury, but he couldn't summon the courage. He skulked

PART II

off to find Michelle to start his shift.

CHAPTER 19

William checked his phone four times in five minutes, waiting on Sarah to leave the house. Their puppy Neville was jumping round his feet, excitedly vying for his attention.

"When are you heading off?" William tried to sound calm.

"Are you wanting to get rid of me?" Sarah leaned over to kiss her husband.

"Of course not, just wondering when your mum is expecting you." He pulled her in for a second kiss as Neville jumped between them.

"She said to drop by anytime, but I'm going now. See you later!"

Neville ran out the door with Sarah following.

With five days to go until the planned swoop, William turned the television on to fill the silence in the house. He still had to call Stevo, again.

They met in Ibiza eight years earlier. William was on a holiday with a group of boys from his college after breaking away from Phil's group, and Steven Coyle – or Stevo as he was known – was on his stag do with some friends. After the trip, they took turns visiting one another when, often, a boozy evening turned into a weekend of carnage. Although they didn't see each other all the time, it was never a surprise when one called the other for a get-together.

Willliam took a beer from the fridge and picked up his mobile to call his friend and make sure everything was on track.

"Hi, William, how are you doing? I was going to call you—"

"Great, mate. *Really* looking forward to it, and the guys are, too. I'm off Saturday, so we could head out for a few beers, seeing as it's last minute, I've booked the Radisson Blu for you for a Friday and Saturday." He hoped he sounded casual.

The room price was a good deal, and he was willing to forfeit some of his cash. It almost made him feel less guilty. Their IVF fund was perilously low, and their debts were mounting.

"Will, I'm not sure—"

PART II

"Don't be daft, pal, get yourself up on Friday afternoon. I've got this favour to ask you. You've no idea how much you'll be helping me if you can get involved with this undercover operation. I can't say too much, obviously, state secrets and all that, but I've got a really cool bit for you, mate. It's pretty exciting."

Stevo laughed. "You want me driving your police van? Strip searching? I am your man, reporting for duty."

William nervously chuckled back. *If only you knew.* "Ha, yeah, something like that."

"Okay, let me get back to you later but should be fine. I'll be in touch."

William said goodbye to his friend and ended the call, then drank his beer in one go, followed by a second. Then, a third.

Stevo told him several times how much he liked Glasgow, so getting him to visit wasn't usually a problem. William's job was interesting, and he was never short of sharing a story or two with his pals.

He was intentionally cryptic with Stevo, hoping the job would sound even more dramatic or enticing than it was. He also hoped Stevo suspected it was to drive by and check out a drinking den or have a pint in a pub they were watching but he wished it was something more exciting— letting him sit in the car during a raid or firing a gun!

With any luck, Stevo's imagination was getting away with him, but sometimes it was fun to dream.

Just as the thought passed through his mind, William's phone buzzed with a text notification and Stevo's name flashed up on the screen.

What time do you need me on Friday bud? Making some plans.

With sweaty palms, William hit the call button again.

Stevo answered laughing. "You desperate to speak to me again?"

Not wanting to confess that he didn't want to commit anything to writing, William told a lie.

"Ah yeah, I thought a call would be quicker. So yeah, mate, we've got this big undercover operation, and I just need you to make

61

a call as a civvie and say you've seen someone acting suspiciously when you get off the train." He cleared his throat, then coughed in an attempt to cover up his quivering voice. "You just say you're making an anonymous call. It'll be cool. Nobody will ask anymore," William added, fearing he was protesting too much.

"Right," Stevo began. "Won't they want to know who I am and why I'm calling? What is this job, William?" He sounded concerned.

"No, no, don't worry," he replied, in a tone of voice much higher than he anticipated. "Nah, look bud, it's more a formality than anything. We've had intel that a bad guy is going to be there, but we need to protect the person who told us. So it's not only a favour, but you're the hero, although they don't know who you are."

Even he felt impressed by the version of the truth he'd spun. "So one call, no details. You just send the cops to Central Station and go about your business."

After a few moments, Stevo sighed. "Okay, seems simple enough. What time can I organise a date for?"

William chuckled and made a noise to show he was thinking and calculating. "If you can call it about 5-ish so it's busy with people, and there's a chance it could have been anyone. So, aye, 5 pm, please, then you can pick up any bird you want."

PART II

CHAPTER 20

When Jamie Cain was visited by the head honcho and given instructions for the Slaven job, he knew there was no getting out of it.

Chick was a good-looking man known for his flashy cars, high-end clothes, and his association with McColl. He was a removal man by trade if it can be called a trade. As far as the tax man was concerned, it was a lucrative enough business that involved a lot of expenses but not so much income that he was paying more tax than he wanted to. Chick was a decision-maker, and those below knew not to question. He was tight with McColl.

"We need to get rid of him, and you need to do it. You're a bit of a pervert. They won't expect this."

"It was one time—"

"You saying no?" Chick narrowed his eyes at Jamie. "Don't fuck this up."

"No' sayin' no. I won't mess up."

"We keep your reputation intact, son. Just remember that. After what you did…"

Jamie would never forget what he did. He knew he had a lucky escape. He often thought about it and Chick's threat triggered the memory he could never suppress.

Once again, taken back to that moment.

One evening, on the night of his cousin's funeral in the Anvil Inn pub close to his home in 2012, things took a turn. His cousin had been stabbed in Bridgeton on a night out after an Old Firm game. Despite a frantic and desperate attempt to stem the blood and get him to Glasgow Royal Infirmary, he was pronounced dead in the ambulance.

One mourner, Fraser Miller, attended the funeral with his girl-friend Chantelle to whom Jamie took a shine. He trapped the girl like an animal, cornering her outside the ladies' toilets. In one hand, a half-drunk pint of lager that swilled and swished round the pint glass; the other, he used to stroke her hair as he slurred his words.

63

"Do you want a wee kiss, darlin'?" he asked, trying to steady himself.

"Eh, Fraser is waiting for me, Jamie," she said, trying to get past him.

Leaning against one wall of the corridor, he put his left arm out, blocking her back. "Aw, come on, Shell, don't be a wee tease," he slurred, lunging at her.

She turned her head to the side, avoiding his beer breath and trying to maintain a distance.

"Let me by." She looked him dead in the eye and tried to push his arm down.

"Shell, babe. Just one wee kiss. You've been driving me mad all night." He kissed her neck, and she shoved him away.

"Don't. Come on. What's wrong with you?"

Jamie lunged at her, ignoring the fear in her eyes. He took a step forward, pushing himself against her, the cold glass pressed into her shoulder and neck. He stood over her with a hand on the wall above her head, stopping her from moving.

"Jamie, move out my way. I don't want to," she told him and lifted her hands in front of her face to stop the drunken man in front of her, planting his drooling lips on her face.

He could feel her heart race and knew she couldn't move.

In the distance was the sound of jeering and music and the drunks. Jamie unbuttoned the top button on her blouse and slid a hand down her body to the hem of her skirt.

She kept her head down as tears slowly dripped from her eyes.

"Shell…" He unbuttoned his trousers and grabbed her hand, gripping it tight.

She let out a gasp, and he put his pint glass to her mouth, silencing her.

"Shell?" Fraser appeared in the corridor behind Jamie. "What the…" His eyes grew wide. "Jamie, get the fuck off her," he shouted, spraying phlegm.

He grabbed Jamie's left shoulder, spinning him round – the glass shattered as it hit the wall behind.

PART II

The men scuffled from side to side as others came in from the bar area.

Fraser shoved Jamie to one side, exposing his unbuttoned trousers, and Chantelle looked dishevelled and scared.

"You are a pervert and a scumbag," Fraser said, pointing directly into Jamie's face and taking his girlfriend under his arm.

The pub fell silent as the couple left.

Jamie always denied that he was up to no good and maintained that the girl had led him on. It was acceptable to be violent, but not towards women.

In the years that followed, Jamie did what he could to prove himself good enough of being gang-worthy. He was utilised for small jobs, and he knew he wasn't respected – always seen as "the creepy guy."

"I mean it." Chick's words interrupted his thoughts. "You're a dead man otherwise. You'll have someone with you but learn how to shoot a fucking gun."

"Wit? I can," Jamie shot back, feeling his voice shaking slightly.

"Don't get wide. We know you like a bit of skirt; this is a man's game." Jamie noticed his clenched fists.

"Right, fine. I'm just saying, I'll do it right."

Jamie knew his creepy reputation made him the choice for this hit. He was a sleaze who wasn't trusted. Nobody would suspect him.

MURDER CENTRAL

CHAPTER 21

Within a few days, Jamie got a chap at his door. He opened it to find associate Martin Cole in his driveway, leaning against the bonnet of his red BMW. Fog hung in the air, lingering at the street light and a faint smell of smoke as though someone was having a bonfire nearby. There was tension between the men, and Jamie knew why Martin was there. Maybe knowing the plan would put him at ease? He hadn't slept properly since he learned what was expected of him.

"Hi, mate. You alright?" Martin stood up and put his hands in his pockets.

"Good aye, you been at the gym?" Jamie was desperate to talk about something other than what he had to.

"Nah, you know me. Shorts every day. Cold is for wimps." He laughed with a playful punch on Jamie's shoulder.

Jamie laughed nervously, but before he could think of anything else, Martin moved to stand closer. He felt Martin's breath on the side of his head when he whispered in his ear, "Friday, it's happenin'. Me, you and Barry Harris, maximum impact. Mark Deacon will drive, and we'll get it done, okay? Enough messing about. This is it, right?" Taking a step back he held his hands together under his chin as though holding a gun.

"Just like that? What about planning? We're fucking killing him, not taking him to Disney." Jamie said, putting his hands on his hips.

"Keep your voice down!" Martin hissed. "There's nothing to talk about. Don't overthink it. Chick wants this done and will come by tomorrow to brief you. But you turn up and shoot the prick. Job done. We can do this." He smacked his hands off one another as though wiping them. "Right pal, see you later."

The gangster lifted a hand in a wave-like gesture and then drove off.

Jamie considered getting in his car and driving off, but he'd get caught. He knew he would. Instead, he entered his house, took a bottle of Jack Daniels from the kitchen, and made his way to his

PART II

room.

I'll change their mind about me, he thought. *Old memories will be replaced soon.*

"Is that you, Jamie?" came his mum's voice from her room. "Who was that outside?"

Sighing, he cleared his throat. "Aye, ma, it's me. Just going to bed. It was just a pal droppin' something off. Night."

"Okay, son. See you in the morning," came the reply from over his dad's snoring.

Jamie cursed the man he blamed for his lifestyle. The "no good waste of space" as his mother called him over the years. With anger burning inside him he couldn't help but think if he had a different upbringing he wouldn't have this impossible task laid on him.

He often wondered what that would have been like, while remembering what his childhood did to him.

Jamie was part of McColl's gang through his family connections, not through choice like the others. His alcoholic, cowardly dad bullied Jamie into a life of crime from an early age. The only control Archie Cain had was using his fist and sharp tongue against his long-suffering wife. A boss in his own home in a marriage of inconvenience to both. Memories that plagued Jamie.

Young Jamie watched the relationship develop over the years. The sly, alcohol-fuelled slaps and partially muffled screaming matches developed into full riots and scenes of violence with fisticuffs on both sides. His father's seemingly over-the-top hand gestures, which just so happened to crash into his wife's eye, head, and arm or back time after time, graduated from an infrequent bruise or scrape to cuts, gouges, and scars.

What was etched into Jamie's memories was being the drug mule to repay debts his father had racked up. He had vivid recollections of playing with another boy from school after Beavers every once in a while. He was sent off for the evening with a packet of buttons, a can of Irn Bru for himself, and a special thank you package for his friend's daddy, who made them chicken dippers and potato faces for dinner. He had been part of a criminal empire since primary school, and didn't think there was ever any other career path.

The gradual escalation of violence towards Jamie's mother sparked a hatred for his father. When he worked, he earned a wage that provided a comfortable life. But it ran out too quickly. It was never long before his dad had stormed off a job, been sacked, or announced the boss was "a jumped up wee prick," or he decided it wasn't for him in one of his many drunken stupors. Each led to money borrowed and owed, promises to repay were made and always with interest added.

Occasionally, Jamie was drafted to "lend a hand" to Uncle Jack, who gave him a bung and passed on some of his treasures to his nephew. Jack was connected to McColl which opened the door for Jamie.

Usually, he managed to get his hands on some of the designer gear. Nobody knew how he did this or where it came from, but Jamie got new clothes. His mother knew better than to ask questions, and his father was just pleased it took the responsibility of providing for his son away from him.

As a child, the role of his uncle's apprentice seemed exciting before he knew what he was doing. His early teen years were particularly difficult when he was a pawn in their warped world. *Why can't I just get a normal job?*, he often thought when Uncle Jack expected him to make deliveries on his mountain bike. He was in fact working for the McColl family.

When he did, he got a can of Tennent's Super Lager and a tenner, but most importantly, the kudos of the adults and the reassurance that his dad would be in a better mood. If he didn't complete the task or, worse, tried to back out, his uncle riled his father up so much his fists were bruised from punching doors and walls as a warmup before laying into his weary wife. Occasionally, Jamie fought him off her, and the men scuffled instead. That was life.

At fifteen, when most kids played football and, at worst, smoked in the park, Jamie watched his dad slap his mum. The anger he felt for his father started to manifest itself as an ugly, heavy aggression that lingered. Permanently.

PART II

***

The next day, Chick passed by Jamie's house with details of the gangster's plans. Chick had it on good authority that Slaven would be on the fifth floor of the car park and that he would be an easy target. He told Jamie that another of their gang, Mark Deacon, would pick everyone up who had been especially selected to carry out the hit. Along with Jamie and Mark, Barry Harris had also been chosen. Barry was young and Mark had some experience but neither were far enough up the food chain to be considered real threats by the other side.

"I'd love to take that smug prick out but the cops know I hate him." Chick cracked his knuckles and pursed his lips just talking about Slaven. Jamie could feel the anger radiating from him.

"Be ready sharp, Deacon can't be seen hanging about anywhere", Chick growled. Jamie nodded, hoping he looked more confident than he felt.

Jamie knew what Josh Slaven was capable of and how high the stakes were. But easy and target were not words associated with this gangster.

What use would protesting do? I'm not getting out of this now.

He was in deep and could do nothing except rely on everything going to plan. He talked himself into believing their actions were not as bad as first thought.

Jamie didn't think about it as murdering a father and husband; this was taking down an evil, vicious bully who had escaped justice for the awful things he had done.

69

CHAPTER 22

With three days to go until plans were to be executed, William and Michelle worked on shift with Davie and Paul.

As William made his excuses to step outside, pretending to need to make a private phone call, he stared hard at Davie, who took the hint and followed him outside with his vape as an excuse.

Davie drew in a deep breath and exhaled, sending a sickly sweet berry flavour into the air. It combed William's nostril hairs, forcing a sneeze from him. There was a clear height difference, but Davie commanded his bullish stance even with his smaller mass.

Before the men exchanged, William heard a voice coming from between two parked cars on the road behind them.

"Yes, fine. Okay. Right…right I have to go now." William turned to see Mel ending a call and walking towards the front door. She stopped in her tracks when she saw him and Davie at the front door.

"Mel? Everything alright babe?" Davie's brows were furrowed.

"Yes, of course. I, eh, I was just on the phone to my mum." William glanced at his colleague who took another inhale from his vape and sent it into the air. His eyes fixed on his partner.

"Okay, wh-"

"Sorry, need to get on babe. See you later." Mel walked past the men, touching Davie's left bicep gently and nodding at William.

He looked at Davie, unsure what he had witnessed and not wanting to dwell on it. His mind was on other matters. Breaking the silence he ignored the awkward exchange he had just seen.

"We're on for Friday, I've called in a favour from a friend, and we just need to act normal now." William moved his weight from foot to foot with his back to the entranceway of the station.

Davie took another draw of his vape and turned to the door to keep an eye on who was coming in and out, or might be listening.

"Which friend?" Davie mumbled, staring ahead.

William sighed, desperate not to weave round any more

PART II

obstacles than he needed to, but he realised why he was asking.

"You tell that wee Manc prick to keep his hands to himself. You hear? He had his fun with Mel, but she's with me." He prodded himself on the chest with his thumbs. "If he doesn't, you will deal with me, and we're already on shaky ground."

Davie leaned forward delivering a sharp prod to William's abdomen. He winced, and a wave of panic crashed over him, a feeling he was starting to notice was a daily occurrence.

He was almost home and free.

Why is he making this more difficult? He's getting paid? Maybe they're in a bad place, they didn't seem happy?

In truth, William had forgotten all about Stevo's dalliance with Melanie last year until that moment. He thought it was just a weekend of wild sex, not that they'd kept in touch. It dawned on him this was likely the Friday date Stevo had planned.

"I'll tell him, aye, don't worry. But mate, he's going to do what we need, then we'll both be quids in."

Davie punched him on the arm playfully but with more force than William expected, and walked back inside, leaving a plume of vapour.

William's shift passed without incident, making it feel like time was standing still.

There was a call scheduled with Phil after work. As William walked to the staff room door, he took his phone out and found Sarah's name from the recently called list. He tapped her name and listened to the ringing tone.

"Hi, you okay?" she asked, the sound of clinking and banging from their kitchen in the background.

"Yeah, long day. I'm going to go for a run and clear my head before I call it a night. I'll see you when I get home?"

"That's fine. Don't overdo it, see you when you're in." Sarah's voice was chipper and warm.

"I won't. See you soon." William's insides felt tight with guilt as he ended the call.

Before he could overthink what he was doing, he placed his

phone and bag in his locker again. He stuffed the other phone he needed into his hoodie pocket and made off out of the police station, walking along Queen Elizabeth Gardens and on to Ballater Place, then Ballater Street, where he broke into a jog, crossing at the traffic lights and turning left onto McNeil Street.

Crossing the River Clyde over the St Andrew's suspension bridge and into Glasgow Green, less than a mile from where the action would take place on Friday night.

Dusk was falling, and the off-duty officer caught his breath. He pulled the burner phone from his pocket, and turned it on. As though rooted to the ground, William stood still, holding it in his right palm and resting his left hand on the back of his neck, counting down the minutes until the phone rang.

Six minutes and twenty-seven seconds.

With sweaty hands, it took three tries to swipe the screen and answer. "Hi?" William said with a dry mouth as though unsure what he expected to hear from the other side.

"Everything better be in place. Do not fuck this up, Billy, it isn't difficult. Be there. Get Tonner in the bag."

William nodded frantically as though standing in front of Phil. For all they were the same height at just over six feet, Phil seemed taller. His stance was naturally intimidating; he instilled fear by doing very little. But if he took aim, he rarely missed. And he made it count.

For a split second, William found himself full of adrenaline. Excited about the illicit plan to trap this gangster, he felt important and powerful. As the intensity of the exhilaration rippled through him, it suddenly drained again and a sickening unease replaced it.

"Got it. It's in the bag."

William jogged round the park once to expel some of the nervous energy, then retraced his steps back to the station, where he picked up his belongings and drove home.

From the smell coming from the kitchen, Sarah was already cooking when he got in. He felt more relaxed than he had in a while. She smiled when he came through the door. The sight elicited instant guilt. Giving her a kiss on the lips, he wrapped his arms around her, but before she could say anything, he gestured up the stairs to their room and said, "Shower!"

Rinsing the soap from his hair, William washed, then suddenly realised he hadn't told Sarah about his plan to have a night out with Stevo on Saturday. She liked his friend and would probably ask why he wasn't staying at their house. If he told her Stevo was staying at a hotel she might assume there was something to worry about, especially after last time.

William had been with Sarah for six years and truly couldn't imagine being with anyone else. But he had been propositioned when he found himself in the room of another female officer with an ulterior motive. While he didn't accept, he was slow to reject her – and on the same night Sarah ended up going to hospital miscarrying their second pregnancy.

They had gotten past his misdemeanour but he felt as though he had cheated and still carried the guilt with him.

Maybe I shouldn't mention Stevo and just call it a night out.

His thoughts reminded him to call Mikey and Tom. With it still on his mind, he pulled out his phone and opened the "Ladzzz" group chat on WhatsApp.

Hi guys, last minute plans but Stevo is in town on Saturday night if you're up for a night out? Nothing wild, few pints and maybe game of pool? Guys only, he'd love to see you.

Plugging the phone in to charge on the bedside cabinet, he left the bedroom to join Sarah for dinner. William had some making up to do and needed to show her some attention.

By the time they went to bed, he had replies from both friends.

Mikey sent a pint emoji with the message:

Sounds good will join for a few.

Tom was already booked out for the night with work people but said,

Will try and come by if I can.

***

MURDER CENTRAL

William's shift the day before the plan was to be carried out took him to court to give evidence. He always treated the process with respect. He didn't know if it was guilt or excitement, but his heart rate skyrocketed as he walked into the High Court on Glasgow's Saltmarket. All at once, he questioned his decision-making abilities given what he had agreed to do in just over twenty-four hours.

What if I get caught? What if Davie reports me? He'd find himself in the dock.

William took himself to the closest toilet in the building to splash his face and calm himself down. There was no way he could give evidence at a trial where three men were on trial for dealing drugs when he was going to be committing a crime.

I'm part of a conspiracy. I am actually accepting a bribe. And I'm paying someone – is that extortion?

William took several deep breaths.

No, this is for the greater good, the public interest, he told himself.

He did not want to bring any children into a world where people like Daniel Tonner were about.

William straightened his uniform, took another deep breath, then made his way to the witness area.

***

As William later climbed into bed, for the last time before life as he knew it would change, he tried to distract himself and think of things that made him happy. And just as the night he was targeted in the street by Phil and told about this mission, he couldn't hug Sarah for fear she'd feel his thumping heart; that same fear resurfaced. He needed to feel her touch on his. Her soft skin and gentle smile comforted him.

She was already drifting to sleep when he slipped between the sheets and slotted his legs between hers, pulling her close into him and resting her back against his chest.

He tucked her hair behind her left ear and ran a hand from her soft earlobe on the side of her face, tracing her jawline, clavicle, onto

PART II

her shoulder and down her arm to her fingertips. William's fingers wove between hers, and he rested their clasped hands on her hip.

Sarah had fallen into a deep sleep, her breaths soft. Her body slowly and rhythmically rose and fell, she was peaceful.

William mimicked her breathing with his slow, deep breaths until he drifted off.

MURDER CENTRAL

CHAPTER 23

William jolted awake as the door slammed when Sarah left for work at 8.30 am. Looking over to the clock, he came to, realising she was away and he was left with his thoughts.

He had wanted to get up at the same time as his wife, make her a cup of tea, and check on her. She was on a phased return after being signed off when she had the third miscarriage. They were now four months on, and following a myriad of health issues, she was almost back full-time.

She doesn't deserve all of this.

William thought about Sarah arriving at the Royal Bank of Scotland for her shift. She had been with the bank since leaving school. William always reminded her that loyalty was unwavering, and they knew that.

The branch in Milngavie opened at 9.30 am, but he knew Sarah liked to be in early to have a coffee and catch up with her friend before dealing with the public. This comforted William, knowing she had someone to confide in.

He hadn't stirred when she left the room.

Did she see the damp bed sheets when she kissed me goodbye, as she always does?

A fresh panic washed over William as the toll of the pressure on him started to show. He had awoken bathed in sweat and with fear in the pit of his stomach realising what day it was.

William had dreamt of everything going to plan, until it wasn't; ideally Tonner will be arrested with drugs and an arsenal of weapons, he will be first police officer on the scene when the call comes in, seeing the gangster led away in cuffs. He will be the hero.

In the dream however, he then gave Davie his cut and put the rest of the money in the pot for IVF. But as they drove Tonner to the police office and took him from the van, he morphed into William's eighteen-year-old self, who ran from the crime scene where Phil took the hit for his crimes. William panicked as he watched

76

PART II

his younger self break down in tears and age before his eyes into the man – the corrupt police officer – he was going to be as of that night. Dread kicked him in the gut. He still had to make it happen, and there was a lot at stake.

Groaning, William got himself ready to start his shift at 2 pm. The plan was to do paperwork for a couple of hours before patrolling. Then, they were likely to be nearby to answer the control room call. It would surely work; it had to. Davie and Paul were on the same shift, so they would be around to deal with other business.

William showered and lounged around the house, replaying how he wanted the evening to go.

Patrol the area, respond first to the call, prevent the car leaving, and track down Tonner.

He thought about the steps to take – over and over.

The rest should take care of itself. It has to work.

William checked his watch at 10 am and watched a few episodes of Suits on Netflix to distract himself. Then packed his sandwich, apple, and a can of Irn-Bru. A typical morning, sticking to routine.

***

As William drove the four miles to work, reality hit him.

Will this be the last time I take this journey? Will I get caught and lose it all? What will Phil do to me if it goes wrong?

He pushed the thoughts out of his head. It would all work; Phil wouldn't have any reason to come after him.

When William reached John Knox Street and passed the Drygate pub, he pulled into the side of the road, swerving onto the kerb. The car behind let out a honk as his car suddenly veered. Turning his Bluetooth off, William held the phone to his ear, making sure no one overheard their conversation. Stevo would be on the train to Glasgow, but hopefully, the call would connect.

"Hey mate, can you hear me?" Stevo answered, clearly on a bustling, jolting train.

"Yeah, I can hear you, mate. You on the shots yet?" William

joked but suddenly realised he didn't want him too drunk. Loose-lipped was good, but slurring his words, his call wouldn't be taken seriously. "All good, coffee for now. Need a clear head for my big cameo later."

His mancunian friend had no idea how much was riding on this. "I'll be in my hotel for about 4.30 pm. I'll have a shower and probably a pint then I'll head to the bar and call?"

William didn't want to sound too serious or worried, but he couldn't take any chances. Sitting at the side of the road, he closed his eyes for a second, praying to a God he didn't believe in that he wasn't pushing his friend too far. But he tried anyway.

"See, just for the sake of completeness and, you know, just making sure we've covered everything, can you make sure you're in view of the car park entrance at Central, please? Just for the call, please? Then go get a few pints on me!"

The aim was to sound cool but convincing. Holding his breath until he got an answer, which came after only a few seconds but felt much longer.

"Yeah, sure. Everything okay, William? I'm not going to find myself on the wrong end of a fist, am I? I'm too pretty to get punched." Stevo laughed but it was clear he was concerned.

That was the final push, and bribery would hopefully sort it.

"Nah mate, all good. Look, you're tee-ing me up to catch a bad guy, but nobody knows it's you or will ever know, so all good. With-hold your number. We get phone-ins all the time. A twenty-second call and it's a white Audi you're reporting then walk across the road to the pub, and you are done. Sound like a plan?"

As a gaggle of giggling women in the background of the train interrupted their conversation, William heard his friend laughing. "Sounds like you've got good company where you are!"

"I do, but I've got plans later, bud. That wee Hot Scot, what's her name again?"

William closed his eyes and mouthed "shit". He almost for-got Davie warned Stevo off. He didn't want to piss on his parade, and anyway, Melanie was a big girl. He decided to issue a friendly

PART II

warning instead. "Ah, Stevo." He laughed. "You don't change. Mel is with wee Davie. Half your height but can throw a punch. And you *are* too pretty, so just be warned."

Stevo exhaled loudly. "Wee minx, she never told me that. Okay, well, dinner never hurt anybody, did it?"

Although they were speaking on the phone, William could tell his friend was grinning.

He continued, "And if she doesn't show, I'll get on Tinder for a Scottish bird who appreciates my good looks and sense of humour."

Despite his nerves, William couldn't help but laugh at his friend's easy-going attitude, which made him grateful for Sarah. The thought of trawling dating apps or scouring bars for women didn't appeal to him. Now, just to keep his nerves in check for a few hours.

"Okay, mate, I'm just at work. Do me proud, enjoy your night, and I'll phone you later. Remember, a white Audi, suspicious behaviour, and you feel intimidated. Use the word *intimidated*. Good luck."

The call was ended before Stevo could ask more questions and William immediately turned his phone off. He couldn't deal with the stress of checking it every ten minutes. He hadn't looked at the phone Phil had given him either. William wanted as much distance as possible between him and what would happen.

His mind wandered back to the last trip he had taken down to see his friend south of the border. Along with Mikey and Tom – his friends from the Ibiza trip – they travelled down for a long weekend. As it seemed to be normal for them, they met another stag do on the train, and joined in with their drinking games. By the time they got off at Manchester Piccadilly, William had a garland round his neck, Tom had a fake sleeve tattoo he had been dared to keep on for the weekend, and Mikey barely knew his name after a few too many tequila shots.

The memory almost made him emotional, and his eyes stung slightly. William valued Stevo's friendship.

One day we'll laugh about this as "the time they went undercover."

79

MURDER CENTRAL

***

With sweaty palms and a dry mouth, the officer strode into the station as Davie and his partner Paul Shaw headed out on patrol.

Paul nodded and smiled as he passed. He had a reputation for being good looking and a nice person, highlighted further by his partner's attitude.

With a menacing grin on his face, Davie met William's gaze as if he knew what William was thinking. By the following day, they shouldn't need to deal with this anymore, and it would all be over.

PART II

CHAPTER 24

With shaking hands, William logged off his computer at 4.15 pm, too tense to concentrate even though he knew nothing would happen for another forty-five minutes. He glanced at his Fitbit as his heartbeat crept to 145 bpm.

Is this adrenaline or just pure unadulterated fear?

On his suggestion, he and Michelle left the station.

As they drove along Templeton Street beside Glasgow Green, they saw a group of teenagers with brightly coloured fluid in a glass bottle.

"Neds with bottles of Mad Dog," Michelle pointed out.

His heart rate began to increase again. This was not what he needed. William pulled into the side of the road mouthing, *Fuck's sake, Michelle.*

Come on, boys, he thought, *give me a break.*

The officers put their hats on as they sauntered towards the group, who made no attempt to conceal their bottles. The most brazen of the group, wearing a royal blue tracksuit, smiled and shouted, "Alright," as William was a matter of feet away.

"Where have you been, lads?" William wasn't even sure if they were paying attention to the two uniformed officers walking towards them. "What are you drinking?"

Another boy in a red tracksuit hit back with "Ribena," sending them all into fits of drunken laughter.

Michelle walked straight to him and removed the bottle from his clutches. "You can't drink in the street or park. Hand it over."

She looked surprised when the boy, who couldn't have been older than fifteen took a final swig and handed her the bottle. The three others did the same and ran off before William and Michelle could do anything, each shouting "Laters," "bye officers," and other inaudible phrases as they laughed, happy they'd gotten away with it.

Michelle turned to him, seemingly confused by his lack of engagement. "I thought you'd have said something."

He shrugged. "Just kids, aren't they? And they were no bother."

William was not wrong, but it wasn't like him. He liked to try and do good, make an impression, and change the world.

They threw the bottles in a nearby bin and wandered back to the car a few paces away. William checked his watch and drove back to the Gorbals and parked at Crown Street without a word.

Michelle left him sitting in the car when she went for a snack and a drink at the Co-Op across the road. When he checked his watch at 4.47 pm, he needed her to be back in the car before the call came in.

At 4.52 pm, he thought his head would explode with the tension. His heart raced. His palms were sweatier than he'd ever experienced.

Come on, Michelle.

He drummed his fingers on the steering wheel. "Come on to fuck and get back in the car," he muttered, then spotted her in the wing mirror walking back to the car.

At that moment, a voice came through the police radio. "Any available call sign to attend NCP at Oswald Street immediately regarding a firearms incident. Suspects have fled the scene. ARV has been authorised to carry out a search of the area."

For a few seconds, time slowed down; the voice coming through his radio was in slow motion. "Firearms incident."

The words echoed in his mind. This wasn't what Stevo was phoning in.

Was he shot? This was not the plan.

He gestured to his radio when Michelle got in the passenger side, and they heard, "Firearms incident" again.

She nodded back at him. "This is not a routine control room call", he muttered, preparing to drive off. "It is going to be a long night".

"What the…Here we go." She groaned and hit her fist on the dashboard, saying, "Foot down, William."

He tore off to the car park, barely able to concentrate with fear. *What am I going to find? What is going to happen? Should I phone*

PART II

Sarah and tell her to go to her mum's?

Before he knew it, he was turning into the car park. He had a feeling the whole plan had gone to shit.

As soon as they drove up the entrance ramp, William saw shocked and distressed-looking people, some disorientated and others upset. As he continued on to the next level, the tension was almost tangible. The Audi that William had been told Daniel Tonner would be driving was parked as expected, but instead of police officers searching the car and arresting the man with drugs, cash, and weapons, it was surrounded by police tape.

A body was in the passenger seat with holes in the windows. It took a second to register what he was looking at, and the carnage around him was the furthest from what he expected.

Get a grip of yourself, he thought.

William saw a woman with two little girls being led across the station floor by two police women. Seeing the look on the two girls' faces, he felt a lump in his throat.

Michelle went to speak to other officers as William looked around. Just then, Davie and Paul pulled into the car park behind him, the city centre on a Friday was swarming with police. William stood for a moment, taking in the scene.

His phone vibrated as Stevo tried to call. He wanted to answer, but now was not the time. Instead he quickly punched a message into the phone and hurriedly sent.

Hi mate, how did it go??

In the bar about to go for dinner. Did the call go to plan? Stevo added a winking face emoji.

Relief flooded through William that his friend was safe. He smiled but caught himself. He couldn't be looking happy at the scene. The news that Stevo was okay meant one less problem to think about, and he'd mop up the mess with Phil later.

Yeah, great, thank you! Catch you later. He quickly typed back.

No time for pleasantries. He had work to do.

William turned to follow Michelle but Sergeant Arthur Black

83

called him over.

"Sergeant, sir…what's going on?" He wiped his forehead and shook his hands out, dispelling some nerves.

The senior officer looked up, brows furrowed, deep in thought. "Josh Slaven has been shot dead. Two gunmen made off in a Peugeot. We've got officers tracing that. Get as many statements as possible but as sensitively as possible."

William rummaged in his pocket for his notepad as the sergeant walked off. Because of the chaos around him, he couldn't decipher what was being said. William wiped a bead of sweat with the back of his hand as it trickled down his face.

Approaching a distressed-looking man William's stomach dropped; he was involved in this. He cleared his throat several times until he found his voice to ask the man what she saw.

He felt an overwhelming dread for what was to come.

William was eventually able to leave at 1 am after taking statements and making notes. His gut told him to hide in the police station instead of facing the consequences.

What if Tonner found out? Is Sarah in danger? What will Davie say when he isn't getting his money?

Thoughts raced round his mind like a hamster on a wheel. A clear question would stand out, and he'd stop and think about it, then it merged and got tangled with the others until another popped up to the surface. In the end, he didn't know the answer to any of them.

When he left the station, he drove for a while, trying to unwind and find a quiet place to stop and deal with Phil. He pulled into the car park at Asda in Govan and turned the engine off to enjoy a minute of total silence save for his own breathing and heartbeat.

He'd given his heart more of a jolt in the past week than he had in a long time. The only time he'd been more scared was hearing Sarah was in hospital when he had been on that night out and not with her.

That night they lost their baby. The overwhelming love for Sarah was the impetus for dealing with this.

PART II

CHAPTER 25

When Friday afternoon arrived, Jamie climbed into the back seat beside Barry when the car stopped abruptly. The front passenger seat was empty.

What happened to Martin? Have the plans changed?

"Where is he?" Jamie spat, sounding aggressive when, in fact, he was terrified.

They hadn't even left his street yet and things were already going wrong.

"Had to take his ma to hospital," Mark shot back, just as aggressively. "Been there since this morning and couldn't get away. He's gutted, but Joan's no well at all, and he's worried she's had a stroke, Becky's with the kids."

A silence fell between them.

Mark turned to face Jamie in the back. "So you ready, princess?" He smiled sarcastically and revved the engine. The driver then turned back to face the front, forced the car into gear and pulled away.

Jamie didn't know if what he felt was panic or exhilaration, or a mixture of both. He tapped his sweaty palms on the tops of his thighs. Time felt like it was slowing down as they weaved through traffic. He'd never set out to murder anyone before, so the sensation he experienced was new. One thing was certain: this was happening.

The very second the car turned into Oswald Street, there was an unmistakable adrenaline spike.

No turning back.

As the engine revved, the tension in the car rose to a discernible level as the men sat silently, like coiled springs.

Jamie saw Mark check his balaclava, covering his identifiable features. He held on to the door handle as they pulled into the entranceway. He watched Mark carefully reach out with his gloved hand to press the button for a ticket to allow entry to the car park and tentatively made his way up the first ramp onto the second

85

floor to not draw immediate attention to the car. Then, as though a switch was flicked, Jamie felt the car jolt as it accelerated, sending the vehicle up the remaining floors in seconds.

It screamed along the fourth floor, turning sharply onto the final ramp, and came to an abrupt halt across the platform, stopping almost nose to nose with the white Audi as expected. The Peugeot blocked the Audi in place.

The atmosphere in the car was now electric; the back doors flew open as "Go! Go!" yelled Mark, his voice echoing throughout the concrete walls.

Jamie was unable to stop himself. His legs carried him out of the car, gun in his hand. From his peripheral vision he saw Barry tumble out of the car on the other side. Seconds later, with his balaclava leaving slits for him to see, his eyes met Josh Slaven's who stared back in terror. He let out a howl Jamie knew he would never forget. Jamie then pulled the trigger. Twice.

Exhilaration pulsated through his veins so hard he thought he might drop the gun. Holding the grip with both hands, there was no time to think. At that moment, Jamie felt powerful. It was euphoric. He looked at Barry, and could tell even with his face covered he was grinning back at him. The adrenaline was palpable.

He heard Mark yell "Come on!" from the driver's seat. Jamie turned and threw himself back into the car, landing almost sideways on the front passenger seat. Barry launched himself across the back seat.

Jamie glanced across at their driver as he straightened himself into the seat. Mark had the wheel round to full lock then manoeuvred them back down the ramps. Jamie felt the speed increase again. He took a deep breath as behind him his associate shouted "WOO HOO" sounding excited.

A phone was thrust into his hand with instructions to let the boss know the job was completed.

Mission completed. They had just taken out Josh Slaven.

No going back now, he thought.

Part III - The aftermath

CHAPTER 26

William rifled in his rucksack for the burner phone then held the power button and his breath. After a moment, the phone buzzed with notifications of missed calls and a voice message.

"It's me. A new number. I need to speak to you. Text me the second you get this, and let's meet."

For a split second, William considered not replying but thought ignoring Phil was probably the worst way to handle this. Having changed out of his police uniform, he continued driving round the city for a while longer.

William found himself at Clydebank Crematorium, where he texted Phil, telling him to meet him at Strathclyde Park, then set off, clueless over what to expect.

He got there first and sat with his lights on so Phil could see him when he arrived. William felt so conflicted. Until now, he had been an upstanding member of the community, a faithful partner, a good friend. Now, he was sneaking around, using his friends, and being blackmailed by his colleague.

William pulled down the visor with the light in the passenger seat to check his hair and the bags under his eyes that stung with exhaustion. He had aged almost overnight with the stress of everything. All because he had been a coward when he was eighteen and ran away from his actions.

Headlights appeared, and the car drew up beside him. The conversation didn't go as badly as he expected, leaving him feeling just as uneasy. Phil still wanted Tonner dealt with, but with Slaven newly murdered, it would keep the police busy, and William could not afford to get deeper into this.

With a temporary reprieve from the gangster, William drove home, pausing as he pulled into the driveway at the front of his house. William stared at his reflection for a few moments. He didn't recognise the man staring back at him. It felt as though he left for work a week ago, not fourteen hours.

Picking up his bag from the passenger seat felt like lugging bricks on his back, and the steps to the front door felt like wading through mud. Getting his legs to walk up the stairs to his house was almost impossible.

Just an extra push to get upstairs and into bed, he told himself. *One, two, three steps to the front door, completed.*

William stepped inside, his body tensing as he closed the door gently using the handle.

Neville ran to his feet to greet him. William sat on the bottom step and gathered the puppy up in his arms. The dog playfully licked his face and neck as his owner hugged him close. "Thanks boy", William felt the soft fur against his cheek. "This is just what I needed".

As the young dog jumped from his lap, William pulled himself to his feet and using all the energy he had left, climbed the stairs gradually, his emotions becoming more difficult to suppress.

The house was deadly silent.

Squinting in the darkness, William entered their bedroom and felt around to find the bed. Unable to face even carrying out a nighttime routine, he stripped off, leaving his clothes in a pile, and climbed into bed.

Lying behind Sarah, her back to him, William positioned himself with a hand on her side allowing it to rise and fall with the movement of her breathing.

Without warning, his stomach tightened, and panic rose to his neck and sat in his throat. The stinging sensation in his eyes was uncontrollable, and as he closed his eyes, tears seeped out and ran down the side of his face and onto his pillow. He lay crying silently until he dozed into sleep.

It was difficult to know how long he had slept. As usual, William was awake when Sarah's alarm went off at 7.30 am. She must have forgotten to turn it off over the weekend.

His wife reached out from under the covers to silence her

phone, knocking it from the bedside cabinet. Sarah grunted but made no effort to retrieve it, instead tucking her hand back under the duvet and pulling it over her head.

William was awake having spent the night drifting in and out of sleep, wrestling with his thoughts. Each time he came to, reality kicked in. Hard.

Tonner got away, Slaven was dead, and William was implicated and agreed to accept cash to help fit someone up, even if they deserved it.

He escaped the consequences of bad choices in his teen years. Would he be so lucky again? The dreams he shared with his wife for a child were getting closer, and he might have ruined that. Ruined the future, the family they always wanted.

Fixing his eyes on his sleeping wife, he stroked her hair. He desperately wanted to give her a child. It had been in touching distance, and now he might lose everything. He needed to speak to Davie, keep him sweet and on board, and most importantly, keep him quiet.

He crept out of bed and took his phone into the ensuite, where he sent Davie a text.

Morning, fancy a coffee??

William wanted to sound casual, and if he was committing anything to writing, he wanted to sound genuine.

Looking in the mirror in the stark lighting, William could see a grey hue clung to his skin. Not yet thirty, he felt a man twenty years his senior; everything felt heavy and his body ached.

William wasn't blessed with the best head of hair, but it appeared to have receded further with more coarse greys poking through from his scalp. He had a milky complexion. Often, he pictured the blonde or red-headed babies he longed to give Sarah. Without his uniform, he'd never be picked out of a line-up as a police officer. An accountant, perhaps, an IT expert, but not an officer of the law. The same law he was breaking.

Get yourself together William, he told himself firmly.

His phone buzzed, and Stevo's name appeared with a message

with a winking emoji.

Hey bud, what time today? What a night.

His hand flew to his forehead as William remembered he had forgotten about his promise to go out later. He hoped Stevo had taken his advice or Melanie had decided not to go out while her roid-rage boyfriend was working at a murder scene across the road from her old flame.

William quickly sent a message to his friend.

Get you at Committee Room 9, that boozer at George Sq at 4?

Almost immediately after that, Davie replied:

Costa Baillieston @ 10.

There was no option but to face this and "man up," as his father always told him.

William slipped back into the bed and shuffled across to where Sarah was. He reached out for her back and traced her body until he found the joint between her arm and side, prising them apart and pushing his hand through and round her middle, pulling himself into her back and holding her tight. Her warmth kept him calm, reminding him to breathe.

Although there was no time to fall back asleep, he wanted to embrace her and take in the quiet time. Her hair, with the faint scent of coconut from her shampoo, had been scraped back into a plait. Her head on the pillow with loose strands of hair escaping after a night of tossing and turning.

Outside, he could hear a car radio blasting Ed Sheeran. Another house nearby chimed loudly when the Ring Doorbell was pushed.

William nestled his face into her neck, enjoying the warmth.

This is what it meant to be in the moment.

PART III

CHAPTER 27

William drove along the M8 motorway to junction nine towards Easterhouse, taking several deep breaths. He and Davie were meeting in a public place. William hadn't done anything wrong, and Davie would surely understand he couldn't give him money he didn't have.

For Christ's sake, he thought, *Davie was on shift with me last night, he saw himself what happened.*

Pulling off at the slip road and right onto Easterhouse Road William drove past Central Car Auctions, over the roundabout and down onto Edinburgh Road. Driving down Buchanan Street in Baillieston he passed the police station. Seeing other officers in the car park made William's stomach flip.

At the bottom of the road, he turned right onto the main street parking across from the coffee shop. Davie was sitting outside, and wearing a cotton tracksuit with his hood up – more like a coke dealer than a cop.

William parked outside Iceland, zapping the lock on his car fob as he crossed the road towards his colleague.

Davie looked concerned.

"Do you want to sit inside?" William pointed to the door.

The sky was grey, or maybe that was just a sign of what was to come, and this was a warning he should heed.

"If we must," Davie stood, then followed him in. "Black coffee, extra shot thanks," and with that, he took himself to a table at the window, looking onto the adjacent street.

William braced himself for a bollocking from Davie as he joined him at the table with drinks.

Best to prepare for the worst.

Silence fell between the men for a few minutes. Davie quietly and casually tipped three sugars into his coffee and took a sip, slurping loudly and meeting William's eyes.

Ready to burst, William spoke first in a low voice. "So last night didn't go to plan. Tonner got away. I've no idea how or what

91

happened with Slaven, and I've not had the cash yet."

He stared back at Davie, trying to decipher his mood.

"Okay," Davie said very definitively. "Not your problem... I understand."

William couldn't believe what he heard, and for a nanosecond, he thought everything would be okay.

Davie took another sip of coffee. "I still need that cash you promised, though."

William was confused. He had just heard him say Phil hadn't given him any money and had seen for himself how the night ended.

"What?" William widened his eyes. "How the fuck am I going to get you that? He didn't give me any?"

Sweat formed on his brows. *Why is he doing this?*

"Davie," he said so loudly, a couple at the table behind turned round. He modified his volume to a loud whisper. "Davie, I don't have that cash—"

"You'll find it," Davie cut in. "Look pal, your mess, your problem. The cash I want, or you'll have more to worry about than debt. My money or your job."

This has to be a bad dream. Why is he turning on me? Did Melanie leave him or something?

As though reading his mind, Davie added, "I told your pal to leave her alone. She fucking met him last night. You were warned. You disrespected me, and you haven't coughed up. Get me the cash, or I will have you done for *all* sorts."

He stood up and sunk the last of his coffee cup, exhaling loudly for effect. "Have a good day, *mate,*" Davie added, walking out of the Costa and up the street.

William could only watch, motionless.

Seconds later, William saw bright dots and became light-headed. For a moment, he thought he was going to faint.

With a degree of caution, he took himself to the toilet and sat with his head between his legs. Hardly a position of dignity for a serving officer, but appropriate for someone who conspired with a gangster, and was being extorted by a colleague. Now he had to try

PART III

and solve a murder while worrying the man who got away would find out about his plan – or kill him first.

MURDER CENTRAL

CHAPTER 28

William wiped his eyes carefully so as not to get shaving foam in them, although at least then he'd have a good excuse for looking rough.

He needed to do something to look more awake. Since being accosted by his gangland friend in the street, William had barely slept.

William pressed on and got himself ready to meet Stevo, then used the walk in the fresh air to the train station to try and wake up. He already planned a night ending in the casino so he could try and win enough to end his worries.

As he waited for the train's arrival to go into the city centre, a thought passed through his mind.

This whole thing would be over if I just stepped in front of this train. It would be quick.

Returning to reality as the train before the one he was waiting for pulled into the station, William ran his fingers through his hair. He looked around, noticing how few people were on the platform for that time on a Saturday.

His breathing quickened, and suddenly, he didn't know what to do with his hands. Thrusting them into his pockets, he walked slowly to the end of the platform.

After the initial shock and grief, everyone would get over this. Phil has too much to lose, he'd never tell. Stepping on to the tracks would end everything.

Children's laughter penetrated his dark thoughts. A man of similar age walked with twin girls, holding them by their hands. They laughed as he made silly faces at them and William's trance was over immediately. How could he possibly think of doing that to Sarah?

Stop being a selfish prat, get yourself together and sort this mess. Everything always comes out in the end. You don't want that to be the lasting memory she has of you.

Suddenly, the train doors beeped and opened in front of him,

94

PART III

and he stepped onto the train. Pressing his earbuds in the Bluetooth connection, he blasted Foo Fighters into his ears. He grappled for his phone in his pocket to turn the volume up further, and his thoughts dissolved into the noise.

When William arrived at the bar in Committee Room 9 near George Square, Stevo was waiting with a cheeky grin and pint for them both.

"Alright, lad. How are you?" He gave his friend a bear hug, slapping him affectionately on the back.

"Thanks for last night," William opened with. He wanted this part out of the way with as few questions as possible.

Stevo's eyes lit up. "No worries, did you get what you needed?"

William looked around the bar as he rubbed his neck.

"Well, bad guy isn't caught yet but appreciate your help. What did you say?"

William was, after all, curious to know. Although, it paled into insignificance, given what happened to Slaven.

"Mate, right. So I just called and said I'd seen a white Audi driving a bit recklessly. I said the behaviour was suspicious and that I was intimidated." Stevo's arms flailed in excitement, almost knocking over the drinks on the bar.

He waved a hand dismissively as if to say don't worry. "I said I'd been walking along the street and thought it was going to hit me. That's when I said just like what you told me to, that I was intimidated", he repeated again. "I said it went by and startled me so much I didn't get a regi plate, but it turned into the Central Station car park, and I was worried. So they should check it out!"

William laughed and patted his friend on the back.

"What the hell went down?" Stevo asked. "The place lit up like Christmas with flashing lights and sirens."

Sipping from his pint, William looked around again, making sure nobody nearby would hear. "So, a gangster got shot," he said, realising immediately his delivery was more matter of fact than his friend was expecting.

Stevo's eyes widened in horror. "Shot dead?" he spluttered.

95

"Someone was killed in the same place you asked me to send the cops to?"

Realising how it sounded, William instantly wanted to ease his friend's mind. "What we were working on had nothing to do with that. That was a shock to everyone. Dodgy bugger being shot at point blank range wasn't how I planned on spending my Friday night shift."

His friend didn't look convinced.

"Seriously, mate, it was a targeted attack," William said, putting a reassuring hand on Stevo's shoulder. "Bloody scary for those who saw it, but nobody else was hurt. Nothing to do with the call you made."

The last part wasn't strictly true, but it was too complicated to explain. He could see Stevo sweating with panic but drawing any connection was not a good idea. To distract him, William ordered another round of pints and steered the conversation to the next dreaded topic.

"Less about my night, you dark horse," William said, gently nudging Stevo's arm, hoping his fear wouldn't seep into his voice as he changed the subject.

Stevo's face relaxed, and a grin swept across it.

"It was a good night then?"

Laughing, Stevo winked at him. "I shouldn't kiss and tell."

Still trying to be relaxed or at least appear that way, he raised his eyebrows. "Come on, spare me the gory details but fill me in." William laughed. He was trying to get the necessary information to help him prepare for Davie coming after him after being told to make sure Mel was left alone. "Did you meet Mel?" He already knew the answer.

"Oh yes." Another smug grin took over, and Stevo was almost giggling. "What a night! She is very...athletic!"

This told William all he needed to know. He had warned his friend. He felt the segue on the subject appeared natural.

"Oh man, you better watch yourself. I told you she had a man, and he's not the type you cross," William said, shaking his head as

PART III

he sipped his pint.

Stevo looked almost proud of his efforts the night before. "Let's just say this hair of the dog is needed, mate," he said, clinking his glass against William's.

Both men took large gulps of beer before Stevo broke the silence again.

"Mel told me her and that guy Davie were casual, and he's a real arsehole to her. I think she's planning to bin him off anyway, not for me or anything, but he doesn't treat her well, she said. Sounds like a proper melt."

It wasn't the answer William wanted to hear, but realistically, he couldn't bear thinking too much about the consequences of his colleague's threat.

The men downed another couple of pints before Mikey turned up to join them for a few more.

Over the next few hours, they put the world to rights over lager, shots, and some reminiscing. They laughed until they cried and, for a few short hours, William's problems melted away. By 2 am, after a couple of hours in the casino and a few angry messages from Mikey's wife, the men parted ways.

William stumbled to the nearest kebab shop before flagging down a taxi to get home. Smelling of stale booze, with sauce down his shirt but feeling happy, he fell asleep on the couch.

A few hours later, he awoke with a start, with Sarah perched on the arm of the chair at his head, cupping a coffee and watching the news. Seeing it was only 8 am on his watch, he grunted and took himself up to bed to sleep off the hangover he could feel creeping over him.

Standing up took all his effort. His legs felt heavy, his heartbeat thumping through his head and ears. He only had a couple of hours until reality kicked in and his troubles emerged.

MURDER CENTRAL

CHAPTER 29

As a freelance reporter, April didn't always know where her job would take her. She sat at her kitchen table and pulled out her laptop to scroll through social media. Police Scotland shared a post on Facebook that Josh Slaven was shot in a car at level five of the car park and that it was being treated as murder, with a phone number for anyone who might have information. The update said there was "no wider danger to the public".

The post was shared more than 350 times. April opened another internet browser and saw coverage on other media outlets including the BBC, Daily Record and the Scottish Sun.

Word is spreading, she thought.

Forensic teams swabbed, scraped, bagged, and photographed everything possible from the scene and officers trawled CCTV for movements of the car that tore off from the scene, her police contact had told her.

Several daily newspapers had commissioned April to track down Josh Slaven's grieving family and try to speak to them. As Slaven had been gunned down and publicly executed, experience told her it was unlikely they would want to talk to anyone, let alone the press.

Death knocks were the worst job. Approaching the heartbroken and angry family of someone killed – especially one who had previously been linked to gangs and violence in the media – was never an easy task, as April knew all too well. But it was the job, and all she could do was be professional and courteous.

April went back on to social media and TikTok where tributes had already been posted by friends and family sharing pictures of Slaven holding his young son and daughter, pictures of him on his twenty-first birthday, at his mother's wedding, and a bunch of photos of him and his wife. They were childhood sweethearts who married at twenty-three after having one child at nineteen and the second the year after their wedding, April pieced together from trawling different social media accounts.

98

PART III

Knowing full well how this was going to go, April phoned her colleague and friend Joseph, the trusted photographer she often worked with. He had a flat in the city centre but didn't drive, so she often collected him and dropped him off again to and from jobs.

She rifled in her bag to make sure she had notepads and a Dictaphone. And a snack, she always had snacks. She pulled out her mobile phone and found Joseph's name in the last dialled call record, tapping the screen and hitting the speaker button to continue scrolling on her laptop until she heard him answer.

"Hi, Joe, you good to doorstep the Slavens with me? Not expecting tea and biscuits, but gets it done."

"No worries, April, just out the shower. I'll be ready in fifteen, get you at Trongate?"

She checked her watch: 10.30 am, it would work. "Great, see you then," she confirmed cheerily, ending the call and scooping up her bag.

Joseph was waiting by the Purple Cat Café across from the Trongate Steeple, with a camera bag on his back, his left hand in his jacket, and his right hand holding a roll-up cigarette. A tall, thin man, his standard attire was outdoor clothing. Gore-Tex Jacket and trousers, neck gaiter – no matter the weather – and a baseball cap.

He looked cautious as he waited, but his eyes lit up, and he smiled as she pulled up beside him, opening the door for him to get in.

"Ready to chap some gangster's door?" He laughed, teasingly.

"Let's go get a door slammed in our face," she quipped back with a smile.

They drove to Slaven's house in Springburn where cars lined the streets on both sides. The cynic in her thought this was to keep the press away.

April parked round the corner so as not to draw too much attention to them. She grabbed her bag; Joseph left his in the car but accompanied her to the door.

As they approached the house, she noticed several CCTV cameras dotted around the top of the house. At the front window, there was some bouquets, and the rumble and murmur of voices and clanging coming from an open window. They looked at each other before April stepped to the front door.

She took a breath, pressed the doorbell, and lifted the letterbox flap, letting it drop with a hard thud.

There were shouts behind the door summoning Laura Slaven before it flew open. Her expression immediately morphed from fluster to fury.

"Good morning Mrs Slaven," April started. "I'm so sorry to—"

Before she could finish her sentence, the angry, grieving wife of the dead gangster said, "Piss off," and slammed the door closed.

April turned to her colleague, who shrugged, and they returned to the car. They had made it away from a gangster's door unscathed, which they had to take as a win. Nonetheless, it was deflating when a story didn't go well.

April wanted to be the one to speak to Slaven's wife, gain her trust, and deliver an article. Her husband may have been a feared and hated gangster, but she was a widowed mother of two whose partner was publicly executed. She sighed. "Fancy a coffee?"

Joseph clipped in his seatbelt. "I thought you'd never ask."

With that, she punched the address for the nearest Costa into her satnav, and they spent the next hour putting the world right over hot drinks, swapping recipe ideas, and talking about upcoming holidays.

April dropped Joseph at his flat before heading back to her place a few miles along the road.

Just as she parked, her phone buzzed with a new message, and immediately, she could see the number wasn't saved.

Hi April, your friendly neighbourhood police officer here. If you're still after info I have a public duty to serve. Free tonight if you can be? Paul

It took a second to figure out who this stranger was and how they got her number. Until the penny dropped.

The handsome police officer from Central Station.

April laughed. It had been a while since she felt flirty and giggly.

PART III

Was that what this was, or was he just a police officer who wanted to pass on relevant information? She would never know if she didn't go.

Hey PC Paul. Always after info, sounds good. Where suits?

A few minutes later, she received Paul's response.

Bar Home at Merchant City, 7 pm. First one's on me

As she put the key in the front door of her flat she heard Oasis' *Live Forever* blasted from the living room. Walking in she saw John hanging washing and immediately felt a pang of guilt for getting excited over meeting the police officer. It was a meeting about what could be the biggest story of her career. It was a work meeting. She reminded herself it was the big story she was excited about.

"Hi. How did your job go?" he asked, looking up at her smiling.

He draped a towel over the clothes horse and came over to greet her, kissing her firmly on the lips.

"Nah, as expected, the door got slammed in our faces."

John gave her a bear hug, he was warm, and she could smell his aftershave.

"Thank you," she said, burying her head in his neck.

There was a pause, and she wasn't sure exactly what would come out.

"I've got a meeting tonight with someone who's got information about the case. Someone with inside knowledge, apparently."

John walked into the kitchen, turning back briefly to respond. "Okay, before or after dinner? I'll go see my brother when you're out, he wants advice on job-hunting apparently."

He did not know she would be meeting another man for a drink.

"Mmm, after, and I reckon we'll probably have a social glass or two, loose lips and all that." She laughed. More nervously than she wanted it to be.

***

Wearing a black skater dress, tights, and biker boots, April wanted to look trustworthy if a little dressed up. She came out of the bathroom

MURDER CENTRAL

wearing makeup, which got John's attention.

"Oh aye, who *are* you meeting?" he joked, but his faux humour struck a nerve.

April slung her bag over her shoulder and made her way to Merchant City; the fresh air on the mile-long walk would do her good.

This might be the first step towards the scoop of the year: who killed Josh Slaven?

PART III

CHAPTER 30

When April walked into the pub, Paul was waiting for her at one of the tall round tables in the middle of the room near the bar. His smile reached his eyes when he noticed her.

She felt something flutter inside her, excitement for what he could fill her in on? April told herself that was all it was.

Wearing a denim shirt and navy chinos, the officer was more casual than their last encounter, but he still carried himself with an air of authority. He shook her hand, a firm handshake, and met her eyes.

April felt a blush creeping up her face. She flustered, immediately reaching for her purse. "What are you drinking...officer?"

"Paul," he said, laughing.

"Yes, Paul," she repeated. "What's your tipple?"

He reached across, took her purse from her hand, and sat it on the table. "I told you, the first round is on me. So, wine, gin...Sambuca? He laughed again.

April joked back, matching his energy. "Well, hopefully, it's a good meeting and we can celebrate with champagne. Until then, I'll stick with a rosé wine. Large, seeing as you're buying."

He walked to the bar which gave her a chance to think rationally for a second.

Tell him you're engaged, and make it clear this is about work, she told herself. *Don't be that person. This is professional.*

Her thoughts were interrupted by a large glass with pale pink liquid plonked before her. She took a huge slug, hoping it would help her feel more at ease.

"So, you happened to be free to come and meet me tonight at short notice?" Paul asked, taking a sip of cider and wearing what she thought was a smug expression.

"I have invested a lot in this story, and if you can help, then I'm happy to work out of hours if needed."

This is my chance to mention John, she thought. *Just slip it into*

103

conversation and it takes any awkwardness away.

"And...well...I'm just fortunate I've got an understanding partner who doesn't mind me working late when I need to," She hastily added.

Paul smiled and took another drink. "Well, that is always a bonus."

She didn't know what to make of that answer. Should she ask if he had a girlfriend? He had no ring on, but that went for nothing, or did it seem too much to ask about his private life? Maybe he'd drop it into conversation when he was ready. He seemed like a decent man, and she wouldn't have been surprised if there was a Mrs Paul.

For now, to get to the matter at hand, she reminded herself.

"So, the reason we're here. Slaven, what do you know and why now?"

Paul looked around, leaned in closer to her, and said in a low voice, "I think one of my colleagues may be involved. I don't have proof, but I have a bad feeling."

April sat back, studying the serious expression on the officer's face. This could be significant information, and he was putting himself on the line sharing it. But she needed more than a feeling to go on.

"A bad feeling?" Lowering her voice midway, aware they were trying to be discreet, she asked, "I get you need instincts in your job, but can you qualify it with anything?" April tried to suppress the excitement that there could be a huge scandal to uncover.

Paul took another, bigger slug of cider and, looking ahead as though deep in thought for a moment, broke the silence with another quiet statement. "William Field has been acting *very* strange. I heard him tell someone he called a favour in and that something was happening on the same night Slaven was shot. I've no idea why. The guy seems decent, but maybe he's got some skeletons he's trying to hide. He looks like he's got the weight of the world on his shoulders just now, more stressed than I've seen him before. It all just seems too suspicious."

April noticed Paul was studying her stern expression as she tried

PART III

to process everything he said.

She stared back at him. "Are you able to find out any more information?" She hoped he could do a little more than pass this on.

"I saw…"

"What? I give you my word this is off the record and confidential, Paul."

April leaned forward onto the table. Paul sat back in his chair and looked up to the ceiling as though he was about to deliver bad news. Mirroring her posture, he leaned in and played with the beer mat in front of him.

"I saw William Field and my police partner Davie Donovan speaking all quietly outside. It might be a coincidence, but they aren't friends. I don't understand why Field would confide in him about anything?"

April raised her eyebrows in surprise and with intrigue.

This police officer, Field, is worth looking into.

Paul nodded slowly as though reading her thoughts.

"I overheard Davie calling William Field a "wee arsehole" too, so I asked him about it, but he told me to mind my own business. Then I heard PC Field having a meltdown in the toilet at the station. He sounded really upset. After seeing them speaking, I didn't want to let on to him that I heard. I've no idea if this is related or helpful, April, but something just doesn't feel right."

He rubbed his eyes vigorously, clasped his hands and rested his chin on them. Even with his brows furrowed, deep in thought and a little anxious, he still looked like a man in control.

After thirty seconds of silence, he said, "I wanted to tell you in case there is something suspicious, but I cannot have this come back to me. It would be career suicide. You know we aren't meant to speak to the press."

"Fine, okay. What can you do?" April asked, fixing her eyes on him intently. She tapped the side of a beer mat on the table, feeling he was holding something back from her.

"I'll keep an eye on Davie too. So far he's just the same wee grumpy man he always is but William Field, find out what you can.

105

And I can tell you when he is next on shift and you can do whatever it is you journalists do to dig around?"

She nodded slowly and took a big gulp of her wine, almost draining the glass.

"Okay," she replied, checking her phone. "And you can refill this while I'm at the ladies' room." She slid the glass towards him as she stood up and strode to the toilet in the far corner of the bar.

She felt her face flush as she sat in the cubicle but was pleased he'd called with potentially interesting information.

April took her phone out and opened Joseph's WhatsApp conversation.

You free tomorrow? Follow up job re Slaven.

When she returned to her seat, a fresh glass of pink wine was waiting for her, and Paul looked more relaxed than he had before.

"Large again? Are you trying to get me drunk?" she joked. Just at that, her phone vibrated loudly in her pocket with an incoming message from Joseph.

Vale. Mañana

Joseph liked to respond in Spanish, which amused her.

"That your fiancé?" Paul asked, taking note of the smile on April's face.

"No, my colleague who'll be taking on the challenge with me," she answered, getting comfortable on the tall stool.

"And no, not trying to get you drunk," he said. "Just showing my appreciation for meeting up with me and listening to my concerns. If there is something going on, I want it sorted, but nowhere near it. I do trust this won't come back to me?"

The police officer's authoritative look had faded, and he looked younger, less rugged and more boyish as worry was all over his face.

"A good journalist never reveals their sources," April replied, just as serious as the question asked.

They spent the next half hour swapping career stories, how they got into their respective jobs, and she learned he was newly single and "not on the lookout," which made her feel less guilty about their meeting. Still, there was a feeling she couldn't shake.

PART III

At 8 pm and three glasses of wine later, it was time to call it a night.

Paul was working the next day too so was heading toward Central Station, but not before offering to walk April to the station on High Street. It was only one stop up the line to get home but she decided the fresh air walking all the way would do her good.

As they stood up to leave, April wasn't sure if a hug was appropriate or if they should stick to a handshake. An hour of drinking, and they somehow felt like old pals. She didn't want any awkwardness if she tried to make one gesture and he went for another, so she waited to see what he did.

Paul slung his jacket over his broad shoulders, zipping it up, then laid a firm hand on her right shoulder. "Good to speak to you, April. Thank you for meeting me. I'm glad we met and spoke about everything. An' I'm really grateful to you for keeping me out of all of this. I'll help where I can, and I look forward to seeing what you find."

April wasn't expecting his touch to last so long, and she didn't know how to respond, so she stood awkwardly – just as she had tried to avoid.

"Thanks for confiding in me. I'll keep you updated on what I find out."

Paul moved his hand to her back and guided her in front of him towards the door.

As they parted ways April felt a sense of hope.

On her walk home April checked social media, more out of habit than anything.

Her thumb hovered over a press release issued an hour earlier by Police Scotland announcing a firearm had been found in the River Avon. Immediately she clicked on the link to read it.

Her heart beating fast, April's gut feeling was this was one of the guns used to shoot the gangster and that any weapons would be tested for DNA.

Scrolling through the announcement the police asked the public to remain vigilant and come forward with any information they

107

thought might be important.

April put her phone in her pocket and crossed her arms. Her head was sore from frowning hard.

If there's any police involvement in this, I want to get to the bottom of it.

PART III

CHAPTER 31

April juggled her bag and a tray carrying a huge scone, tea, and strong black coffee as she made her way to the table at the Asda cafe in Govan.

Joseph looked up from his book, casually keeping the table as she navigated through the busy cafe and a small toddler roaming around. Joseph smiled at her, took his glasses off, and unloaded the tray onto the table.

"According to a reliable source, William Field is working from 2 pm until 10 pm today. I don't think we can just sit outside the police station, can we?"

April smeared clotted cream on the baked good and then topped it with strawberry jam. Taking a huge bite, she looked across at her colleague. He stared back at her with a look that suggested the answer was no.

She raised her eyebrows and took another bite, expecting him to answer. "Can we, or is it too suspicious?" she asked, maintaining eye contact. April took a slug from her mug of tea.

Joseph shook his head and set his mug down firmly. "No, we cannot. Sitting outside a cop shop all day then following a car when it leaves will be very suspicious, dear. What's plan B?"

April rummaged through her bag for her mobile and sent Paul a message.

Hi, will you see Field today?

Laying her phone on her lap, April picked up her scone, ready to take another bite, when she felt a vibration and saw a message appear. Wiping her hand on her trousers, April tapped the screen to read it.

Don't think so. We're on patrol for another hour until 7 pm and haven't seen him yet. Good luck.

She let out a long sigh. There were only four hours to kill until the police officers finished their shift.

"Right, we'll go by McColl's place to see if there's any movement

109

MURDER CENTRAL

there, maybe swing past a few others in the area. Then we'll head to the Gorbals just in time for Field finishing so we don't arouse suspicion and just see if he goes anywhere other than home?"

Joseph nodded, draining his coffee mug. "Sure, sounds like a plan. Do we really think we're going to find anything significant?"

April asked with widened eyes, "Where is your sense of adventure? We can always hope. Apparently, he's a total arse, and there's something really fishy. Maybe he took a hit out on Slaven because he owed him money, or he hurt someone he knows. Stranger things have happened."

Smiling at her as she spoke enthusiastically, Joseph stood and zipped his jacket. "I bet you didn't think you'd be doing this when you left university?"

April laughed, "No, I thought I'd be reporting on community council meetings and school fayres." She slung her bag over her right shoulder. "But this is *way* more fun."

***

Over the next few hours, they drove by gangsters' houses, starting with McColl's, a few streets away from the supermarket and that of his associates. April welcomed the chance to stretch her legs before getting into the car after sitting so long in the supermarket cafe.

She was grateful she had such a good working relationship with Joseph, especially on jobs involving hours together in a car. They could talk about anything without any awkward conversation.

McColl's house was in complete darkness, not even so much as a light on – even the streetlight was out, and after fifteen minutes of sitting idly outside, they moved on. They completed a whistle-stop tour of the south of the city, ticking off three of the associates they thought might be working with William Field to secure Josh Slaven's demise.

April had no sooner pulled up on the opposite side of the wide street outside of one of McColl's men's addresses when a black Audi swung into the driveway. A hooded figure got out of the driver's

PART III

side, slammed the car door behind him and did the same to the front door of his home. The bang made April jump slightly, and she glanced at Joseph, who was watching with eyebrows raised.

She let out a short laugh. "He's in a great mood!"

April turned the engine off to kill the lights in the car. There were three stops they had to make, three guys linked to McColl. Each was known for anything from bullying to serious assault and a few punch-ups in between convictions. They had each done time but not a significant stretch, and they were fiercely loyal to McColl.

"Do you think they've noticed us?" April stared across to the house.

Joseph tried to stretch, but his tall frame didn't have much room in her car. "Doubt it." He stifled a yawn. "We've been sitting in darkness for half an hour, and he looked distracted by something when he went inside."

April glanced at her watch, convinced the numbers should be further on than they were. Time was dragging with nothing going on.

Her thoughts were interrupted by the exhaust audible miles away, and the noise grew closer as a blue Golf came to an abrupt stop outside one of the houses they wanted to check out. Looking closely at the car, she nudged Joseph to state the obvious to him that this might be significant.

Seconds later, one of the men they were watching charged out of the front door and got into the back of the Golf while on his phone. The car stood still for a few moments, then began to do a three-point turn.

Does this prove anything? April thought.

Instinctively, she turned her engine on. "Let's follow them."

She looked at Joseph to confirm it was the right thing to do. Her heart rate quickened, and her mouth was suddenly drier. "We won't stop, but we'll see where they go?"

He nodded slowly, clipping his seatbelt into place. "No stopping, but we'll follow. Just take your time and keep a bit of distance."

She followed the car but not too closely. It took them from the

MURDER CENTRAL

house they were staking out, to one a mile and a half away. Another man they didn't recognise got out of that house and into the car, which remained parked across the driveway.

April drove past, turning into the next available street. She breathed a sigh of relief that there had been no interaction.

"This could mean anything." Joseph prepared a roll-up cigarette.

Leaning her head on the driver's window, she glanced at him. "I know, if it's significant, then it's certainly not obvious. I'll try and find out if any connections to McColl live at the house they've stopped at."

Joseph shrugged and nodded at her words, concentrating on the paper and tobacco in his hands. When he finished he shot her a sympathetic look. They weren't uncovering anything revelatory.

Sighing, she started driving again, making sure not to drive back past the house the Golf stopped at.

"Right, let's head to this police station and see if Field offers us anything obvious."

Panic swelled in April's throat when she saw a Golf behind her flashing at her moments later. "No…" she said, unable to hide her fear.

It flashed a second time then she realised she didn't have her lights on. Turning the dial to turn them back on, embarrassed she had been too caught up in the drama to notice.

Laughing with relief, she tapped the button to activate her hazard lights for a moment, signalling her thanks to the car behind, realising it was different from the one they had followed.

They pulled up on Cumberland Street, parking parallel to the entrance. It was a busy enough area with cars coming and going, so they hoped it wouldn't seem too suspicious or draw attention to themselves. There was less than half an hour to go until they expected their subject to leave; time appeared to go backwards.

In the remaining few minutes until they expected to see Field, the tension began to build. The adrenaline pumped, and April wiped her palms on her trousers. They were a little moist at the prospect of uncovering something significant that could help lead to the cause

112

PART III

of Slaven's death.

Joseph's watch beeped twice, alerting them that it was 10 pm.

They watched the front door of the police station silently, willing something to happen.

April checked her phone again; Paul had sent her a few Facebook pictures of William Field earlier so she knew who to look out for. She had committed them to memory but wanted a last-minute check.

A few minutes later, two male officers emerged from the building, but it was obvious neither was the man they were waiting on.

Almost immediately afterwards, Paul left the building. He looked around the street before crossing, but April couldn't be sure if he didn't see her or simply didn't let on, certain he looked directly at her. She watched him as he remained impassive and walked to a black BMW parked near the door to the police station.

April picked up a water bottle but threw it in the back seat, realising it was empty, then drummed her fingers on the steering wheel.

Joseph opened the passenger door, throwing his legs outside, but remained seated. "I need to stretch. I'm not cut out for sitting in a car all day."

April, scared to get out in case it drew attention to the car, put her seat back instead to allow her much shorter legs to stretch out. She heard the crushing of empty bottles and paper cups accumulated from their many hours of work. She sighed loudly.

"This is normal, right?"

April rubbed her eyes hard, not caring if she smudged her mascara. She manoeuvred her seat back to the regular position and pressed her forehead on the window.

"Paperwork and stuff. Must take a while, and they can't just walk away," she said, answering her question.

Moments later, a man and woman came into sight, walking out. April recognised PC Field's face instantly. Without thinking, she grabbed Joseph's sleeve to get his attention.

The photographer moved his legs back into the car and turned to face the police officer, leaving the door open so as not to startle

113

anyone as April whispered, "Shush."

They watched as PC Field said goodbye to his colleague and crossed the road to a car parked under the streetlight, casually throwing a rucksack on to the passenger seat, then walking round to get in the driver's side.

This is it, April thought. *Let's see what you do.*

Within thirty seconds, he pulled away from the street, driving towards Caledonia Road and off towards the M74 motorway at Polmadie. She hung back a few seconds before following on and tried to stay a few cars behind, hoping to blend in with the other motorists and praying he had other things on his mind distracting him from the journalists following behind.

It was a Friday evening in Glasgow on a busy road. It shouldn't be too suspicious. Keeping her distance, April followed the black car to the A725 cut-off at Bellshill and onto the industrial estate, where he pulled up in a quiet street and turned his engine off.

April stopped momentarily at the junction but upon seeing him stop, she pulled over on the main road with a view into the street where Field was parked. She, too, turned her engine off. April's heart rate increased rapidly being the only car in the street, but she had sight of their subject in her rear-view mirror.

"Are we too close?" All she could see was the light of a mobile phone as she squinted at her mirror, trying to get a clearer view of the police officer.

"We definitely are close." Joseph's voice sounded shaky and unsure.

Field held the phone to his ear for a few moments. April put her seat back, preparing to hide, and instructed Joseph to do the same. She watched Field rummaging around in the car, then he sat in darkness for another five minutes. Field soon drove off, and instead of turning back the way he had come he drove past April's car.

She held her breath and turned to look at Joseph leaning back in his seat. Instinct told her to do something to hide her face.

The brake light in Field's car came on, and the vehicle stopped momentarily. With Joseph horizontally in the passenger seat, she

PART III

closed her eyes and put her head on the steering wheel. Wishing she'd thrown herself back to conceal herself easier on the lowered seat as panic rose from her stomach.

What if he notices my car and saw us waiting on him?? We aren't doing anything wrong. If he is linked to Slaven's death, he might get to me before I expose him. April's thoughts ran wild.

She stared at her hands under the steering wheel. After what felt like ten minutes, April lifted her head. Her mind was so busy wandering she picked off her gel nail polish. She didn't notice until Joseph said her name that Field had driven off. There was nothing concrete to go on, but something didn't feel right about this.

April pulled her phone out and texted Paul.

Bellshill industrial estate, made a call then drove off.

As April drove Joseph home, they sat in silence. It wasn't awkward, but she was exhausted and just wanted to get home.

When she did get in, John was dozing on the sofa to the sound of Opal Hunters. April nestled beside him, underneath the blanket on the two-seater sofa, causing him to stir.

"How did it go?" he murmured, lifting his arm and enveloping her underneath without opening his eyes.

It took a second to feel his warmth and listen to his deep breaths as he fell back into a slumber.

April felt her phone vibrate, it was a response from Paul.

Will see what I can find out more tomorrow, thnx for heads up

"I'll tell you about it tomorrow", April murmured.

Where is all of this going to lead us? She sighed loudly. Surely nobody saw us tonight. It will be okay, April reassured herself.

115

CHAPTER 32

April shoved the last Pringles into her mouth as she pressed the remote control to tell Netflix she was still watching Modern Family. As she leaned over to put the empty tube on the floor, she saw Paul's name flash on her phone.

Finally! she thought.

It had been almost a week since he'd contacted her. He read the last message she'd sent, following her mission at the Gorbals police station, asking how things were at work. She huffed as she swiped her screen to read the message; her eyes widened in shock at the words.

In hospital, got attacked after work, knocked out and a few broken bones but alive. Best lying low for a while.

April immediately panicked; her hand flew to her mouth as she let out a groan. She couldn't help but think this was a response to her passing to Paul what she had seen at the industrial estate.

Surely, Field must be behind this?

If he was connected to the Slaven attack or the McColl's in any way, she didn't want anyone else getting hurt as a result, and she certainly didn't want that coming back to her.

For now, they had nothing else to go on. She'd have to sit tight and hope the police caught whoever was responsible before revenge attacks.

Typing as fast as she could while Paul still showed online, she texted him:

Was this because I saw PC Field making a call?

The message was read straight away, and he began typing but stopped again and disappeared offline.

April couldn't put Paul out of her mind. With everything she did, her thoughts drifted back to his message.

She tossed and turned that night, seeing every hour on the clock.

As she woke to the sound of her alarm at 8 am, April realised she

PART III

must have dozed off at some point. Dragging herself to the kitchen on autopilot, she flicked the switch on the kettle and made a large, strong coffee. She was commissioned to carry out a door knock by several newspapers in Fife: a woman was suing her employer for sex discrimination.

April repeatedly checked to see if Paul had replied or was online, but there was a deadly silence. She hardly knew him and yet felt strangely protective after hearing he was hurt.

During the interview, April put all of her worries to the back of her mind and afterwards found a Wetherspoons pub with WIFI to transcribe and file her copy as quickly as possible.

Something in the pit of her stomach made her feel anxious, but she suppressed it until the drive home. Finishing an article and hearing that it was time to clock off and drive home was always a good feeling.

Before she set off, she checked her phone again and saw a message had arrived five minutes earlier.

Forget about everything just now

April read it, and threw the phone across the car; it hit the passenger seat door and fell into the footwell.

Pulling away from the car park, April repeated the message in her head. It was blunt and vague, crushing any hopes of them uncovering potential police corruption.

Field didn't look like he had it in him to attack another officer. Maybe he had McColl's mob do something to act as a warning shot.

Did someone see my car? Surely not, or I'd have known about it by now.

April's eyes glanced down at the speedometer as it slowly crept up. Realising she'd driven a few miles without paying attention, April checked herself.

I'll worry about this when I'm home.

She turned up the volume on the radio and focused on the drive home.

Do not think about Paul.

117

CHAPTER 33

William could see that it took every ounce of energy for Paul to shift into a comfortable position in his hospital bed. He watched as the injured officer with his bashed face and broken bones tried to manoeuvre himself.

William was at the Royal Infirmary hospital for the second time that day after being chased away earlier by nurses who said Paul needed to sleep.

"This is very important." He protested when he returned with Michelle.

"We need to speak to him as soon as possible to find out what happened and who did this to him." The nurse didn't look pleased but allowed them in. After hearing Paul was attacked outside the police station the night before, the boss had instructed William not to return without a statement.

As he took a seat and reached for his notepad, he looked up to see Paul reach to touch his bloodied and battered nose, wincing with the pain. Resting his hands on his thighs, William saw the cuts and bruises from when Paul, he presumed, had tried to ward off the blows by his attackers.

Poised and ready to take notes he watched on as Paul sighed, nodded and told the officers what he could remember. William held his breath as his colleague spoke. Was this anything to do with Slaven's death? It might not have had anything to do with him but suddenly he found himself feeling guilty. William noted down the details as Paul relayed them.

"I finished my shift at 10 pm and was just leaving the office. I left at the same time as Davie Donovan. I watched him get into his car and drive off, and it was then I felt a thud on my back, which knocked me forward onto my knees. There was a person in front of me dressed in black with a balaclava, and he hit me on the head, hard, with something heavy."

William's head snapped up when he heard Paul stop talking.

PART III

His breathing was laboured. "Are you okay, mate?" he sat forward putting a hand on Paul's shoulder. A wave of panic washed over William. The injured officer nodded back at him and rubbed his face. After a couple of seconds Paul nodded at William again. Taking a deep breath of his own, William sat back in his seat. "As long as you're okay to continue. Then we'll leave you alone." He glanced at a worried looking Michelle who met his gaze. He continued to write as Paul relayed more details of the attack.

"The hit, it knocked me to the ground. I felt my face make contact with the pavement, and blood was trickling down my throat. I tried to move, to get to my feet, blood falling from my mouth. I could see a pool of my blood on the ground, and my mouth filled up with it again."

William saw Paul lift a hand to gesture to his neck, but his face scrunched up as he dropped his hand again. "There was a third blow to my head and neck area, but I didn't see who did it. I heard someone shouting, 'Hey' a few times and then felt a breath on my face and something licking me. I assume it was a dog, but then I passed out."

As Paul coughed, William checked his watch wondering how long it would be until they were out of the ward. He struggled to shake a niggling feeling of guilt. Looking exhausted by the effort, Paul put his head back on the pillow, taking further deep breaths.

William looked on, patiently waiting with his own head beginning to throb.

After another couple of seconds Paul began speaking again. "I came to when the paramedics arrived, although I felt really disorientated. A dog was barking, and I heard a man saying he saw me being attacked and that whoever did it ran off. I felt myself being strapped to a gurney and lifted into the ambulance. I could still taste blood. There was commotion and people taking my top off and pulling at me, attaching wires and tubes and things." He waved dismissively, showing the wires he was now attached to.

"I felt the ambulance moving through the streets. I felt it speed up and heard the sirens. I tried to stay awake, but I couldn't. I tried to listen to all the voices around me, but it was too much. Then, I woke up in here. Have you any idea who did this to me?"

William saw Paul's jaw visibly stiffen as he stared back without any answers.

"We're looking into everything, Paul" he said, hoping to sound comforting. He got to his feet and put a hand on Paul's shoulder. "Take care mate, rest up and make the most of all the painkillers."

As he walked to his car to go home that night William felt his chest tighten. A niggling pain crept up his left arm and travelled to his chest. Seconds later he struggled to breathe. With his car a few yards away William kept walking even though his legs were starting to fail him. Throwing himself into the driver side he allowed the sensation to take over.

Am I having a heart attack?

William pulled his phone out from his pocket and pulled up Sarah's name but quickly decided not to phone her. The tightening in his chest intensified and he forced himself to take deep breaths, lowering the windows to let fresh air in.

Deep breaths, take deep breaths, this will pass.

He typed in 999 on the keypad as a precaution. After a couple of minutes the pain and tightness began to ease. Beads of sweat ran down his temples as relief flooded his body.

"I can't keep doing this."

PART III

CHAPTER 34

William signed himself off sick with a virus. Being off would buy him a week to sort his head out and figure out how best to deal with everything, and Davie. He was avoiding his workmate for as long as he could, but working the same shifts would only make it more difficult. William couldn't give him what he didn't have.

"I'll just try and sleep it off," he told Sarah as she made dinner. He poured a glass of water and gently grazed her back with his hand as he sloped off to bed. Sleep would make everything better.

Within a few hours, as his wife slept beside him, William's mind wandered back to his last conversation with Phil, a call he made at an industrial estate a few couple of nights earlier. He made a point of going to random parts of the city, away from his work and his house when making calls in case the device's movements were ever tracked. During the call, the gangster had eventually given him a reprieve but made it clear he wanted to revisit the Daniel Tonner situation.

For all his fears about his job, his marriage, and his life, William somehow managed to persuade his gangster acquaintance to trust him and wait until the time was right to swoop on Tonner. They also arranged another late-night meeting at Strathclyde Park.

He climbed out of bed, pulling on joggers and a hoodie as the time on his alarm clock showed 2 am. He crept into the hallway and scribbled a note saying he was going a drive to clear his mind, which he carefully left on Sarah's bedside table. If she woke up and realised he was gone she'd panic.

You are crazy to think you'll get away with this.

"Trust me," he assured Phil during their covert meeting. "Cops are watching both sides like hawks. I won't be able to pull it off just yet. You want this done properly, eh?" William asked with bated breath.

The low temperature exposed William's fast breaths. He folded and unfolded his arms then cracked his knuckles. He tapped his hands on his sides and hugged his body with his arms.

Silence hung in the air.

With his voice shaking, William added, "This will be worth the wait. I'll do what needs to be done."

To his astonishment, Phil agreed. "You better make this work, Billy." He stared intently at him.

William almost asked Phil to write it down and sign it so it could be referred to later. Instead, he nodded vigorously and left before his gangster friend changed his mind. William drove home feeling more upbeat than he had in a while.

Maybe it was everything that was going on within the group. Maybe Phil had grown a conscience or suffered a bang on the head. William shook his head at the thought. Not that William didn't need the cash, but he couldn't handle the extra pressure with the police activity surrounding Slaven's murder. Now he just had to tackle Davie and get him off his back for the foreseeable.

***

That night, as he and Sarah were getting ready for dinner with her parents, he was momentarily paralysed with fear. He clung to the wall of the shower as water poured over him, his mind wandering to the events of the small hours that morning.

When did I become this person? Sneaking about during the night with gangsters?

Sarah banging on the door snapped him out of his self-pity trance.

"We need to leave in ten minutes, babe. Mum texted to say they're on their way and we don't want to be late." She almost sang the words on the other side of the bathroom door.

William heard the joy in his wife's voice.

Make this a good night for your wife. Get out of your own head.

He decided to take the bull by the horns and call Davie, to alleviate some of the stress so he could focus all his attention on his family tonight. He wrapped a towel round himself and took a deep breath, walking into the hallway.

PART III

He heard Sarah banging about in the kitchen. "I'll be ready in five," William shouted downstairs.

Knowing Paul had been attacked outside the police station would be his excuse for getting in touch. William picked up his phone as it charged on his bedside table, and he tried to make the call. He put his shirt on to distract himself from the nervous feeling coursing through him while he waited for the voicemail.

Feeling unsure but determined to give himself the best chance of relaxing tonight, he left a voice message.

"Hi mate, do me a solid, eh? Phone me before 6 pm if you get this before then. Have you heard how Paul is? He didn't look great when me and Michelle took his statement. If you see him, pass on my best, and eh, I'll speak to you—"

William's phone buzzed before he could finish. It was Davie calling him back. Relieved and panicked, he ended his call and answered.

"Hi, Davie mate, I was just leaving you a message. How's Paul? Any sign of him getting home?"

There were muffled noises at Davie's end.

"Aye, he's in a bad way, off for a bit. Probably told someone off for dropping litter or parking squint in the street. You…eh, you calling about the cash I'm due?"

With his shirt only half-buttoned, William was too distracted to carry out both tasks at once. There was no mistaking the aggression in Davie's voice.

William wondered fleetingly if his colleague had always sounded this way, even as a teenager, or if something had changed that made his tone one of permanent irritation and anger.

"Well, about that. The situation has changed, and it's been called off now," he lied.

William had practised in his head saying this, hoping it would be enough to persuade Davie to back off.

"Oh aye…" Davie said, unconvinced. "Your gangster pal has had a change of heart?" He laughed. "Come on, pal, I know I look stupid, but I'm not thick enough to believe he's suddenly developed

123

MURDER CENTRAL

a fondness or, worse, a conscience. What the fuck are you playing at?"

The panic rose in William and sat in his chest. He switched hands to dry his palm from the sweat between the creases. His heart thumped hard, and for a few seconds, he didn't register what Davie had said. He caught himself and snapped back to the moment to take control.

William cleared his throat. "Look, Davie, I'm sorry, and I'll get you your cash when I get it, but what they asked me to do isn't happening right now, so I can't do anything. See you later and pass my best to Paul."

Without missing a beat, Davie retorted, "Eh, so I heard the gaffer wants to speak to you about Slaven. Mel told me her shift heard your name came up. So aye, catch up later."

There was a sudden silence and William looked at his screen to discover the call had ended.

Why does the gaffer want to speak to me? I had nothing to do with Slaven's death. If this is a sick joke from Davie to make me squirm, it's working.

From downstairs, Sarah shouted again, sounding less patient than before.

He smacked the palm of his hand on the bed, hoping the covers would cushion the sound. "Two minutes. I'll be ready in two minutes," he shouted back, with equally little patience.

Within an hour, they were sitting in Brown's restaurant overlooking George Square with Sarah's parents. William sat with his arm across the back of his wife's chair, silently admiring her as she spoke passionately about a topic he wasn't even tuned into listening to. He nodded to show participation. Until dread swept over him again.

The waitress put his dish in front of him, but he paid little attention to the food, nudging chips around the plate with his fork. He hummed and smiled with acknowledgement as the other three chatted without a care. He took a few mouthfuls of food, not tasting what he was eating. William was with them in body, but his mind was miles away.

He jumped at the noise of cutlery being dropped from the table behind them. The noise sent shockwaves through his body, leaving him with the tight feeling in his chest again.

"Are you okay?" Sarah looked at him with concern on her face. She put a hand on his lap which helped ease the gripping sensation across his body.

"Yes, of course." William wiped his brow and laughed, rubbing the top of her hand with his. "I just wasn't expecting such a clatter. Excuse me, while I visit the toilet" he pushed his chair back and softly touched Sarah's shoulder before walking away.

When they got home that night, he took himself off to bed with a "migraine," but Sarah followed him upstairs.

They silently got ready for bed. It was still light outside as she drew the curtains and slipped between the sheets before him.

William got into bed and kissed her goodnight, flipped his phone face down, turned his back to his wife, and lay silently, knowing he wasn't going to sleep.

Sarah sighed. He held his breath, sensing she was about to say something.

He knew she noticed his out-of-character behaviour and how jumpy he was every time his mobile phone made a noise or vibrated. Sometimes, he'd be startled by a phantom vibration or noise on the television he thought was a notification. Her happy exterior, he realised, was masking the pain she must be feeling seeing him withdraw from her.

William closed his eyes tighter in the hope they might avoid a conversation he didn't want.

"What's wrong, William? You're not yourself, and you never come anywhere near me?"

He could feel the tension in her voice and hated that he was making her feel anything but completely loved and adored – which was exactly how he felt. "Work is just busy. There's a lot going on with the investigation and…" He scrambled around for something that didn't sound so pathetic. "A colleague was attacked so there's a lot of tension in the station."

He turned to face his wife, studying her crestfallen face.

"You're so secretive these days. I would never look through your phone, but William, you are *so* absent-minded. You have been for a while now, and I don't know what to do." She caught herself before her voice broke.

William reached an arm over to calm and comfort his worried wife. The truth would not bring her any solace. In fact, it would only panic her further, but he needed to do more to cover his worries and alleviate hers.

Silence fell between them before Sarah blurted out, "Are you having an affair?"

Her eyes swam with tears, and she stared at the window on the opposite wall.

William had not seen that coming, so terrified his innocent wife would be caught up in his crazy mess that he hadn't taken stock that his behaviour was so alarming she thought he was being unfaithful. He pushed himself to sit upright, then moved across the bed to pull her close to him. "Sarah, no. Absolutely not, I would never. No, definitely not – I swear. It's just work, nothing else."

He tightened his grip on her, comforting both himself and her.

William felt her small frame in his arms lightly shaking as she cried silent tears. If he wasn't already feeling guilty, his eyes stung with his salty tears.

He swallowed hard and leaned down to kiss his wife's hair, dabbing at his face with her pyjama top. He would reinforce his position with Davie and call in to check on Paul. Perhaps he'd get a steer on how to deal with angry Davie.

I will sort everything, he vowed to himself.

PART III

CHAPTER 35

At just twenty years old he was one of McColl's youngest lackeys. Barry Harris was a well-built, manual labourer for the kingpin. With sallow skin and thick dark hair gelled back, he was often mistaken for being Eastern European. He laughed when others in the group teased him, gradually fuelling his anger, biting his tongue each time. He was at the bottom of the food chain in this gang.

A delivery driver for a Chinese takeaway in the evenings and carrying out the odd drug run, Barry was often driving and running around following orders. A heavy foot found him on the wrong side of two police officers hiding in a layby. The speed they clocked him driving at, along with the mouthful of abuse, landed him in the dock – again – and coupled with a string of unpaid parking fines and a grumpy sheriff, he found himself in Polmont Young Offenders' Institute for a time after Slaven's murder but before any arrests were made.

"Don't be a grass" was the phrase etched into his brain. For as long as he could remember, he lived by the mantra "don't rat anyone out". He never, for a second, thought it would be what got him in bother, another lag landing *him* in it.

The exhilaration was still cascading through his veins when his cell door was closed behind him. It was two weeks after the murder, though nobody knew about his involvement. Yet. Barry was under strict instructions by McColl to keep his head down and a low profile while inside. In truth, he struggled with any rules and authority.

It was only three days into his sentence when a younger thug joined him in his cell. A nineteen year-old first timer.

"Alright pal, what you in for?" Barry swaggered up to the boy. "First timer?"

Narrowing his already pin-size dark eyes, he said "Assault and robbery" There was a slight pause, "With a knife." He stood straighter and puffed his chest out. "Aye, first time banged up."

Barry smirked at the boy, only a year younger than him but

127

with less prison experience.

He rubbed along nicely with the younger boy for a few days. Barry even shared some of his previous prison tales and experience – as a member of a gang. The younger lad seemed to even show interest in what he had to say.

What started off as banter in the food area of the jail a week after meeting, escalated quickly. The teenager began to annoy Barry. He couldn't put his finger on how exactly but looking at the rat-like face was making him angry. And the more the young boy spoke, Barry felt himself become enraged. When stories started being shared between the prisoners, the teenager grinned at Barry. He felt the fury in him instantly build.

"Aw chill out Bazza, can I call you Bazza?" The teenager looked at him and winked.

"No you fucking can't," Barry shot back.

"Well Mr Harris, shall I call you that instead? I'll be out before you, so I'd be happy to go see your Mrs for you. Pass on a message." He giggled at his own joke, looking around the other three inmates hoping for some backup.

Barry stared straight ahead, his jaw stiffened. He clenched his fist. "She'd eat you up pal," Barry said laughing, his nails digging into his tightly fisted hands. The teenager leaned forward until his nose touched his cell mate's and his eyes blurred into one.

Why is he pushing me? Barry tried to calm himself.

"I'll pass on a message if you want, mucka. Let her know you're thinking about her, or give her something to think about." He laughed and punched Barry's arm.

"He really wants to wind me up," Barry muttered, unable to stop himself reacting. No sooner had the words been uttered, Barry found himself taking hold of the teenager. He couldn't stop himself. He was so tightly wound up, like a coiled spring ready to release all pent up fury. Barry felt unable to control his temper as the anger rose listening to the taunts about the one person he desperately wanted to see. The change in his mood was too much to bear and it took over. Within seconds he had pinned the mouthy teen to the wall

PART III

with his right forearm over his throat, spitting his words so hard saliva spouted from his mouth.

"Touch anyone I know, or so much as look at them, you will find yourself keeping Slaven company. I've done it once, I'll do it again. Understand?"

Realising where he was as he held the young lad against the concrete, he clenched and unclenched his fists in an effort to try and calm himself and not react further. But when it came to his family he struggled, he missed Katie, he was wound up, frustrated and on the brink.

The teenager blinked twice back at him, unable to move from under Barry's grip but nodded. It was the last time he spoke to Barry without being spoken to first. But, it was the moment Barry put himself at the scene of the country's most high profile murder inquiry.

In the weeks that followed the food hall incident, Barry walked around like a peacock, strutting about thinking how he'd put the young lad in his place. It had felt good. It turned out that at the same time, his young cell mate was working up the courage to commit the *ultimate* crime, and grass him in. The teenager took the opportunity to benefit from the situation and arrange a plea bargain for another upcoming case, in exchange for some very important information. Barry felt sick when he heard this was the witness statement that finally put someone at the crime scene for Slaven.

Just say you were trying to scare him, he told himself. Deny it until there's proof.

"I just said that to get him to shut up," he protested when confronted with the information. Feeling stupid for cracking that was soon replaced with fear. The last thing he was told by McColl was to keep his head down.

"I had nothin' to do with it, I swear!" his voice squeaky and high pitched when under pressure by police. But by then he knew he was front and centre of the investigation, someone the police could focus on.

CHAPTER 36

The stress of returning to work caused William extreme sweats and nightmares, so much he feared he had brought on a real illness in place of his fake one.

Panic attacks and even hallucinations crept into his mind in the small hours. The night terrors paralysed him so much he feared he wouldn't wake up.

He had felt Sarah's touch during the night, wiping the sweat from his head. He heard her up, pacing to the toilet and back more than usual. He was even sure he had heard her crying on one occasion. It was this that almost sent William over the edge.

Counting the hours on his alarm clock, he crawled into the bathroom to hyperventilate to avoid disturbing his already worried partner. Soon after, he vomited so much that he was convinced he had ripped the lining in his stomach.

Putting his uniform back on took every ounce of energy he could muster. Maybe that was karma for throwing a sickie the previous week and avoiding the inevitable. Or it was the fear gripping him over his future living within him like a gremlin playing havoc with his insides.

"Are you feeling better, babe?" Sarah looked worried, laying a hand on his cold, clammy forehead. She ran her fingers through his hair and kissed the crown of his head as he sat on the bottom stair to put his shoes on.

"Not the best, but needs must. Surely, I'm coming out the other end of whatever this is by now." William took her hands in his and squeezed them, then kissed her gently on her forehead.

***

When he arrived at the police station, William parked, got out of the car, and made his way into the staff room. He had no sooner put his lunch in the fridge when Sergeant Black walked into the

PART III

room behind him.

"Field," he said in a stern tone, "my office, now."

The sergeant turned on his heel and disappeared out of the room.

Davie sauntered in, smiling smugly at William. "Apparently he wants to see you, mate." Behind him was Mel, she stood back out of William's path. She looked at him with what he thought was a sympathetic expression and he wondered what Davie had told her.

Unable to find any words or energy to scowl, William skulked into the Sergeant's office.

"Yes, sir?" he asked meekly.

This cannot be real, he thought. *Why the hell is this happening? Only Phil and Davie know what is going on.*

"Sit down, Field."

William shifted uncomfortably. "If it's all the same, sir, I'd rather stand." He didn't want to sound disrespectful, but if he sat, he might break down.

"Field, it's not a request. Sit your arse down."

William sat swallowing hard to try and bury the burning ball of anxiety working its way up his chest and into his throat.

"There's been a report made that you knew Slaven's whereabouts on the night he got murdered."

He felt a sharp pain in his chest as the words echoed round his mind.

What had Davie done? Why did he shop me – Phil will kill me.

"There is a suggestion you informed McColl's gang, helping to set up the hit," the Sergeant continued.

William froze. He ran his tongue around his mouth desperately trying to moisten his mouth and find words. A high pitched sound took over his mind for what seemed like an eternity but must only have been seconds and dots appeared before his eyes. Blinking he focused on his hands resting on the table in front of him to stop him from passing out. He was unable to fully formulate any thoughts and have his brain deliver the words. William hadn't been grassed up for trying to snare Daniel Tonner, instead he had been accused

131

MURDER CENTRAL

of conspiring to murder Slaven.

"You'll be suspended on full pay, and you'll be under investigation."

He didn't know whether to cry or pass out. Both seemed equally possible. How could this be happening?

"Boss, no. This isn't true at all. Who has said this? They've—"

Sergeant Black put a hand up to stop him going any further. "Field, this is a serious allegation. One of my officers is put at the centre of one of the country's biggest murders. You'll be suspended, and you'll be investigated. Get your stuff. You'll be questioned later."

***

The drive home was a blur, William's vision slightly impaired by the sweat dripping down his face. By the time he parked, he barely remembered the journey.

William stopped short of his house to give himself time to compose himself.

Why is this happening? Has Phil tried to set me up? What the hell do I tell Sarah?

He took several deep breaths, his fingers gripping the steering wheel as he counted slowly as thoughts swirled round his head. He turned the radio off with his left hand, his forefinger and thumb of his right hand, tapping on the steering wheel. William decided to tell Sarah he was still unwell to buy himself a day or so when he could think more clearly.

With the house empty when he entered, he dumped his work bag on the coffee table and grabbed the burner phone from it to contact Phil, then took himself out for a drive to turn it on somewhere far away from his house. His usual protocol.

I can't afford to slip up now.

William decided he would also try and get another doctor's appointment when he was out to make his absence more legitimate. He mulled over the idea that his old pal might be responsible for the mess he was in, but it just didn't make sense. Phil had even

132

PART III

more at stake.

He drove for a while before realising how far he'd gone. Pulling up in a quiet street in Dalkeith some 50 miles away from Glasgow, he turned on the burner phone. There were no messages.

William needed to speak to Phil about this.

The phone rang twice, and surprisingly, Phil picked up.

"You got news about Slaven?" he asked without so much as a hello.

Confused, William wondered if this was a test. "No, well, not about what happened. Are you setting me up here?" His voice cracked, forcing him to clear his throat.

William was terrified of the answer and didn't want to sound like he was taking Phil on, but he was running out of options.

"What the fuck are you talking about?" Phil's voice was low and growly.

"I've just been told I'm suspended and under investigation because someone told the gaffer I'm involved in Slaven's murder. *Me*! And I can't even tell them what I *do* know. Tell me this isn't payback, mate? Are you stitching me up?"

Phil laughed properly and heartily. "Fuck sake Billy, you're up to your eyes in it. Who have you pissed off? As if I've got the time to set you up, you know my target, pal. Sorry, I can't help. No intel on who shot Slaven then?"

William didn't want to risk upsetting his gangster friend further, but he wasn't in the mood, and he couldn't do much to investigate now. "All I did was collect some statements from folk, pulled some CCTV that shows the car driving but no ID on anyone. I can't sniff about it now; they think it was my intel!"

"Seriously? After everything, you think I'd do this?"

William realised this wasn't Phil's doing. "Of course, sorry. Right, I'm just stressed. Like really fucking stressed, mate," he said, almost childlike.

"Get it together, Billy, do not crumble now! Keep me posted if you hear anything on McColl's lot and how they got to Slaven. Keep your head up and your mouth shut." Phil almost sounded

MURDER CENTRAL

like he cared.

But William knew the main goal was to cover his own back. It felt like a bad dream, up to his neck in corruption and now accused of being involved in a gangland murder.

Is this my penance for running off all those years ago?

PART III

CHAPTER 37

As William flicked through the hundreds of television channels to find something to capture his attention, he jumped at the sound of his mobile phone ringing.

"It's Sergeant Black. I need you to come in tomorrow. Sergeant Callum King will carry out your interview at 11 am sharp. You can bring someone if you want."

Struggling not to complain or show his bad mood at having this hanging over him, he said, "Fine, I'll be there."

"William? It's protocol; we need to do this."

He rolled his eyes and took a breath. "Yes, boss."

Sarah was growing suspicious, asking questions about his lingering illness the past couple of days. William insisted it was a line from the doctor keeping him off the second week, although he'd been unable to get an appointment. He was keeping that up his sleeve for the next week, just in case.

***

When he arrived to talk to Sergeant King, William found it difficult to be spoken to like a suspect. He wasn't called as much, but he'd conducted enough interviews to know.

"William, we've been given some information that suggests you had intelligence about Slaven's movements."

"Is that a question, sir?"

"Well, did you know he would be at the car park?" The Sergeant raised his eyebrows.

"I can't believe you think I was involved. Where has this come from?" William asked, incredulous.

"Someone on another shift has provided some messages they claim to have been sent by you," the Sergeant said sheepishly, pushing several documents towards William with text messages.

William couldn't believe what he was seeing. The messages had

135

MURDER CENTRAL

all the relevant information with phrases including, "He's a goner"
and "You no where to find him."

Of the ten or so messages, one was signed off, "Thanks, W."

"Who am I meant to have been messaging?" William shouted,
throwing the papers across the table at his superior.

"Field, we have to investigate. This is why I'm asking — explain
what it is if you can."

"*I* have to explain?" His frustration was bubbling over. "This
isn't how we investigate crimes, boss. We gather information, and
we see what it proves. We don't expect the innocent to prove that!"
He was starting to lose his rag. Is *this a setup?* William couldn't help
but think it was.

"I did *not* send those messages, I don't know who the other
number is, and I've not got a fucking explanation because I didn't
send them."

He sat back in his chair with his hands behind his head, breathing heavily.

The sergeant rubbed his temples and looked at William sym-
pathetically. "Okay, are you willing to have your phone examined?
I'm sorry to ask but—"

"Fine," William snapped. "Here," he said, sliding his phone
across the table. "Do what you like. You won't tell me who gave
you this pish, but whoever it is, I'd do them for wasting police time.
What's next?"

"We'll speak to your colleagues, due diligence and all that,"
Sergeant King muttered.

Suddenly, a wave of fear crashed over him, crushing his chest
and momentarily deafening him.

"Is there anything else you want to add, Field?" Sergeant King
said for a second time, penetrating the mind fog that descended.

"No, boss, I just want to be back at work. Whoever has fed you
this bullshit is out for me – for some crazy reason. But I didn't know
about Slaven or order any hits on him. I am an officer!" William
felt a pang of guilt at the last statement, but even doing what he did
was for the right reasons.

136

PART III

***

Hours later, William's heart rate shot up as he ran away from the same scene in the park as when he was eighteen, this time in uniform. William ran and tripped just as masked men began to catch up with him. Terrified of what they would do, he covered his head and yelled – or tried to.

A guttural noise escaped his throat. It was all William could muster.

They were on him, shaking him as he lay in the foetal position on the ground. Their hands on him, shaking him vigorously. Seconds later, he heard Sarah's voice slowly becoming more focused.

"William!" she cried. "William, are you okay? Please, tell me you're okay, talk to me!"

He came to with her nails gripping him as though he was going to fall off a cliff. Turning to face her, he saw the terrified look in her eyes. William took a deep breath, realising it was a nightmare, he was home and he was safe.

"Yes, I'm fine." He panted. "Sorry, I woke you." He mopped the sweat from his forehead.

"Woke me? You scared me half to death. You were shouting and making noises. I've been trying to waken you for the last few minutes! William, what on earth is going on?"

William looked deep into Sarah's eyes. "I am so, so sorry," he said.

"What for?" She looked scared.

He took a deep breath and told her.

William told her everything.

MURDER CENTRAL

CHAPTER 38

Barry Harris had no sooner been released from his short stay behind bars for his driving charge when he was hauled out of bed at 5.30 am on a Saturday by officers and taken to Helen Street police station for questioning.

This is all for show, Barry thought. *They could have done this when I was inside.*

He was questioned by police for nine long hours about Slaven's murder, though he only offered "no comment" responses.

Sitting in the interview room he couldn't believe he was caught up in this. All because he stupidly ran his mouth off. He wouldn't be so daft now; he'd be giving up *no* information.

"We've got evidence, Barry", he was told. "We've searched your house, your phone and gathered DNA."

Convinced they were trying to spook him or force a confession, he kept his head down. He repeated "no comment" so much that the police knew his response before he said it.

"Did Michael McColl put you up to this? We know he did" the officer pressed. Barry kept this head down.

"What's in this for you, Barry?"

"No-"

"Yes, no comment. We know. But this is your chance to explain, tell us what really happened. This is a serious murder enquiry not some minor driving offence we're talking about."

He hadn't changed his position. Every time he thought of answering he heard McColl's voice reminding him to say nothing.

"You admitted what you did when you were in Polmont. You threatened to kill someone or rather 'do to them what you did to Slaven', didn't you?"

Shame and embarrassment flooded Barry.

"If you go down for this you'll be spending decades behind bars. You can help us and we'll look after you." He felt the officer's eyes on him even though he refused to make eye contact.

138

PART III

"You were working alongside Jamie Cain, weren't you Barry? Were you offered money?"

Barry looked at the officer, silently.

"We know Mark Deacon was with you, did he give you instructions? Who planned the hit?"

"No comment." Barry sighed, throwing his head back and leaning back on his chair.

Opening up a laptop the police officer tapped on the keyboard for a few moments and turned the screen round to face Barry. "Watch this please."

He played a video of a Peugeot hurtling along the road, the date showing the day Josh Slaven was murdered. Barry watched intently. It did show the car he'd been in speeding along a road. *There's nothing linking this to you, keep quiet.*

"Are you driving that car, Barry? You're in it anyway, aren't you?"

He stared at the screen as the police officer hit play, replaying the footage again.

"You can help yourself by helping us."

Barry looked at the officer sitting across from him. "No comment.

"Make this easy for yourself". The officer leaned back in his chair, clicking his pen.

They're just trying to intimidate you. Keep quiet.

"We know this isn't all you. Your partners in crime, pardon the pun, we know they're involved Barry. You won't be telling us anything that we don't know.

Barry knew they weren't innocent. They just hadn't been caught.

"If you help us, we'll help you."

He'd go down for life before admitting anything that would land anyone in trouble. But it didn't help him. Barry's legs almost gave way when he heard the words "charged with murder", he didn't take in anything else about the allegations. He heard something about being kept behind bars over the weekend to go before a sheriff on Monday afternoon. The voices sounded like they were underwater. An unexpected fear swept over him and sweat trickled down

MURDER CENTRAL

his temples.

I'm going away for life.

His thoughts were interrupted by his lawyer guiding him away from the interview room.

"Barry...Barry?"

His lawyer looked blurry through the tears in his eyes.

"Try not to panic."

***

Barry was taken back to Polmont. He felt like he'd never been away. He had to try and ignore all the speculation amongst inmates about what really happened. Although he wouldn't admit it, he was fearful of McColl's wrath.

A small-time gangster, Barry knew he was picked for the job along with the others because they were the small fish in the group. Since his last stint inside and his foolish behaviour trying to act hard, he hadn't even left the house. By avoiding everything and everyone he was able to ignore what he said while inside. The hairs on his neck stood up when he thought of McColl and what would happen to him if the boss found out. Slaven wouldn't be the only dead man. Barry wasn't sure who he feared more, McColl and his boys or a lifetime behind bars.

Others inside the Young Offenders' asked him if he was involved. If he was the one who shot Slaven.

"Was it you big man? Slaven had it coming."

"Well done. I heard he deserved it."

"Better stay on your good side, pal", one inmate even joked in the dining hall one day.

But Barry couldn't act like a hard man anymore and accept the honour. He trusted nobody. Some of the others in Polmont said Mark Deacon's, and Jamie Cain's arrests were a shock to Clarke's gang. Other than some minor drug charges and the odd speeding offence, they had no other convictions and weren't the frontrunners of the gang.

PART III

That was why they were selected. If they had it in them to murder in broad daylight, what were the others capable of? Barry could hear McColl's voice say the words.

The rumour-mill in the cafeteria was that Martin Cole was in Dubai, but nobody could be sure. Barry heard some ill-thought-out social media posts by his wife Becky suggested a fancy apartment in the United Arab Emirates, but they had since been taken down, and there was no concrete proof of where they were. Nobody had heard from them or admitted as much.

After hearing this, Barry punched a wall, thinking the whole plan was unravelling. Then slapped himself to remind him to keep his cool.

MURDER CENTRAL

CHAPTER 39

William was on tenterhooks after his interview with Sergeant King. For weeks, he couldn't relax. Sarah tried to appease him, but he could tell she was worried too. Then came the call he was expecting but dreading. He held his breath, answering the phone.

"We've carried out a full investigation, Field. You're free to return to work. The allegations made were serious but we've concluded there isn't enough proof to substantiate them. Sergeant King has reported back there should be no disciplinary action and you are not found to have carried out anything illegal or any wrongdoing. This will all be sent to you in writing."

William's shoulders dropped, and his heart pounded. "Sir—"

"And you should know there's been arrests made in the Slaven case. Three of McColl's gang were charged today and will be in court on Monday."

William listened as the senior officer explained who was charged and with what. When it was his turn to talk, he couldn't help but be snarky. "Are you expecting me back in as though nothing has happened? I've been through the mill."

There was a pause. Sergeant Black sighed. "Unless you have a reason to be at home, and we will support you if you do, then yes, I expect you back at work."

Clenching one hand, anger rising in his stomach, William also knew not to push it. He wasn't completely innocent. He was involved in a plan to have a drug dealer arrested.

"Yes, boss. Okay, I'll be in on Monday."

William was relieved and furious.

How dare someone set me up?

Everything pointed to Davie, but given everything, William couldn't bring himself to talk to anyone. He had persuaded his doctor to sign him off with stress. Now, he had to return.

Since his confession to Sarah, they had opened up about many things. She told him she had put his behaviour down to be a delayed

142

PART III

response to losing their babies, along with the stress of the job catching up with him. This weighed even more heavily on his conscience, as his behaviour was about himself and not their relationship. He hated keeping secrets and explained over and over that he felt there was nothing to gain from sharing his shameful behaviour with her when she was supposed to be keeping her blood pressure low and taking care of herself.

He hoped his news might release some tension.

After ending the call with his boss, William immediately hit Sarah's name in his last dialled list.

"Hi, William, you okay? I'm a bit busy—"

"Yes, babe, sorry. I just wanted to let you know…my name's been cleared at work. The gaffer called. They've nothing on me. I'm good to go back."

"That's great news. Well done." Her voice sounded flat.

William rubbed his face, pacing up and down the living room.

"Thanks, okay, I'll see you when you get home. Won't keep you." He paused, then said, "Love you."

Another silence fell. He felt awkward. Then Sarah said, "You too, see you later."

He knew he had hurt her. William needed to fix this. Honesty wasn't enough, he had to show her how sorry he was.

***

As Sarah's car pulled into the driveway, William lit the candles on the table and poured the wine. He had made an extra special effort to show how sorry he was.

They ate mostly in silence until she asked about the men arrested.

"Three members of a gang have been charged with murder. They reckon there were two gunmen and a getaway driver. The gaffer says they're also charged with getting rid of the guns and the car. There were three guns so they think another person was involved"

She nodded along with everything he said.

143

"They might have thought they covered their tracks, but we get them in the end," William added.

His wife shot him a look that he interpreted as not to be so judgemental.

To keep himself on the right side of the wrong people, William took himself for a drive to send a message to Phil to make sure he knew everything. He almost sent it from his house but, the police officer in him told him to still be careful. He needed to make sure his phone was nowhere near his family. Phil would have heard the news about the gang, but after their last frosty interaction, he wanted to be clear.

Driving to the Showcase cinema car park in Coatbridge, he turned on the burner phone and texted.

McColl's lot have been lifted. Harris, Cain and Deacon, Martin Cole thought to be abroad now but involved.

William sat in the car for longer than planned, enjoying the silence. He sat for so long that he forgot why he was there in the first place.

His phone buzzed, taking William by surprise.

Hope they rot in hell.

PART III

CHAPTER 40

Since seeing the news break that men were charged, April looked forward to finally getting a story out of this, albeit the gritty details wouldn't be known for some time.

She went to the local Sheriff Court on the day of their appearance to see what was happening with Barry Harris, Mark Deacon and Jamie Cain. By then, she knew the other names of those said to be involved.

Not who I expected, she thought when she heard through a number of sources.

She had covered court cases involving all of them but minor offences that only made it as stories because of their gangland connections. Others higher up the food chain had reputations as being fierce enforcers.

As she walked past the Clutha Pub with the court building in sight, her phone rang. It was a new start at one of the papers asking if she would be covering the case.

"Yes, I'll be there in a few moments. That's right, it's the Sheriff Court today. All the guys that will end up going on trial before a jury are going through a private hearing today to begin with." April explained to the young journalist that the trial would eventually be heard at the high court but not to worry about that yet.

By the time the men were due to appear in the dock later in the afternoon, it was common knowledge, according to social media, who the suspects were. But with the criminal justice process underway, the press were very limited in what they could write. This would give April time to gather and write all of the background for when things blew up at the trial. It was a shocking and bloody assassination in Glasgow at a busy train station in front of terrified commuters who saw a man shot dead at point blank range. This would be a story people would talk about for decades to come.

Eager to get any information, April hung around in the basement corridor of the building at the door of the courtroom where

145

MURDER CENTRAL

the men accused would attend their private hearing. No members of the public or the press were allowed in at this stage.

She was stationed beside the wives and partners waiting on their loved ones who had been kept in over the weekend being released from incarceration after their brief court appearances and a night or two without a shower. Some anxious relatives paced up and down, asking every lawyer who passed if they knew anything. Others sat stewing, ready to create a disturbance the second their beloved emerged carrying their belongings in a plastic bag.

April had countless occasions over the years observing those freed after a stint in the cells.

Watching people waiting, she recalled one of the more bizarre sights she once saw, a scruffy man clutching nothing more than a multi-pack of cheesy Wotsits crisps and an apple. Another had a single training shoe and a toothbrush, and his pal wandered out wearing a Christmas jumper – in summer.

A reporter of several years, she knew the court well and who to keep in with. She stood staring at her phone, wondering when she would get out of the bowels of the building and if it would still be daylight.

"Oh, it's the fourth estate," a voice said from behind. "April, how are you doing? Not seen you in a while."

She turned to see a familiar gentleman striding towards her with folders of paperwork in one hand and a coffee cup in the other.

Derek Kinnaird was a regular around the Sheriff Court, known for representing gangsters and their associates. He was also a friendly face who gave April the time of day; both had an understanding of one another's jobs, and she knew when not to overstep the mark.

"Ah, Mr Kinnaird. I was wondering when I was going to see you. Are you heading into court anytime soon?"

He nodded towards the top file in his left hand. "Won't be long now, just waiting on one of the other lawyers and we'll get this done."

She might not overstep the mark, but she sometimes put a toe over...

PART III

"What's the script here?" she asked quietly.

He took a sip of his coffee, raised his eyebrows, and laughed. "I can't speak without my client's permission, and you know that."

"When it suits!" She laughed back. "Okay, well, usual process?"

He nodded as he took another swig of coffee, brushing past her into the private courtroom.

As she waited outside patiently, another lawyer slipped into court, fixing his ripped black robe flailing behind him as he walked with purpose. The third and final lawyer then dived in behind him.

She knew the proceedings never took long when they finally got underway, and not wanting to let anyone sneak by her, April made her way to the door of interview room two, that allowed her to look through the glass panel into the corridor of the cells to watch for Kinnaird leaving.

As expected, twenty minutes later, still carrying his coffee cup, he emerged and followed her into the small room, closing the door behind him.

"It's some charges, probably as you expect, and all remanded in custody," he said, without any second thought, that he was representing a murder accused.

He pulled out his mobile phone and started tapping away as April scribbled down all the charges in her scrawny shorthand that only she understood. All men were charged with murdering Slaven by shooting him multiple times in the head and chest and of trying to destroy evidence by throwing the guns away and setting fire to the getaway car. They were also accused of possessing firearms and speeding.

"A speeding charge?" She looked up from the page, furrowing her brows.

"Apparently caught on CCTV doing in excess of 100mph that night." Kinnaird didn't look up from his mobile.

"Your guys are probably happier to be inside now they're linked to Slaven's murder," April commented, knowing the gangland mentality.

"I couldn't possibly comment," the lawyer said wryly. "That all

147

okay for you? And remember, Kinnaird is spelled h-a-n-d-s-o-m-e," and chuckled at his joke.

April shook her head at the poor comedic effort made and returned the piece of paper with all of the details. "Thanks, Derek."

Before she could ask any more questions, Kinnaird's mobile rang, and he answered while gathering the folders of documents and the now empty coffee cup and waved as he raced out the door and down the corridor.

April returned to her car parked on Carlton Place outside the row of lawyer's offices and quickly typed up the story on her iPad. Articles at this stage were short and simple, explaining the charges only. No gangland connections, previous incidents or opinions on anyone. All men were charged with a string of charges including murder, they didn't enter any pleas of guilty or not guilty as was normal at this stage in the process and they were all remanded to stay behind bars until they next appeared in court. She added the subject: Men appear in court over Slaven murder.

It was the story of the day and just the beginning.

As she was getting ready to leave the street, she saw the BBC satellite truck pull into position at the bottom of the steps leading to the court building. She'd be home in time to listen to the journalists reading her stories from the news wires; it was always funny to hear her written words read on the evening news, often with her only yards away from their camera.

The excitement of the story and what was to come, put April in the mood for a drink. She stopped at Tesco on the way home to pick up wine, then drove the short distance to her flat.

Opening the door, she kicked her shoes off and threw her keys on the table in the hallway. The evening news was coming on the television as she entered the living room.

"On tonight's news at six, three men have appeared in court over the death of gangland figure Josh Slaven, who was found dead in a Glasgow car park…"

April walked into the kitchen where John was making dinner and hugged him from behind. It felt as though they hadn't spoken

PART III

properly in a long time. There was no distance, but she missed him, being close to him, especially with all the worry about this case.

She hadn't told him about Paul's attack and that he had withdrawn from her. She didn't have anything to hide but also didn't know how to explain why she was so concerned, her involvement, and why she hadn't told him anything at the time.

"That your story on TV?" John's hand paused on the spoon, stirring a pot of bubbling food.

"Yes, that's mine." She rolled her eyes. "What's for dinner?"

"Chilli tonight. Do you think they're guilty then? Got to be them hasn't it, rival gangs? That Slaven was a bad guy; he had it coming."

"Don't let any of them hear you say that," April quipped. "But yes, I'm confident they did. Let's see what comes out. There's got to be more to it; something feels off. I have a feeling there's more to it."

She wanted to open up about the police officer and her theory he was connected, but she fell short. By this point, her mind had wandered elsewhere. She needed to make up for some lost time with her partner.

"How long until dinner?" April sat at the dining table while she poured a glass of red.

John stopped stirring, turning his head to face her. "I could do with relaxing a bit. Do you need to relax?"

She looked him in the eyes as she sipped wine.

Holding her gaze, John took a sip.

April stood and leaned her bottom on the edge of the table, still holding her glass. Leaning forwards, she slowly stretched her left hand and reached behind him to turn off the gas on the cooker. She smiled at him, then turned on her heel and walked out the door. Without hesitation, he followed closely behind her.

***

The same news bulletin was on in William's house while he ate dinner with Sarah.

149

"These must be the guys we're talking about?" she asked between mouthfuls of steak pie.

He didn't want her to think about the evil in the world, not least because of his loose involvement.

"Yeah, but that's the last they'll see daylight for a while," he told his partner, wondering if that was the case.

He turned on Netflix, which seemed more appropriate for the dinner table than gangland shootings. This had taken up so much of their life already.

***

Elsewhere another message was sent.

Boys R banged up. Shame but you fly with the crows you get shot. Martin Cole fucked off for good. Thinks he's so clever, he better act it. Everyone no's better than to say more. 2 much 2 loose. Debt will be sorted soon.

The phone vibrated, and the message was opened but left on read. The plan was working; it seemed foolproof, and now, they just had to bide their time.

PART III

CHAPTER 41

Chick's phone blew up with messages and calls about the court appearance. He had warned them to be quiet and trusted they wouldn't mess up the plan.

Will there actually even be enough evidence anyway?, he thought.

Each of the steps they planned played out again in his mind. The stolen car, the shots fired, the weapon ditched, the fire. It had been very public, but nobody had seen their faces. Balaclavas were a godsend. He had to trust they had carried it out as instructed. He had given very specific instructions

The car was stolen, but it was destroyed. They wore gloves and chucked the guns. Surely, they were cleared of any prints?

Circumstantial wouldn't be enough, would it? Chick's mind started to spin. *We've thought of everything. The guys will be fine. They know why they've been picked. Collateral damage.*

His phone rang; it was McColl, but he couldn't begin to deal with the boss just then.

The messages continued to come in from others in the know.

What happened, mate?

What have cops got on them?

Are cops just bluffing?

Seconds later, his phone lit up, vibrating against the glass coffee table in his living room. He ignored it for a second time, but it rattled him, and he didn't know what to tell the old man.

Before he could think about it again, the phone rang for a third time. Chick grunted loudly. The rage in him rose, and he wanted to answer it and shout, "Fuck off!" but he knew better. Instead, he took a breath and hit the green icon on the screen.

"This was meant to be foolproof?" came the gruff voice. Remarkably calm.

Chick clenched his jaw even more. It took all his effort not to groan loudly with frustration again. He'd rather the old man just shouted and took his anger out on him – it might even make Chick

151

feel better.

"It was. It is. It was planned, and it was sorted." He sounded a little pathetic and caught himself. He wasn't one to apologise or grovel, it showed weakness, and that was not what they did.

"Well, clearly it *wasn't*." The final word was delivered through gritted teeth, and Chick could almost feel the spittle hit the phone.

"It'll be fine. Of course, they think it's our guys, but it'll be fine. There's nothing on them, It's polis bullshit."

Silence fell between the men. Chick could feel the pressure building as a bead of sweat trickled down his back. He repeated the assertion to his boss, "It will be *fine.*"

He could hear heavy breathing down the phone and, for a split second, panicked that the old man was having a heart attack due to the stress. It had been Chick's call to do this after all, he just couldn't get his hands dirty.

After what seemed like an eternity, McColl muttered, "You better fucking hope so."

When the old man said nothing more, Chick glanced at his phone and the call had ended. The phone was red hot from all the activity in the past half an hour.

Another ten messages arrived since he'd been on the phone. He threw it across the room; it hit the wall and fell. *I covered everything,* he reminded himself again.

A strange sensation he wasn't used to, took over his body. It wasn't until a few seconds later he realised what it was. Fear.

PART III

CHAPTER 42

Mark Deacon lay on his back, staring at the ceiling of his cell, wondering where life had gone wrong. At what point in his twenty-six years on the planet did it all take a turn for the worst.

I am on remand for the murder of one of Scotland's biggest gangsters, he thought. *All because I was desperate to get in with the big boys.* He hit the wall with his fists.

Mark's mind wandered back to when and how this all started, how he was given attention by the older gang members on his twenty-first birthday in the local pub after two decades of feeling useless.

What better time than now to reminisce, I've got no plans.

Mark had always been smaller than average for his age. He was picked last for sports at school because he wasn't very athletic, acted up in class because he wasn't academic, and didn't have the patience to learn. When he reached his teens, he shaved his bright red, curly hair off - he could never get a style that suited him. Instead, he sported a 'number one' all over, grew a beard, and used his uncle's punch bag to build some muscle – which eventually got him noticed.

He had enjoyed the flattery, the benefits, and the respect that came with being associated with McColl's crowd. But he also knew his ranking.

Why did I let myself get caught up in the drama? When Chick instructed him to carry out the hit, it wasn't so much a request as an order – saying no was not allowed.

For the past five years, he'd been riding on the coattails of the bigger boys who pulled in the funds. He picked up and dropped off packages and kept look-out occasionally, but Mark had never been expected to do the heavy lifting.

There were many perks with only minor responsibilities. It seemed like a good deal. He was prepped for this, it seemed. They'd been grooming him. Now he dreaded having to speak to his gran about what was happening to him.

For a second, he welled up at the thought of the frail,

MURDER CENTRAL

eighty-three-year-old woman who had so much hope for him. It was she who raised him while his mum worked round the clock, a cleaner by day and a barmaid at night.

His Gran tried to make ends meet for them at the flat they shared in Hillington to help his mum, who was a single mum after his dad died when Mark was young. He never knew the full story and the subject was changed anytime it was mentioned. As long as he could remember his mum worked, and his gran stepped in after school and in the evenings when she was needed. She lived one street away and relied on her gangly grandson to reach goods out of the cupboard for his "wee granny."

When he was thirteen and wasn't doing well at school, Mark started skipping days and hanging out at friends' houses.

Prison is making me sentimental, he thought, wiping tears before they trickled down his face. He laughed at how soft he was acting but sat up on his cell bed, allowing his mind to wander again.

At sixteen, he caught the attention of the police when he fell in with McColl's crowd and would catch the bus to drink at their local pub until he was fully inaugurated at twenty-one.

His mind turned back to his family. He always kissed his gran on the forehead and told her not to worry, ignoring the pain he caused her when he crashed out the door on a Friday and didn't return until Sunday.

It wasn't the first night Mark made a late-night call to say he'd be spending the night in the cells or that her beloved grandson had been returned home by the police. Gran kept a lot of her thoughts to herself.

Mark suppressed most of his feelings of shame and guilt, choosing not to think about his Granny Liz, who would be so disappointed. She might not tell him and she would always support him, but he'd see it in her eyes. Her wee Mark accused of murder, she would be utterly heartbroken.

Mark replayed what happened time and time again, unable to think about anything else. On the night of the hit, he collected the stolen car at nearby shops, drove to collect the others, and on to the

154

PART III

NCP car park—all as per the strict instructions from Chick.

He remembered thinking at that point, *Must do as I'm told.*

Mark played Chick's voice on a loop during the car journey there. *Cover your faces, go to the NCP, use the guns under the seat, then get rid of the weapons together, wear gloves, destroy the car.*

The instructions had been drilled into them and repeated over and over. It had seemed flawless. It had seemed quite simple the more Chick said it.

Mark rocked back and forth in his small cell as fear took over. He was charged with murder.

There were so many people, we didn't expect so many people.

Sweat trickled down his back and temples as he relived the scene. He was always told, "If you do anything with enough conviction, you will be in charge of the situation."

It seemed logical at the time, but now, the only thing that seemed to have any conviction was the guilty verdict that would be decided at the end of his criminal trial.

Afterwards, Mark hadn't said a word about it to anyone, not even Chick. And he didn't think any of the other guys would be stupid enough to blab. But *he* wasn't the one who came up with the plan to kill anyone, not like he was accused of. And he didn't even steal the car, he just collected it. None of this was his idea.

Despite what he had done, he actually felt sorry for the dozens of witnesses who stumbled across the bloody scene at the train station. They witnessed the cold-blooded assassination in broad daylight. But the decisions weren't his to make, and the consequences were…well, the other option would be to suffer consequences and have the bullet in *his* head. That much was perfectly clear.

Being part of that group, he felt untouchable. Someone bigger and more important than him could always help get him out of bother. Mark slammed his hands on either side of him, the impact on the rubber mattress stinging his palms. He stood up and paced around the small cell pausing at each wall to bang a fist against it. *They're making me the fall guy.* After a few more lengths of the cell, he sat back down with his fists and jaw clenched. He threw his

155

head against the wall, harder than he expected, sending waves of pain through his skull. He had invested time in this group, and he looked up to Chick – even respected him.

We got rid of the weapons, we torched the car, we did as we were told.

It was out of his hands. He knew he couldn't speak out, so he accepted what was coming. And then he wept. Loud, salty tears poured from his eyes as he sobbed.

***

Racing thoughts kept Mark awake all night before he had to get up for a meeting with his solicitor, Derek Kinnaird. Chick used him before. The man was known within their circle as the go-to brief. Never admit anything, Mark told himself. More strict instructions he had been given.

Don't rat and don't confess, he thought over and over as the hours ticked by slowly.

Mr Kinnaird looked like a lawyer, Mark thought when he clapped eyes on him in their meeting room. Charcoal grey suit, white shirt tucked in albeit creased, and a navy and white striped tie round his neck held together in a loose Windsor knot.

"Right, Mr Deacon. It appears you are part of the criminal gang that's believed to be responsible for the murder of Mr Slaven." Kinnaird crossed his arms and looked at his client over the top of his glasses that had now slipped down the bridge of his nose.

"A witness puts you with Mr Cain earlier that day, phone records put you with him – or so say the prosecution – and you're supposedly on CCTV."

Mark could feel the temperature rise in the room. He shifted uncomfortably in the chair, and he couldn't say anything. He knew it wasn't worth saying a thing even if he wanted to.

"Your DNA was also found on clothing found in your friend's house, and other DNA of theirs was found on items in your house."

The solicitor sighed and picked up one of the documents before

PART III

him.

"I cannot represent you Mr Deacon, if you do not give me any instructions. It is for the Crown to prove your guilt, but I need you to work with me." He stared at Mark who didn't know if he was coming across as arrogant or if his fear was apparent. Beads of sweat made their way down the crack of his arse, and he shifted again, trying to soak it up with his joggers in one swift action that didn't give anything away.

He stared at the paperwork and shrugged. "Wisnae me," he said before hastily adding, "Sir." Mark wanted his lawyer on his side but didn't know how to work with him without speaking.

"Eh, so, am not guilty. Wisnae me," he advanced again, trying to sound convincing.

The lawyer looked at his watch and then momentarily took his mobile phone out from a pocket "Okay, Mr Deacon, I have another appointment. We will revisit the CCTV evidence and phone evidence. Please think carefully and work with me here. You are facing a murder charge."

Mark nodded. He was in over his head and didn't know what to say. But he had plenty of time to think about it.

He was to be kept in jail until the trial, remanded, with plenty of time to mull over the events of that night.

I'll think about this, and nothing else.

CHAPTER 43

It took months for the trial to get underway, which caused more stress than witness Helen McKenzie could ever imagine. Months of pre-trial hearings and delays saw it postponed, including several checks for Martin Cole, until finally, almost eleven months after the incident, the three accused were transported to the High Court from their respective prisons.

The press pack on the first day of the trial gathered excitedly at the front of the building. Dozens of photographers and established reporters, veterans in their field, waited with pad in hand for what would be explosive and dramatic evidence.

Helen hadn't slept properly since her court summons dropped through the letterbox weeks earlier. She had been reassured several times that she would have someone with her at all times, she wasn't in any danger, and that all she had to do was tell the truth about what she remembered that day. From watching courtroom dramas on television, she had an idea of what to expect. Grand courtrooms with posh lawyers wearing wigs and fifteen strangers staring at her. And the men in the dock who were on trial for murder.

Murderers, she thought.

These men were accused of killing a man, and she was a witness. What her children had seen at such a young age, they were traumatised. Not even ten years old and her daughters saw someone murdered. She carried guilt of them being with her when this happened, unable to shield them from the horror.

She took a deep breath as she sat in the waiting area and looked at her watch – 11.49 am. She had been sitting there since 9 am when she arrived as the court building opened early so that nobody saw her. Helen had been warned of the "paparazzi' as they had been referred to by her friend Elizabeth. She replayed that conversation in her head as she waited.

"Just make sure you get in really early before they arrive, and they'll be more interested in those walking in after you. I mean, you're quite an insignificant witness anyway, aren't you? Well not, not important but not like the main one are you? Like, important but not vital? Obviously you're important but I mean, don't worry. That's what I mean." Elizabeth had smiled, unconvincing.

"Helen McKenzie?"

She looked up and saw a woman in a gown holding a paper. Helen nodded, fidgeting with her neck scarf.

"Come with me, please," the woman said with an encouraging smile.

The woman led Helen to a heavy mahogany-coloured door, which the lady in the gown pushed open, and they stepped into the brightly lit courtroom. She guided Helen to the witness stand.

The judge, a rather jolly-looking man with a thick Glasgow accent, offered her a glass of water then reminded her to speak clearly and slowly, to let the court know if she needed a break, and he guided her through taking the oath.

Helen swore to tell the truth, the whole truth, and nothing but the truth.

A woman sitting with her back to Helen got up from the table in the middle of the court mumbling something to the judge as she stood. Turning round to look at the jury, she then carried a pile of papers to the side of the seats where the fifteen strangers sat, and rested them on the edge of the jury box. She smiled.

She has a kind face, Helen thought.

Looking at the woman – who must've been middle-aged as she was – Helen wondered what the most traumatic thing she had ever witnessed was. Surely this job must've forced her to come face to face with evil.

Helen, whose life was dedicated to her children, suddenly felt overwhelmed with fear. She had failed her girls that day. Since then, they had clung to her like little monkeys, terrified to be without her. Both girls had nightmares, and Ella's progressed to night terrors and bedwetting.

The Advocate Depute, prosecuting the case, dropped her pile of notes and a heavy book, which fell with a thud that echoed,

159

snapping Helen out of the safety bubble and trance-like state she drifted into. She pulled her suit jacket down and clasped then unclasped her hands and cleared her throat.

She felt the eyes of the men on trial boring through her. It sent a shiver up her knowing they were watching and listening to her.

"Good morning," the prosecutor said, fixing her notes again. "Can you tell the court your full name, please?"

"Helen Marie McKenzie."

"How old are you?"

"I am forty-two, forty-three next month."

"For the purposes of these proceedings your address is noted as care of Police Scotland."

She glanced nervously at the judge, unsure how she was supposed to respond; nobody had prepared her for personal questions.

"You don't need to give your personal address, Mrs McKenzie," he assured, nodding at her and then at the woman in the wig.

Despite not quite understanding what was going on, she nodded, too.

"What do you do for a living?"

"I'm a sales assistant in a supermarket. Part-time since my daughters started school."

The woman in the wig smiled, and Helen felt her shoulders drop slightly as she tugged at her jacket and clasped her hands again. They were starting to get clammy now.

"Tell me what you were doing on March ninth, last year, please," the woman in the wig asked.

The dull feeling in the pit of Helen's stomach got heavier, and her tongue suddenly felt thicker. She took a gulp from the glass of water in front of her, inadvertently making a loud slurping noise.

"I was in the town with my daughters. I had some clothes to return and they had each been promised a toy. We drove into the NCP. I have a season pass for there – well, my friend does, and I used that... and there's always spaces.

"We did what we had to do and stopped at McDonalds at the four corners where Argyle Street meets Union Street, then walked back to Central Station and went into the entrance under the bridge and into the lift."

She paused, looking around and waiting for those in wigs scribbling notes to gesture so that she could continue.

The lady in the wig made a face Helen thought was a smile and said, "Go on."

Pulling at her jacket again, Helen took a deep breath. "We got out of the lift and walked up the platform. The girls were walking in front, skipping and dancing. But I took their hands, one on either side. I just don't like them on their own when there's train tracks and cars about. Often, people are in a hurry to get to the station. They've been knocked to the ground by impatient people before, so I thought it safer to just take their hands."

She caught herself as she began to ramble and looked up to see the judge with his eyebrows raised and pen poised. Turning back to the lady in the wig, who nodded, Helen took another deep breath.

"Sorry, I'm nervous," she offered, then said, "We walked into the car park from the train platform."

Helen didn't expect to be so emotional at this part, so she grabbed the water in front of her again.

"Take your time, Mrs McKenzie," the Advocate Depute said. "Take your time, and talk us through what happened when you got to the car park."

Helen put the cup down and tucked a loose hair behind her ears.

"I saw two cars, a white Audi on my right with two men standing in front of it, each holding guns—" She stifled a cry, remembering the horrific sight before her. Collecting herself, she continued, "I felt like my feet were stuck to the floor, and I'd stumbled onto a movie set. The men had balaclavas on and dark clothes, possibly tracksuits? They fired the guns right at the windscreen of the white car."

She gasped and widened her eyes.

"What did you do, Mrs McKenzie?" the lawyer asked her.

As though snapping out of a trance, she stared back, tears

MURDER CENTRAL

streaming down her face as she recalled how terrified she felt.

"I grabbed my girls and jumped behind a nearby car. I just wanted out of the way of the shots."

Helen quickly wiped her tears with a handkerchief from the box before her.

"What did you think was happening, Mrs McKenzie?"

"I...I—"

"Objection! Speculation, My Lord. The witness cannot speak to that." The man was on his feet.

The prosecutor nodded at the judge and, without exchanging any words with him, turned back to Helen, who was confused by the theatrical interjection.

"Mrs McKenzie, what did you understand was happening in the car park based on what you saw?"

Still feeling confused, Helen slowly replied, "That the two men with guns were shooting someone in the Audi, the white car."

"Did you see who was in the car?"

"No," Helen said. But quickly added, "I just saw two men, people, well, men, wearing black, shooting, and I hid. I just wanted to get my girls..."

She took a moment to stop a huge sob from escaping, taking care to be clear.

"I just wanted to get my girls out of the way. It all happened so fast. I pulled them onto the ground with me and just waited. I heard doors slamming and a car driving off, but we just sat there. I didn't want to move."

Helen pressed her eyes hard with the tissue in her hand now crumbled and wet from mopping her damp cheeks moments earlier.

She never expected to be so emotional and tearful.

After what felt like minutes, the prosecutor asked how long she remained crouched with her daughters.

"I don't know how long, can't even guess. I just held my girls close and prayed they would leave us alone. Then a kind lady offered the girls some chocolate until the police turned up and told us we were safe."

162

PART III

Helen let out a cry this time, unable to contain it. Glancing at the jury box, she saw fifteen strangers staring back at her. One woman in the front row, who must've been the same age as her, looked tearful.

Maybe she has children, Helen thought.

A young adult in the back row looked completely unaffected and, dare she think it – bored. Most displayed a look of concern with some furiously scribbling notes, while some just looked shocked.

"Thank you, Mrs McKenzie. Please stay where you are. There will be more questions for you." The prosecutor nodded at Helen, then the judge as she collected her folders of paper and glided across the court – her black gown flailing behind her – as she took her seat on her side of the table in the courtroom.

A tall, older man with a noticeable stature and white hair poking out from under his wig – that had seen better days – and a grubby-looking gown cleared his throat as he took to his feet and made his way to the lectern opposite Helen. "Thank you, M'Lud," he said, nodding to the judge, then rifling through papers in front of him.

"Good afternoon Mrs McKenzie," he muttered without looking up.

He flicked through the pile of papers before him, scoring words out and highlighting others. The man looked up, smiled, or perhaps grimaced was a better description, and fixed his wig.

"I represent Mr. Cain," he said, gesturing to the dock where the men sat, and until then, Helen had avoided looking. She knew they were sitting a mere few yards from her and the thought sent tingles down her spine. She bristled on hearing a name being mentioned by the lawyer.

"You told the court of hearing gunshots, diving out of sight, and fearing for your children's lives? Have I understood you correctly?"

Helen nodded and tugged at her jacket, shifting her weight in her seat.

"For the benefit of the recording, please speak."

"Ah, sorry. Yes, that's correct," Helen squeaked, not intending

163

her answer to come out so meekly.

With a concerned look, Jamie Cain's defence solicitor said, "That must have been terrifying, Mrs McKenzie."

Again, she nodded as another hot lump formed and made its way back up her throat, but she managed to let out the sound "Mmmhmm...yes."

Sounding very matter-of-fact, leaning forward on the lectern nonchalantly, the lawyer sighed. "My client accepts that is how you feel. He knows how scary you must have found this situation and is very empathetic..."

There was a pause as he took a slight breath, followed by a longer silence.

"But," he continued, "from your evidence, you appear to accept that you did not see this man." He leaned on the lectern and gestured to his client with a head flick.

"No....I mean, yes I accept that. I saw people but not faces."

"Because in the moment, such was your level of fear and concern for your daughters, you immediately hid from the masked individuals, not taking in what was going on. And therefore, unable to see what was happening? Have I understood this correctly, too?"

"Yes, sir."

The rotund lawyer looked at her over his glasses before looking back at the judge. "No further questions."

Helen could have cried with relief when she was thanked and discharged from her duty. But the solace was short-lived as she emerged from the building to the baying mob of press photographers and journalists.

Without a second to realise what was happening, the sound of whirring and clicking hit her as cameras flashed and recorded her.

"Mrs McKenzie, how are you?"

"Mrs McKenzie, can you stop for a quick chat?"

"Mrs McKenzie..."

"Mrs McKenzie!"

Instinctively, she pulled her hood up and marched towards King Street car park. Helen broke into a jog and crossed the road

PART III

to the car park with her name ringing in her ears, until eventually it stopped.

MURDER CENTRAL

CHAPTER 44

Listening to the terrified woman giving evidence April couldn't help but feel sympathy for what the witness had seen and heard. She listened intently in court taking notes of everything. On day one of the trial, there would be an appetite for anything said about such a high-profile matter.

The journalist took down all her notes carefully and precisely, marking the quotes as she heard them, planning to return to use them again. This truly was like something out of a film: gangland shooting, terror, murder, and fear.

For months the story had gone quiet. Until the conclusion of the trial there was little else that could be written. There was no word from Paul although April still hoped she would hear from him.

Before calling the next witness, the prosecutor and all of the QCs representing the three accused presented as one, a document to the court with a note of all the evidence in the case that was agreed and wouldn't be contested. This was much of the information gathered by police officers to save them from coming to court to confirm they were responsible for taking statements or locating CCTV. It was evidence that was pre-determined and should be considered by the jury as fact, not decide if it was true or not.

April noted down the details that it was agreed Mr Slaven died after being shot in the head and body and that the bullets and cartridges were retrieved at the scene.

Everybody knew that, but now it was official: he was murdered.

Seeing as Martin Cole was away and with no sign of returning, it also came as no surprise that special defences were put forward by those in the dock claiming that he was responsible, which was why he fled.

Typical, April thought. *He left them in the shit. They owed him nothing – so much for loyalty.*

The clerk continued reading out details, this information would be useful at the end of the trial. If they were convicted, every single

PART III

detail would be lapped up, and how the three accused were seen in each other's company on a number of occasions in months and weeks leading up to the murder. Thick as thieves, as the old cliché went.

None of them can deny this, April thought. *I bet their lawyers will say that this wasn't relevant and didn't prove they were murderers,* she predicted.

April watched the prosecutor call the next witness, Janice Moffat, a forty-five-year-old accountant who was returning home from her job at Morgan Stanley. She had left the building on Waterloo Street around 4.40 pm, shortly before the fatal attack.

"If I hadn't stood talking to my friend Evelyn outside Marks and Spencer in the train station, I might have been on my way home at that time!" she told the court, sounding almost tearful.

April listened to Mrs Moffat tell the court that she walked to the car park in good spirits, having had a catch-up with her friend. Then, instead of getting into her Renault Megane and listening to Robbie Williams on her drive home to Bearsden, she walked in on the scene of a crime just in time to see the driver of the Audi scramble out of the car and disappear through the door behind him.

Daniel Tonner, one of the low level gang members working for Clarke was with Slaven that day, that must have been him running, April thought. *I bet he got schtick for leaving his mate.*

"I didn't see how tall or small the person was or the colour of their hair, just that a person ran out of a white car, slamming the door behind them just as another car blocked it in." Mrs Moffat mopped her brow and took a sip of water.

April looked at the jury, who were all listening intently.

"Just as I was walking by to go to my own car on the same level, I noticed passengers getting out of the car that was doing the blocking and heard gunshots being fired. Shots from guns! Like something out of a film! I ran to my car and threw myself on the back seat and waited until the police arrived." She dabbed tears from her eyes.

"Are you okay Mrs Moffat? the judge asked.

She nodded, smiling weakly at him as jurors furiously scribbled

167

MURDER CENTRAL

notes.

April copied them, making sure she had all the dramatic sound bites.

She circled the notes she had just made to remind her to use this passage when she wrote her article.

She noticed during Mrs Moffat's evidence that Barry glanced at the jury for the first time. There were six middle-aged women and three middle-aged men.

With little to cross-examine her on, she wasn't asked many questions by others. April thought the fear in Barry's face was so obvious, he would have been as well having a speech bubble above his head saying "Guilty."

Whether by coincidence or because she noticed it too, his QC Laura Eccles, a petite blonde known for her sharp mind – sharp tongue — and successful defending, rose to her feet. Unlike her male counterparts with their tattered presentations, Miss Eccles was immaculate. Her blonde bob sat perfectly under her wig, and her gown was a deep black as though she wore a new one every day in contrast to the faded charcoal of her peers.

Miss Eccles pulled it over her shoulders as she stood up, leaving it trailing only slightly along the ground, just covering the stilettos she effortlessly glided around on. She was a straight-talker who liked to cut through nonsense and deal in facts. April found her fascinating to watch.

"Mrs Moffat," said Miss Eccles with a smile but to the point, skipping pleasantries, "we all understand how awful this was for you to witness such a terrifying incident and how scared you were. However, you didn't get a look at the person who ran away from the parked Audi. Is that correct?"

Mrs Moffat shook her head.

The QC added, "For the record, the witness is shaking her head, indicating no. Please speak for the benefit of the recording," the lawyer said without breaking stride.

Leaning onto the lectern, pointing directly at her client while maintaining eye contact with the witness, Miss Eccles continued,

168

PART III

"Did you see Mr Harris that day at the scene, please?"

Awkwardly, the witness looked over at the dock. She avoided all eye contact with the men accused of being gangsters until that point.

"No," Mrs Moffat replied firmly.

"To be very clear, did you see *anyone* in this courtroom today there on the day in question, Mrs Moffat?" the fiery lawyer shot back.

The accountant, whether for effect or because of the question she was asked, took a moment to scour the room, studying the faces of people facing her. April felt her face flush as the witness made eye contact with her.

"No," she said again just as firmly.

"Thank you, Mrs Moffat," Miss Eccles replied with a curt smile. "No further questions, My Lord."

She floated back to her seat on her stilt-like shoes.

This is the general defence, April thought. "*Making it clear to the jury that despite seeing the horrific shooting, they cannot say it was the men on trial who were responsible.*

The prosecutor said she had one further question. April sat ready to take the final piece of the woman's evidence.

"How has witnessing this incident affected you, Mrs Moffat?"

There was a pause for a few seconds. The witness sighed and glanced at the three men in the dock before looking back at the judge.

"I have a teenage daughter, an eighteen-year-old who is now terrified to let me go out on my own," Mrs Moffat told Mrs Park, the prosecutor, as she clutched a handkerchief. "It's usually the other way, me worrying about her, and I don't want to scare her. How do I tell her that I was already stressed about her going out into town but that now, seeing what I've seen, I'd love nothing more than to keep her at home forever. I want to prevent her from ever seeing anything like the horror I saw that day."

***

169

MURDER CENTRAL

Before she knew it, it was 1 pm and time for April to find a quiet corner during the lunch hour and send the first instalment evidence to the news editors who were waiting impatiently. Eyewitness accounts detailing the fear and horror of the public killing should be enough to whet their appetites for what was to come.

April saw the other reporters from the broadcast outlets reading over and practising their script for the camera. They dusted their suits as they paced and talked to themselves, preparing to share the news on the television live from outside the court building.

She dug out a crumpled foil-covered sandwich and munched it, barely stopping for breath. Then swilled water from a bottle round her mouth to wash it down and blew away the crumbs that had gathered on her keyboard.

Her mobile had already started to ring, news editors asking where her copy was, but they would need to wait. The more calls she answered, the longer it would take to hit send.

April turned her focus back to the screen as the tannoy announced the trial was restarting.

"Her Majesty's advocate against Mark Deacon, Barry Harris, and Jamie Cain."

Not wanting to miss anything, April frantically re-read her article of drama and eyewitness testimony aloud, quietly double-checking each of the quotes with her notes and ensuring that all details were accurate. Then, she hit send and slammed her laptop shut.

Pulling her phone out to make sure it was still on silent, she shoved it and her laptop back into her bag, then fished out her notepad and the stash of pens so everything was at hand.

April pushed the heavy oak door open, stepped into the courtroom, and silently took her seat, allowing herself to get back into the writing zone.

170

PART III

CHAPTER 45

A businessman called Gordon Brooke was the final witness on the first day of the trial. April's ears perked up when she heard the man say he had given a statement to PC William Field on the day of the shooting.

"I should have been on the train. I had to drop my elderly mother at a hair appointment. So it was just as easy to drive to Glasgow than to try and get the train. I wouldn't have seen anything if it had been any other day," he told the prosecutor, misty-eyed.

Like those before him, he was unable to identify the shooters but was struck by the unadulterated violence that saw a man executed before it was even dark without care towards who saw or could have been caught in the crossfire.

"They just opened fire like they were shooting at a dart-board."

A strange comment caught April's attention as she scribbled down his evidence. The witness, looking pale and scared as though the memory of reliving the moment was painful said, "They just… fired shots at a man who couldn't escape. It was like they had been taken over by the devil himself."

Well, thought April, *this will be tomorrow's headline.*

Mr Brooke was thanked for his time and, again, like the witnesses before him, had to concede he didn't see the faces of the shooters or the driver of the car and couldn't identify anyone involved.

It was a somewhat anticlimactic end to the evidence, but the sound bites had already done damage; his words lingered over the jury box, slowly seeping into their subconscious.

That brought the first day's evidence to a close. The lawyers round the table breathed a sigh of relief. Everything went as smoothly as it could when the evidence finally got underway. There were still fifteen members of the jury, no technical issues, and nobody had been held in contempt of court.

Now, they just had to do it all over again the next day.

171

April grabbed a seat outside the courtroom in the public foyer in a position where nobody could walk behind and read what was on her screen, but she could still watch what was going on. It was a bizarre situation during a trial; all sides involved in the case – the family of the victim and the relatives of those on trial sat separately in the courtroom.

She watched police officers keeping a watchful eye, maintaining the peace but ready to react if there was any trouble.

Watching everyone leaving at the same time reminded April of an occasion a year earlier when she was in the basement of Glasgow Sheriff Court. She heard shouting and screaming from the floor above. Hurrying up to the reception of the biggest court in Europe, she was met with a scene of total chaos – two feuding families being held back from one another. Some were held against the nearest wall by officers with their batons drawn, the police shoved others to the ground while a number were kicked out of the building.

Never a dull moment in this job, she thought.

Snapping out of her daydream, she turned back to her screen to thrash out the second story of the day.

Alleged murderers were "possessed by the devil", court hears was the subject and heading.

She bashed out a few hundred words which she triple-checked for accuracy. April sent it and allowed herself to breathe again.

First day done, what will tomorrow bring?

PART III

CHAPTER 46

To April's and other media members' surprise, Daniel Tonner was called as a witness. Sheepishly, he took to the witness stand with his head down as much as possible. With the help of the judge, he took the oath, swearing to tell the truth.

They really expect him to tell the truth about that day? April sat with her pen poised, very curious about what he would say.

Prosecutor Sheila Park returned to the lectern almost with a spring in her step. "Can you tell the court your full name, please."

"Daniel Tonner," he muttered, barely audible.

"Mr Tonner, I'm afraid you need to speak up. Please speak into the microphone in front of you," she told him.

April laughed inwardly, she had covered other court cases involving Tonner.

This isn't Tonner's first time in a court and he knows how to speak into a microphone giving evidence.

"Sorry. Aye." He nodded, keeping his eyes down.

"How old are you, Mr Tonner?"

"Twenty-seven."

"Speak up!" she repeated.

He shouted, "Twenty-seven!" which prompted sniggers from some of the jury.

This wasn't his first rodeo in a court, but he wasn't used to being put on the spot as a witness, April noted, watching him intently.

"What do you do for a living?" Mrs Park asked.

This time, he replied in a quieter but audible voice, "Between jobs the now. Lookin' for work."

April knew he wouldn't want to explain to the court what his off-the-books job involved and why he didn't pay taxes. For once, he wasn't on trial.

"What were you doing on March ninth, Mr Tonner?" she asked very matter-of-fact.

"Eh, cannae mind," he mumbled again.

173

MURDER CENTRAL

The prosecutor sighed, glancing over at the judge, who stared back at her.

Staring directly at Tonner, she spoke slower, pronouncing every word. "I think you can, Mr Tonner. Take a moment and think, cast your mind back. Where were you on March ninth?"

He shuffled from side to side and looked at the judge who was visibly irritated by his behaviour by this time.

"Eh…" Daniel looked at the men in the dock with a look April thought showed fear.

Looking back at Mrs Park, he said, "I was out and about with… eh…with Josh Slaven." He suddenly seemed sad with glazed eyes, not emotions April thought he would show.

Surely he wouldn't want to show the men in the dock that they were getting to him?

"What were you doing with Mr Slaven that day?"

April watched intently, *This is the detail we need,* she thought.

"Just…driving about. I was out for something to do, and Josh was with me for company." He said it with a straight face, staring directly at the prosecutor.

Mrs Park flicked through her papers, then asked, "What happened when you were out with Mr Slaven that day?"

"We were in the car park in the town, I eh…Josh was meeting someone. Then a car turned up, and it blocked us in, which was pure weird, so I just ran—" His voice shook as it broke off, and he looked at the jury.

April followed his glance to the fifteen strangers taking notes.

Are they going to believe him?

Mrs Park paused for a second, seemingly allowing the witness to squirm in the box across the courtroom and for him to feel all eyes on him. "Are you aware there were a number of weapons, a sub-stantial sum of cash and drugs within the vehicle?"

At this stage the Judge coughed before intervening. "Mr Tonner, you are not obliged to give an answer which may incriminate you in any criminal matters. You can answer as you see fit." The judge nodded at the prosecutor, signalling for her to continue.

174

PART III

"Yes, of course, Mr Tonner," Mrs Park said in a matter-of-fact tone. "However the question remains, please do answer as you see fit."

Shifting from foot to foot the witness stared at the judge, then the prosecutor and briefly towards the dock where the three men sat. "I don't really wantae answer."

I wonder why, April thought looking around the room at the reaction. Jurors exchanged glances and some made notes.

"Very well. But you ran away when you saw the car stop?" she asked with a raised eyebrow as though asking an innocent question.

"Aye, I mean, yes miss…"

Sniggers erupted around the court, making Daniel's face flush. He hurriedly added, "I was getting out the motor anyway, and then the car pulled up dead fast and blocked me in an' ah panicked and just ran. I, eh, thought Josh was behind me, so ran doon the stairs and then a heard bangs like a gun or the car backfiring or that it was a gun an' just ran."

Another silence fell across the courtroom.

He's rambling, April thought as she looked round; all eyes were fixed on him.

As a gang member who liked to flex his muscles and make people feel small, he looked like he was shrinking by the minute.

"Did you see anyone in the car that blocked you in?" Mrs Park asked.

Immediately and, with confidence, Daniel emphatically said, "No."

It was the perfect segue into the questions everyone anticipated.

April and her broadcast journalist colleagues leaned forward in the press box, desperate not to miss a word of the exchange as it heated up. She hoped gangland connections were mentioned – however fleeting – for the jury to hear and make for an exciting and dramatic story from the day's evidence.

Once it's said in open court and they hear it, we can write it, April silently urged.

"Did Mr Slaven have any enemies, Mr Tonner?" Mrs Park

175

MURDER CENTRAL

asked.

April watched the muscles in his jaw tighten. This was the answer everyone was waiting for. He could be the star witness who explained Slaven was a hated man who was only nice to his friends and family. He had a list of enemies the length of his arm, and all of the men on trial couldn't stand him and felt threatened.

"Dunno, ah thought he was a good guy."

April knew he was lying.

Rolling her eyes and leaning forward on the lectern, Mrs Park asked, "Are you sure, Mr Tonner? There was nobody that you knew of who might have a vendetta against your friend?"

"Mmmm, no. He was a good friend."

Daniel had to have known he didn't sound convincing. April shook her head.

"Mr Tonner, your friend was close with a man called Thomas Clarke, is that right?" The lawyer was clearly starting to lose patience and wanted to get something that proved Slaven was a gangster gunned down by his rivals, showing motive for his cold-blooded murder.

"Yes, he knows him – knew him," Daniel said tentatively.

She wondered what went through the prosecutor's mind. Her task was cut out for her. Mrs Park had to establish the evidence and convince fifteen strangers of organised crime and how the three men were linked to it.

Anyone listening to this would think it was the plot of a film: masked men shoot someone at point-blank range in a car park attached to a busy train station. April could see her articles hit the spotlight.

"Are you aware of a person called Michael McColl?"

April anticipated this move. Ms Park had to be feeling quite smug that she had to spoon-feed him to make a fool of himself.

"Naw, don't know him."

His forehead glistened with sweat as the words came out.

Of course, he knows McColl was behind the shooting, but he isn't a grass, and he's too scared of what will happen to him. April's thoughts

PART III

swirled.

"Please put production twenty-six before Mr Tonner and place it on the viewer for jurors to see," the prosecutor said.

A staff member handed Daniel a picture then took a copy of it and placed it on the projector for everyone in the court to view on screens.

"You were seen on CCTV on Hope Street having left Mr Slaven and run off. You were captured here on a telephone call. Who were you talking to?"

April watched with anticipation.

"It was a very stressful night. I can't remember who I phoned," Daniel said with a serious expression.

She almost looked as though she was going to laugh at him, but instead, Mrs Park smiled and nodded. "And what happened to your phone?"

"Ah, well, dunno. I lost it somewhere, think I left it on a bus." He shrugged.

Moments later as Mrs Park looked through her papers, Daniel lifted his hand as though asking a question at school. April shuffled forward to make sure she didn't miss anything.

"I am the one asking the questions, Mr Tonner." The prosecutor peered at him over her glasses.

Looking sheepish Daniel cleared his throat. "I, eh, I need the toilet. Can I go please?" he mumbled.

The judge called a tea break, giving everyone fifteen minutes to grab a cup of tea and stretch their legs.

Buying himself time, April thought as she made her way out of the court room.

Following her coverage the previous day, she had earned commissions from two more newspapers to cover the trial for them, so her wages for the next few weeks would hopefully be generous.

April quickly typed, "Day 2, Tonner claims he can't remember details of shooting due to stress! Thanks, A," which she fired off to papers waiting to hear from her.

This would, she hoped, keep the baying news editors happy

177

until she sent the articles.

Her phone vibrated in her pocket, pulling it out she saw Joseph's name flash up.

Tonner's picture in the bag.

She felt a flash of relief, knowing there was a picture to go with the story. April sent back a smiley face emoji to acknowledge his message and made her way back to the court when the case was called again over the Tannoy.

PART III

CHAPTER 47

The scrawny teenager who shared a cell in the Young Offenders' Institute with Barry told the court he was threatened during their time inside.

Not looking good for you, April thought, listening to the details.

She looked over at Barry sitting with his head down during all of the evidence.

"You had a particularly fraught exchange with Mr Harris, didn't you?" Mrs Park asked.

"We were in a cell, 'course we fell oot," he answered deadpan.

The prosecutor dramatically rolled her eyes and adjusted her wig. "You told prison guards, and later the police, about an incident involving you and Mr Harris. Please tell us about that incident."

Moving from foot to foot in the witness box, and rubbing a hand over his shaven head, the witness looked nervous. "He said he'd hurt me if I kept winding him up?"

"Please tell us *exactly* what happened. We can always look at what you told the police at the time when I'm sure your memory was much better."

The teenager hesitated, then said, "I was annoying him about his girlfriend, and he pushed me against a wall and said that he'd kill me like he did Slaven."

Mrs Park searched her notes and asked for an image from the list of evidence to be displayed on the big screen for the witness, the jury, and members of the public and the press to see.

A moment later, a close-up image of a very dead Josh Slaven covered in bullet holes in the front seat of the white Audi was on the screen. There was a gasp from two women in the jury and stifled sobs from some people in the public gallery, which April thought was Slaven's mum and sister.

The young witness looked completely shell-shocked.

"Mr Harris is on trial, accused of murdering this gentleman who, as you can see here, died a horrible death. When you had an altercation with Mr Harris, what did he say to you that caused you to give a statement to the police?" Mrs Park asked loudly.

"He told me that if ah… eh…if ah didnae shut up and stop annoying him, eh, that, eh, he would make sure ah kept Slaven company. Eh, he said he'd already done that to him, and he'd do it again."

Barry stared wide-eyed at the image then glowered at the witness.

The young man glanced sideways to the man he'd just claimed admitted killing the dead gangster still on the screen.

If looks could kill he'd have dropped down dead on the spot, April thought.

With a satisfied look, Mrs Park picked up her papers and smiled at the witness. "Thank you for your time."

The court macer stood behind the judge and bellowed, "All rise."

Everyone in the old courtroom stood and waited for the judge to be led up to his chambers.

April rushed to the cafeteria to boot up her laptop and file the evidence so far – including the juicy soundbites of the supposed confession by Barry.

She finished her copy, adding "Ends" to the bottom to signify its end, read it over for a fourth and final time, and sent it to the relevant news desks.

No sooner had she shut her laptop, she heard a notification on her phone. It was a message from Paul, a name she never expected to see again. Raising her eyebrows she tapped in her passcode to unlock the screen.

There is more to this than you know. He'll kill me if he knows I'm doing this but we need to talk. Please meet me at McChuills at 7.

The message didn't immediately make any sense to her, which she assumed was intentional.

April was intrigued by Paul's very cryptic message, especially after months of no communication. She wasn't surprised there was more to it and felt a spike of adrenaline at the thought of uncovering

PART III

more shocking details about this case.

She called home to say she'd be late and went to McDonald's on Argyle Street to grab dinner before meeting Paul at the pub. Drinking midweek wouldn't end well if she had no food, and after the day's evidence, she was having a wine or four.

April ordered a drink for each of them when she arrived at the pub. She knew there was more to it than had come out in the evidence. Paul was finally coming through now though, and she trusted him.

While waiting, she scrolled through BBC and STV news websites, reading their versions of the first court day. It was dramatic, and anyone reading at home would be shocked by the guns and death.

As a journalist, April couldn't think about it too much. It made her question humanity and got into her head. She had to focus on the job at hand.

Over an hour later, there was still no sign of her police contact. April got herself another drink; she didn't want to bombard him after the frosty response in their last communication.

By 8.15 pm, there was still no sign. Staring at his name on her phone screen and without overthinking it, she hit the call button.

It rang twice, then someone picked up. The voice wasn't Paul's.

"Hello?" she said more of a question than the opening to a conversation.

April held her breath, panicked. Her mouth instantly felt dry and she heard her heartbeat in her ears. Who was this, and where was Paul?

There was a muffled sound, then the voice, clear again, said, "Paul can't come out tonight, darling. He's a bit under the weather."

Confused, she asked, "Put him on the phone, please? I'm a friend of his." April was not nearly as calm as she hoped but she expected the background noise of the pub would mask her shaky voice.

She heard a muffled noise. Then two voices but couldn't make out anything that was said. The first voice spoke to her again.

181

MURDER CENTRAL

"Yes, doll. He told me about you and how you like to…*talk.* Maybe leave him alone for a while."

April stared at her screen. Whoever that was had ended the call. *What the hell just happened?*

April drained her glass of rose wine and left the pub. She had no idea what to do.

She phoned Joseph to tell him as she walked home, giving her time to think. As she explained what had happened she constantly looked behind her. Should she report it to the police? Paul *was* police. It made no sense.

Thinking about this, April found herself chewing her nails so much that one of her fingertips started to bleed.

This is bad. I know it.

"Fuck-ing hell," Joseph drew the words out as he said them like he was trying to figure out what was going on at the same time as speaking. "What are you going to do? Who the hell was on the phone, and what's your man got on them?"

"I've no idea but there's obviously a lot more to this than we think."

Those were the same questions April had asked herself on a loop since the line went dead. So many questions and absolutely none of the answers, and now she didn't know when she'd next get Paul on his own to find out what he knew or who he was involved with.

As she approached her flat, she said goodbye to Joseph, promising to call him again the following day if she had any ideas about what she would do or if she heard from Paul by some miracle. She suspected he would have been threatened within an inch of his life and would not be divulging any more information.

April kicked her shoes off, changed into her pyjamas, and sat down intending to watch Love Island.

Within minutes, she was looking up all of the day's witnesses and connected parties on social media, trying to marry up any possible connections to figure out what Paul would tell her and do her own digging for what may not come out in court.

Two hours later and thirteen years deep into various gangland

182

PART III

girlfriends' Facebook pictures, she decided to call it a night.

As she took herself to bed, a single thought circled her mind. *I need to speak to Paul.*

MURDER CENTRAL

CHAPTER 48

Checking her phone for the umpteenth time, April couldn't shake the feeling something was wrong. Paul hadn't been online on WhatsApp since the day before. Her stomach lurched each time she looked at their conversation, hoping for any sign of activity.

Gathering her things from the kitchen table, April returned to court for another day of evidence. She would need to deal with Paul later.

Terrence Hughes was the witness April was eager to hear from. He took to the stand mid-morning in his usual manner, confident – borderline cocky – with a crisp tailored suit. April had watched this behaviour before.

Mr Hughes was an expert witness, well versed in giving evidence and very good at delivering it; he knew that too. A thirty-five-year-old bachelor who was dubbed "Court Casanova" with a reputation as a player. April heard he was the flashy kind who had a reputation for using women. The rumours were that a few thought they'd change him.

April recalled hearing one trainee who almost made it to a second date, but the new girl soon got the message when her colleague was collected the following week from their office.

Mr Hughes, with his slick back sandy blonde hair and overpowering aftershave, took the oath. It didn't take long to get to the good stuff. April was expecting him to be part of the trial that nailed these gangster types and get his name in the papers. He previously confessed to April that he thrived on the adrenaline and having the spotlight on him. It was amazing what people shared with her at times.

So she knew that feeling all eyes on him made him feel powerful and fed his ever-growing ego. Some people got their kicks from lines of coke in the toilet – occasionally, a lethargic lawyer would slope off to a loo and return with a renewed sense of fire in their belly. Perhaps they'd just had a double espresso, but she often thought

184

PART III

the flat surfaces in the toilets would likely shock any toxicologist.

Mr Hughes didn't appear to need any powdered substance to help him puff his chest like a peacock. His drug was a room full of people hanging on his every word. It made April laugh to watch the performance.

Often, the younger male members of the jury would roll their eyes; he was everything they knew women, and some men, didn't want in a partner but that some *would* ultimately fall for his charm and charisma.

When he was sure all eyes were on him, he took delight in showing off his knowledge of how cell site analysis worked.

"On the face of it, it's quite dull," he said candidly, leaning forward and speaking directly into the microphone. "But, it's cool when it helps to solve crime."

Mrs Park smiled at the witness. He might be crucial to the trial, but she clearly loathed giving this man a platform.

Her case appeared to be coming together nicely, but it was all circumstantial. April watched on, knowing the prosecutor needed to pin concrete evidence on these guys.

Mr Hughes scanned the jury box as though searching. His frown morphed into a smile. As April looked over, she saw his gaze was met by a blonde-haired juror in the front row. It appeared he had his target audience.

"As an expert witness used in cases where officers want me to analyse mobile phones, I am asked to determine if there are any patterns." He ran a hand over his head as though slicking back his already perfectly groomed hair.

April watched the girl in the jury nod, scribbling notes as she listened. The impact he had on people was quite impressive.

Glancing back to Mrs Park, who nodded and looked at the clock to encourage him to speak more quickly, April thought she saw him wink back but couldn't be sure.

Adjusting the microphone to speak directly into it, he paused before continuing to describe how important his work was. "I check which numbers have been called on devices that have been seized

MURDER CENTRAL

by the police and if they are thought to be associated with anyone.

"I also identify which cell masts the devices have communicated with, which can put phones in a particular area. I know it sounds boring, but it can be very revealing." He smiled at another member of the jury. An older woman in the second row this time.

April shook her head at his ego.

He went on to explain that, in this case, he examined phone communication between the relevant phones and identified potentially important information before drawing conclusions about what all the information meant.

On seeing some juror's eyes glaze over and others become restless, the judge called for a break. They needed a chance to take in the technical information before they lost interest.

April was grateful for the break. She thought jurors wouldn't realise it yet, but it was interesting. It would heat up when he got into the meaty evidence about *who* was *where* at certain times.

Lawyers managed to string out the break for an extra ten minutes, smoking outside the court with their wigs and gowns and looking the theatrical part.

April sat on the wall outside, taking in the fresh air, watching what was going on around her. Paul still hadn't been online. She was worried but didn't know what to do. They weren't friends, but she couldn't shake the feeling that something had happened to him.

What is going on?

Testing the water, she typed out a text.

Hi, how's it going? When's your next day off?

An open question that required an answer but nothing suspicious. It seemed safe. Without thinking much more, she hit 'send.' The message was delivered, and she put her phone away.

Staring at the screen wouldn't help, and she needed to get into court mode again.

The if-he-was-chocolate-he'd-eat-himself witness had obviously been called for a reason, but April relied on more than what she'd heard so far to get an interesting angle for her story today. She needed him to get to the exciting evidence fast. Such was his

186

PART III

arrogant demeanour; April could never remember his name despite listening to his evidence in several trials. What she remembered was that Mr Suave, as she thought of him, was about to deliver some tasty lines that would give her a story for the day and help send these gangsters to prison.

Just as the thought crossed her mind, she heard the sound of the Tannoy and the clerk calling for the trial to recommence.

Enjoying the limelight and having topped up his already pungent aftershave, Mr Hughes stood tall like he was collecting an award, ready to thank his adoring audience at the lectern.

MURDER CENTRAL

CHAPTER 49

Looking exhausted, Mrs Park rifled through her paperwork. "Can you tell us what you concluded about the devices you examined in this case, Mr Hughes?"

Clearing his throat and taking a sip of water, he straightened his jacket and smiled at the judge. "I examined several devices that have been linked to the men who are on trial today." He nodded at the dock where they sat, staring ahead of them with blank expressions. "I very carefully combed through all parts of the phones provided to me, checking messages exchanged between numbers and determining which areas the phones were used in and when." He smiled at the dock as though taking glee in exposing their involvement.

"Thank you, Mr Hughes. What did that show?"

"Most of the time, the phones attributed to each of the men were in or near to where they live." He paused again to give everyone time to finish their notes and return their gaze to him. "I identified the phone masts that picked up signals when the calls and text messages were sent and received from the devices, which made it possible to ascertain where the users were at any given time. It's all in the report."

Mrs Park asked for another production to be put before Mr Hughes, and a document was given to him, which he confirmed was the report he had written. The prosecutor then took him to a section he had written about Mark Deacon.

April glanced at the man on trial. At the sound of his name, he broke from his trance and dropped his head as though praying.

"Why do you say this is a phone Mr Deacon used, please," Mrs Park asked.

Looking back at the jury, Mr Hughes said, "This phone we are talking about, it was picked up by a number of phone masts at the same time as another mobile phone, one that was registered to Mr Deacon. And, for weeks before the incident and for a few weeks after it, both phones were found to be in the vicinity of each other

188

PART III

and in the area Mr Deacon resides."

The jury appeared to find this interesting, shifting in their seats with some jotting down notes. April also noticed the prosecutor, Mrs Park, pick up on this, too.

"Tell us, Mr Hughes, was there anything of significance on this second mobile phone which is attributed to Mr Deacon, one of the men on trial?"

The expert witness cleared his throat again. "The phone had less activity after the murder. However, one message sent to that phone was a screenshot from another unknown number. It con-tained information about Mr Slaven's movements on March ninth, the day he was murdered."

To make sure she drove the point home, the prosecutor asked quietly, "You are telling this court that the phone, believed to be Mr Deacon's, received a message with a screen grab from another number. That screen grab contained information about Mr Slaven's whereabouts on the day he was killed? Thus informing Mr Deacon?"

Nodding forcefully, he replied, "Yes, ma'am, that's exactly correct."

"Would you please read out the information contained in that message?"

Mr Hughes squinted at the report, "It said 'Good authority he'll be there at 4.55. You didn't get it from me.' Or at least that is my interpretation given the poor spelling and punctuation." He laughed.

"What can you tell us about this message, Mr Hughes?"

He cleared his throat and turned his body to the judge to con-fidently answer, "This phone, the one attributed to Mr Deacon, received this screenshot of this message on the morning Mr Slaven was killed."

The jury remained gripped. Mr Hughes cleared his throat.

"There are also calls between the numbers identified as being linked to Mr Deacon and other two accused. The calls between the numbers were picked up by cell masts near their homes."

"And the message you speak of in the screen grab, can you reveal when that was sent?"

189

MURDER CENTRAL

Mr Hughes nodded, seeming delighted to delve into the minutia of his role and explain why this evidence was crucial. It was clear he felt important. Looking smug, he said, "Yes, the screengrab was from a WhatsApp message and it clearly shows the word 'yesterday' above."

"What else can you tell us about the data recovered from this particular phone?"

"There were a couple of cryptic messages that appeared inconsequential, therefore not relevant for the report compiled," he said, nodding at the judge then the jury before turning back to the prosecutor.

"What do you mean by cryptic?"

Looking around the room before settling his gaze and smiling at the jury, Mr Hughes said, "Messages that have no context: often a thumbs up emoji or some sort of funny video. Some short videos from popular culture, which I interpreted as in-jokes. There were no other messages to indicate conspiracy."

Taking her glasses off, Mrs Park rested one of the legs in her mouth momentarily. "Was there anything else of significance relating to this investigation and in particular that made you think this phone was connected to the alleged murder, Mr Hughes?"

Looking particularly pleased with himself, Mr Hughes replied, "A text sent shortly before the shooting used language that was indicative of violence, it claimed Mr Slaven - quote 'deserved it'".

Mrs Park continued, "What makes you so sure the conversation was about this incident?"

"The timing and location put the number attributed to the phone in the city centre, near the scene of the murder."

Jurors shuffled in their seats. Some nodded, and others unconsciously responded with raised eyebrows and puffed cheeks. Others stole glances towards the men in the dock. The trio sat, ashen, staring ahead.

Hughes added, "A call was also made to the number five minutes before Mr Slaven was shot, also while it was in the vicinity of the city centre. Then, it was picked up as making a call back to that

190

PART III

number on an area of the M74. The number dialled at this point from this phone is no longer in use and could not be traced."

An interesting, albeit technical, point, April thought.

With another smug look, Mr Hughes took in how invested the jury was in everything he said.

Mr Suave is single-handedly working towards securing a guilty verdict, April thought.

"To summarise" — he leaned forward again — "between the phones recovered and the activity between them, there are six numbers involved in communicating with each other. One number, the one that sent the details about Mr Slaven's movements, is not attributed to anyone in this case. Four of the numbers with regular communication relate to the three men charged."

Mrs Park asked, "There is a number believed to belong to another man, Martin Cole. Can you tell us why that number is attributed to him, please?"

Again nodding, like a toy Churchill dog on a car dashboard as the prosecutor asked the question, Mr Hughes said, "Of course. We know that Mr Cole is currently not in the UK and the date of his departure is the last date this particular phone was active."

The prosecutor said, "Mr Hughes, do you have any doubt that the phone in question, which received communication and was in the city centre at the time, is connected to this incident?"

"None at all—"

"Objection!" A lawyer from the defence table bellowed, jumping to his feet almost knocking his wig off. "Speculation by the witness. He is here as an expert to present his findings, not to gossip."

Before the judge could intervene, Mrs Park raised her right hand.

"Okay, question withdrawn. I'll ask this: Is it possible that Mr Deacon received the message about Mr Slaven's whereabouts, communicated with Mr Cain and Mr Harris using the other numbers, then was later in contact with someone else? A person or suspect whose identity we don't know, while he was in the city centre before going to murder Mr Slaven?" She looked at the angry lawyer who

MURDER CENTRAL

objected and then turned to the witness. Slowly, she said, "Is this a *possibility?*"

Straightening his jacket and leaning down to make sure everyone heard his answer, he replied, "Yes, that is all *very* possible."

"Thank you, Mr Hughes. You've been very helpful."

Mrs Park took her seat as Mark's QC – with even more stains on his threadbare gown than his learned friend beside him – took to the lectern. April had watched them interact in other cases.

She presumed Mr Kinnaird must have hired him because of his reputation for winning murder cases.

"Mr Hughes, we meet again. You have examined a phone the police believe is connected to my client, and you believe it is, too, am I right?"

Smiling, almost grimacing, and tapping his hand on the microphone stand, Mr Hughes said, "Yes, sir. As with Mr Harris, a mobile phone was repeatedly found to be in the vicinity of *your* client's registered phone intermittently on the lead up to the day of Mr Slaven's death."

The lawyer, an elderly man, rested his small round glasses at the end of his nose. He had a pure white beard that wasn't fully formed and white straw-like hair poking out from under his wig.

"You'll be aware, Mr Hughes, that my client Mr Deacon explains this phone doesn't belong to him but to a relative he spends a lot of time with. Putting that device near to his own on regular occasions. So isn't it possible the phone in question isn't Mr Deacon's phone?"

"I understand that is his position. However, I can only comment on the information given to me and what I have found during my examination. The police believe that phone belongs to him, and my analysis backs this up. It shows it spent a lot of time near Mr Deacon's own iPhone. Furthermore, the phone in question communicated on a number of occasions with the others identified as being relevant to this case." Mr Hughes's jaw muscles tightened as he delivered the last few words of his answer.

"Thank you for that very detailed explanation, Mr Hughes,

192

PART III

but if you could keep your answer as succinct as the question. Is it *possible* it isn't my client's phone? The lawyer was almost laughing, suggesting the witness couldn't possibly be correct.

Mr Hughes smiled again. This time, it appeared forced. He sucked air through his teeth and answered directly to the judge, "Yes, it is possible, but I believe that to be very unlike—"

"Thank you, Mr Hughes. Your opinion isn't necessary, just the answer to the question, which I understand to be that it is a possibility that the phone we are discussing in evidence in relation to my client, may not actually belong to him. No further questions."

The end of his evidence was a natural time to end evidence for the morning, the judge decided.

April stood when instructed to by the court macer.

When Terrence Hughes finally stepped out of the court, it was clear how stiff his shoulders were, as he worked to release the tension. April saw him bump into another blonde lawyer on his way out.

"Interesting evidence, Terry. Think they've been done?" the girl in the suit and stiletto heels asked him.

Standing straighter and smiling at her, he leaned in and said something April couldn't make out. In hushed tones, Mr Hughes and the lawyer spoke as they typed away on their phones.

Swapping numbers, April thought.

He gently touched the lawyer on her arm before parting ways and making a sign with his thumb and pinkie at his ear as though gesturing to call him.

April watched as he walked off with a spring in his step.

193

MURDER CENTRAL

CHAPTER 50

April rapped her fingers on the back of the empty seat in front of her. Up next they would hear evidence from experienced forensic expert Marion McManus. The final witness in this case before the jury determined if the men on trial were guilty or not.

It could be the final nail in the coffin for the defence case and see the prosecutor storm to victory. The men would be branded gangsters, feared by rivals, and held in esteem within their own ranks, but most importantly – a guilty verdict might be the catalyst for further deadly revenge attacks.

With fifteen years of experience, Mrs McManus was asked to confirm her job role and handed the report she had compiled for the case to answer questions about.

"Everybody has DNA. It's found in a person's cells, which can be on someone's skin, fingerprints, and body fluids. Everybody's DNA is unique to them. It can be transferred onto items by touch and leave behind a trace," the scientist told the jury, touching the lectern before her and holding her hand up for effect.

"Developments over the years have allowed this data to be extracted from objects and so, scientists can build DNA profiles. Experts then match with profiles taken from people to draw conclusions about their involvement in certain matters."

The jury seemed to hang on her every word.

Mrs Park dived into the questions, getting to the heart of the matter about the murder.

"You were asked to analyse some items found by the police during their search of a number of addresses and of productions seized that they believe to be of importance?"

Mrs McManus, a dour-faced woman, peered over her glasses at the prosecutor, letting out an "Mhm."

Taking that as her answer, Mrs Park asked, "What did you analyse, and what did you find?"

"We examined some items of clothing, a bag containing a gun

194

PART III

found at the River Avon and two mobile phones."

Mrs Park demonstrated her expertise in many serious and high-profile cases without being flustered. April watched the prosecutor rub her eyes and adjust her wig several times over the course of ten minutes. *Perhaps she feels more pressure*, she thought, *this gang are prolific.*

"If we look at the clothing first of all, what was examined please?" Mrs Park ticked something off in her notes.

This part will have to be spelled out for everyone to understand, April thought.

Checking they were both talking about the same thing, Mrs McManus checked her first item on the document, nodding as she read it. She put the paper down, clasping her hands over the top.

"Yes, we were asked to examine a pair of jogging bottoms found in Mr Harris' house. On the garment just to the right of the crotch area, we found DNA profiles matching Mr Harris and Mr Deacon. None of the men reside together, nor was there anything to suggest they were in a relationship, and so it was thought that it might be of relevance," the witness answered, moving her glasses again.

"Was there anything else relevant about this garment, not in relation to DNA but through your analysis?"

April thought the prosecutor now looked especially tense. If she didn't know better, she'd go as far as to say Mrs Park was mildly excited by this line of questioning.

She glanced at the jury box beside the prosecutor; all appeared to still be gripped. Several leaned forward as if to better hear the science expert like they were part of a CSI court scene, like was on the television.

Mrs McManus seemed to notice this too, directing her answer to them. "Yes," she said deadpan. "There was gunshot residue found on the waistband, and that matched the residue found at the scene."

One lady in the jury gasped loudly only to throw her hand to her mouth in embarrassment, as though the noise also took her by surprise.

Bingo, thought April. *It's going to be difficult to wriggle out of*

195

MURDER CENTRAL

this one.

The blows didn't stop there, Mrs Park landed punch after punch in her fight for justice.

"What else did you examine, please?"

Staring down at the document again, the scientist adjusted her glasses again and said, "Ah yes, we also tested a black hoodie top found in a wardrobe at Mr Deacon's house. It too had gun residue, although smaller particles."

Rookie mistake, thought April, *why did he not destroy it?*

There were murmurings and tuts from the public gallery, from the family of Slaven. As the evidence unravelled, they became more unsettled as a clearer picture of their loved one's death was coming to fruition.

"Quiet, please," the police officer watching from the back of the court uttered.

Looking across to the gallery, Mrs Park waited for quiet. "Is there anything else you can tell us about your analysis of the black hooded jumper discovered in Mr Deacon's home?"

This time, Mrs McManus removed her glasses. She looked at the family supporting one another and directed her answer to the judge.

"When we analysed the garment, we also found a tiny amount of blood spatter which contained a DNA profile matching Mr Slaven."

Almost immediately, there was a wail as Slaven's widow broke down before being removed from the courtroom.

April heard someone behind her connected to one of the accused whisper, "It's not like she's just hearing he died for the first time. At least his death was fast."

A police officer loudly shushed the insensitive chatter.

With the sobbing woman out of the court and quietness back in place, Mrs Park returned to her questions. "How certain are you that this is the blood of Mr Slaven?"

The expert replied candidly, "There is one in a billion chance that the blood is from someone other than Mr Slaven."

Seemingly satisfied with the answer, the prosecutor moved on

PART III

to the gun to find out what analysis of that revealed.

"When we analysed this, we extracted DNA profiles that matched Mr Cain and a man called Martin Cole. We know he is not on trial just now," Mrs McManus said.

This was a great piece of evidence, and April was getting itchy feet to get out of court and get all of this down for today's story. She also had the urge to update Paul. His name still hadn't popped up in her notifications. Mrs Park adjusted her wig. "You mentioned mobile phones, Mrs McManus. What did you find, please?"

Even she was starting to tire with her line of questioning.

Watching her, April could only imagine the stress she put herself under to nail this case. The jury couldn't read about all the ins and outs at this stage, but everyone involved in this case knew it was one of the biggest stories of the decade. Sheila Park was quoted in the newspapers, and her picture was taken outside court, her every word written down and repeated in news bulletins. There was no doubt a lot was riding on this.

The answer broke April's trance, bringing her back to the present.

"Yes, we examined two mobile phones found in Mr Deacon's house. One had DNA also matching Mr Deacon and Mr Cain, and the other had a mixture of profiles matching the same two gentlemen and Mr Cole."

This was enough to secure April's story. She excused herself as she shuffled out of the row of seats and ran back to the cafeteria in the court building to start writing. She thrashed out her article, whizzing through it at lightning speed – or so it felt – ignoring calls from the news desks that insisted on pestering her as she tried to make headway.

April was stopped in her tracks when she overheard two police officers speaking about a colleague called Paul – found dead at home. Her stomach dropped, and she felt sick; in no way could it be her Paul.

He wasn't *her* Paul, but she felt like she'd been punched in the gut. Tears tumbled from her eyes, splattering on the keyboard in front of her. Barely thinking about her story, she fiercely wiped her face and bulldozed into the conversation of the two strangers beside her.

"I'm so sorry to bother you. I overheard you said your colleague has died? My apologies. That's awful. Can I trouble you to tell me his name, please? I have a horrible feeling I may know him."

As she said the words, she was aware of how bonkers she sounded, barging into a somewhat private, albeit quite loud, conversation about a dead colleague.

Was she so paranoid that she thought any mention of a police officer called Paul was him?

Standing beside the table the men were sitting at, it dawned on her that she was being insensitive. Fishing in her pocket, she pulled out her mobile and scrolled to Paul's picture attached to his WhatsApp account, demonstrating she knew him.

The officer to her right-hand side, who looked distressed, offered information. "Yes, it's Paul Shaw. He was found dead at his house."

"What happened?" April could barely get the words out.

With tears in his eyes, the same officer said, "There were a lot of pills and a note we were told."

Her eyes widened. *Shit,* she thought, *suicide?* "I'm so sorry, this is horrific. Thank you for telling me. Sorry again…"

April took a few steps backwards towards her workstation. She wasn't far off finishing her story, and had no other option but to carry on. He wasn't a relative or technically even a friend, but she felt utterly bereft. As though she'd lost someone close.

Usually, one to check two or three times before she sent her articles, April hurriedly pressed the send button to the newspaper that commissioned her.

As she packed up, she returned to his workmates. "Apologies again, sorry I should have asked. I'll be sending a card for PC Shaw. If you have a note of where he stays…sorry where he stayed so I can put it through his door for his family, whoever will be checking his house… We only ever saw each other in town or at work."

They had met once in Merchant City, so it wasn't a total lie.

PART III

She looked each of the men in the eye, hoping she was convincing enough to persuade two officers of the law to give out their dead friend's address. Whether it was grief, shock, or that she was so persuasive, the helpful policeman again searched for his mobile and pulled it out of his pocket. He gave her an address in Rutherglen.

Thanking them profusely, April picked up her bag and laptop and made her way home to decide what was best to do.

There is no way he died by suicide, April told herself, convinced it was true.

CHAPTER 51

April glanced at her bedside clock; 2 am and no matter how heavy her head and eyelids felt sleep wouldn't come. The news of Paul's death hit her hard. She couldn't get him out of her head. Tears dripped from her eyes every time she thought of him. Visions of how he might have been found circled her mind. Each time her thoughts wandered to him surrounded by pills, a niggle in the pit of her stomach made her question it.

As the clock clicked to 3 am, she took herself to the toilet, careful not to turn on the light and wake John.

By 5 am, April could think of nothing else. She re-read all of their messages. Her mind wandered back to their meeting in the pub. Paul did not kill himself; April was certain of that.

When her alarm went off, she was still awake. Beside her, John stirred and groaned, reaching a hand over to rub her arm, as he often did when she was awake before him.

"You seemed really unsettled last night", he nuzzled his head on her shoulder and stroked her arm.

"Mmmm", April put her hand over his as it grazed her, enjoying the warmth from him against her skin. She wasn't sure how to respond. He wouldn't understand.

"What's wrong? I thought I heard you crying but when I said your name you must've been asleep", he kissed her shoulder and leaned over to kiss her cheek.

Guilt crept over her, April felt bad for being so upset over Paul's death and for not explaining the situation to John. Even though he wasn't the jealous type, it didn't feel like something she could share. April looked at her sleepy fiance.

He might think it suspicious that I'm so sad about the death of someone I barely know.

She leaned over and kissed his forehead, "Must just have been a bad dream after hearing some bad news yesterday. Someone I know from court passed away, someone I knew quite well".

PART III

Before he could ask any more questions April slipped her arm out from under her fiance and swung her legs on to the floor, pushing herself off the bed and into the bathroom.

***

With the trial in its final day, the prosecutor, Mrs Park tried to persuade the jury to find the men guilty. While the defence counsel for each of the men on trial argued there wasn't enough evidence to convict their clients. By the end of it, the court was still none the wiser, uncertain who the driver was or the shooters.

The three lawyers argued there was no concrete evidence. That they were simply in a social group in one another's cars and houses, which would explain the transfer of DNA and even the gun residue, blaming Martin Cole for that. It was crucial, they all said, that despite so many people witnessing the horrific incident, nobody could identify the perpetrators.

When the judge directed the jury, April took herself on a mission.

On the lunch break, she drove to Paul's address in Rutherglen. Sat outside, she studied the house, imagining his last night there. Something felt so wrong.

The news of Paul's untimely death ignited the desire to do more, uncover the truth, and hold those who needed it to account. This was why she did this job: exposing those who were wronging others.

April exited her car, striding towards his front door.

If his body was removed by police and a private ambulance, maybe they didn't lock the door?

Staring at the door April pulled her jumper over her hands and slowly reached out to touch the gold handle. *Who was the last person to touch this?* Holding her breath she gently pushed down to try and open it. Immediate resistance; it was locked. April exhaled loudly, and groaned. Her shoulders dropping as she stood back to scan the house.

As if it was really going to be open, she thought.

201

Her eyes travelled down the side of the house to a gate. She crept down the driveway round to the back of the house, she unlatched the gate and stepped into the small but well-kept garden. Looking around for a way to get into the house, she stepped over some potted plants and searched the ground underneath her. A robin, perched on a birdbath caught her attention and she noticed empty birdfeeders. Behind that there were some boxes with planters and what looked like some wilted herbs.

The robin flew off as she took a few steps closer to the wooden planter and lifted it.

He lived alone, surely there was a spare hidden somewhere, she thought.

Two rocks fell as she picked the unsteady wooden structure up. April picked them up to put them back and as she did, she heard one rattle.

Bingo. She slid it open to reveal two small keys. April couldn't believe her luck but faced a decision: Would she go inside?

She wouldn't forgive herself if she let this go. There was something sinister behind Paul's death.

If he didn't take his own life, then someone else did.

The first key she tried opened the back door. It was eerie walking into the house where she knew the young officer had died. Days earlier, he'd been a man, recovering from an attack. Now he was gone. Despite knowing nobody was in, she crept round the house trying not to make a noise.

The feeling of guilt was intense, but April's moral compass was stronger. If she found nothing, she'd leave again and forget about everything. But if there was something to find, she vowed to herself and Paul's memory that she would do something. April was certain the phone call at the pub had something to do with this. She needed to find out.

A cup lay at the side of the sink and empty crisp packets in the bin. It didn't feel like the house of a dead person, and she almost believed he could walk back in at any moment. April felt remarkably calm for someone who'd let herself into the house of a man she

PART III

hardly knew and who – as far as everyone else was concerned – had killed himself thirty-six hours earlier.

She walked through the kitchen and living room, although there was nothing obvious to look at nor check, no drawers – very minimalistic, with a distinct lack of soft furnishings or pictures. There was nothing obvious, although she surmised the police or family would have removed anything of note if it had been lying around. But then it might have been suspicious and not ruled as a suicide so quickly?

There must be something elsewhere.

With that, April went upstairs to his bedroom. Wandering round, there was a colossal sadness that filled the entire room. The silence was deafening. She had to sit on his bed to stop herself from keeling over. Trying to compose herself, she took a breath.

She looked around, taking in her surroundings. April opened the top drawer of his bedside cabinet and had a rummage. She felt she was invading his privacy but was too far into her mission to turn back now. There, she found an Ian Rankin book, Men's Health magazine, a box of condoms, and a box of paracetamol. But tucked away, underneath, was another key.

April felt like she was in a sick game show where each key unlocked the next instalment of a nightmare instead of a prize.

She checked the drawers inside his wardrobe – even on top of it but there were no clues, nor was there anything that suggested anything untoward. She got down on her hands and knees and looked under his bed. April pulled out a folder with personal letters, bank statements, and pension policies. There were boxes of clothes and socks neatly stored. Then, she noticed a red box against the wall the bed was pushed against. She pulled it out, her heart racing.

Is this what I'm looking for? She asked herself.

With her heartbeat ringing in her ears she looked at the key she just found in the drawer. Her palms sweated as she slowly put the key to the lock. She took a few breaths, holding the last then inserted the key "YES!" she shrieked when she heard the click of the lock opening. April repeatedly thanked the higher power she wasn't

203

even sure she believed was there.

April placed her hand on either side of the lid. *Do I want to do this?* Immediately her mind took her back to the phone call at McChuills when someone answered Paul's phone. Without a second thought, she opened the box.

Inside was a pile of papers, pictures, and a USB stick. April sat the box on the bed and pulled out all the contents, a mixture of hope and fear pulsing through her.

She flicked through the papers; they were copies of text messages. Her eyes widened in horror. Everything she was reading was far more sinister than she thought. The pictures were copies, screenshots of messages between Paul and a man called Davie. The messages showed Paul challenging the other man about his attitude and what he'd been speaking to someone named William about and threatening to tell the truth.

The penny dropped that Davie was a colleague and a police officer threatening Paul.

What did you get yourself mixed up in? April thought.

In a chilling message, Davie told Paul:

I'll end you, keep your nose out and stay in your lane. Youv no idea what your dealing with.

Some of the messages were only a week old. She assumed Paul had backed up chat logs to create a dossier. He never got the chance to do anything before he supposedly took his own life, but only weeks after he was brutally attacked.

Maybe that was the plan the first time? It must have been Davie who answered his phone that night.

Pictures printed were stills from his ring doorbell showing a man – she presumed to be Davie – at Paul's door on two occasions.

The messages alone were damning, but the dossier nailed Davie as an aggressor at best and, at worst, a murderer.

There must be more footage on the doorbell camera that showed who was really at the house?

April put everything back in the box, including the USB stick, and took it with her. She wanted time to go through everything

PART III

herself before she spoke to the police. She was convinced Davie was the man who answered Paul's phone, who was behind the attack and she was convinced he had staged the suicide. Davie was so threatened by Paul doing the right thing, he told Paul he'd put an end to everything.

Knowing she too would be captured on the camera, April retraced her steps, leaving through the back door, locking it, returning the key back to the stone safe and going back home.

Her drive back was on autopilot, unable to process what she'd uncovered.

She was convinced Paul had discovered Davie was doing something illegal, something to do with Slaven, and when he threatened to expose him, he killed Paul and made it look like a suicide. Paul thought William was to be watched when they last met, but he wanted to speak to her again just the other day. This reinforced the idea that Davie answered Paul's phone when she tried to speak to him. April had her chat logs and could pinpoint when he would have been there.

She had some digging to do. *I will prove that Davie was behind Paul's death.*

April drove home and was wiped emotionally. She wasn't in the mood to explain everything to John.

Where would I even start? She thought as she made her way up the stairs in her close to the top floor.

Instead, she sloped off to bed to try and catch up on some sleep. She needed a clear head to make sense of the dossier she discovered. She knew she would be returning to the court for the verdict so had to act fast.

At 4 am, after a few hours of nightmares and feeling anxious, April reached for her laptop on the floor to take a quick look at the USB.

It has to be relevant, she thought, *or it wouldn't have been with the other information.*

In true police style, there were further copies of all the text conversations.

205

Good man, Paul, she thought as she read through the messages.

Some didn't make sense out of context, while others were outright threatening. Davie would **"finish him"** and **"make him shut up for good."** Some messages she couldn't quite understand due to spelling mistakes and poor grammar, but she got the jist. Nothing linked these extra people to the case of Slaven so far as the evidence and everything pointed to McColl's men. It didn't make sense.

In another folder, she found more stills from the ring doorbell and doorbell footage of who she believed was Davie at Paul's door. Paul had saved two clips. One of Davie arriving at Paul's the night before his attack at his work, and another showed him leaving. She froze briefly, terrified of what she was about to view.

Beside her, John stirred in bed. Scared to wake him, she quickly shut the lid of her laptop to stop the light from escaping.

April climbed out of bed quietly, taking her laptop into the living room, where she could watch the footage properly and with some volume.

Clicking on the first video, it opened to show a stocky man with shaven hair turning up at the door. He tried the handle and then banged hard when it was locked. He stood back from the door, looking up at the house with an angry expression, then he went out of sight towards the front window. The man paced past the camera, round to the back, and more banging could be heard.

April could make out raised voices a few moments later, then the sound of a door banging hard. A pain shot through April's chest.

She saw the date the video was saved was after Paul's discharge from hospital. He was going to expose Davie.

April's heart rate quickened as she opened the second clip. It captured Davie walking back up the garden path away from the back door. She paused the footage, she knew she was definitely caught on camera too.

Will they believe I'm trying to help? What if someone sees this before I speak to the police? April's thoughts raced and she felt sweat trickle down her brow. This was all too much to deal with.

Sitting back on the settee, April took some deep breaths to

PART III

calm herself.

This will all be explained, she thought. *Everyone thinks Paul killed himself and I am going to help catch his killer.*

Looking back at the laptop, she hit the button to restart the clip again. Davie shouted back towards the house, "Try it!" and something that sounded like, "You're a dead man," as he stormed off. A car door slammed twice, and a car engine revved out of sight and drove off.

April's blood ran cold. She had been convinced something wasn't right, and her gut instinct was correct.

"Paul didn't kill himself."

MURDER CENTRAL

CHAPTER 52

As April put on her makeup and brushed her hair, she didn't feel refreshed or ready to take on the day but knew there was no choice. The jury in the Slaven trial was expected to return a verdict that morning. Until then, she went to the Gorbals to get to the bottom of things.

April had contacts at the court and had asked a couple of people to let her know when the verdict was in so she could make her way across the bridge at the Gorbals to the High Court. It was only ten minutes away. First, she had to make a pit stop.

She parked on Errol Gardens, near the local library, and walked the couple of hundred yards in the opposite direction to the police station. It was a long shot, but given the connection Paul drew with PC Field and the Slaven case, she thought he might know something, and frankly, there was nothing to lose.

She entered the precinct and asked for PC Field at the counter. The officer she spoke to was immediately wary as he asked who she was.

"I'm April…Mc..eh… April, I want to speak to him about Josh Slaven. I believe I can help, but it needs to be him." She said all of the right things to be taken seriously, and the confused and concerned-looking police officer asked her to take seat.

After a few minutes, he re-emerged, followed closely by William. She immediately recognised his face after her night with Joseph outside the police office staking him out and following him. He looked older up close and had grown a beard since then. He was probably younger than he appeared given the dark circles under his eyes and gaunt look he wore.

"Hi…April? I'm PC William Field," he stated quite firmly. "Please come with me."

He led her into an interview room, closing the door behind them. William held a hand out and nodded, gesturing for her to sit at the table. April had never been in a police interview room before.

208

PART III

She felt a little excitement to see how it worked from the inside.

After a few seconds, she zoned back to the task at hand as her excitement morphed into nerves. Not usually one for feeling anxious, she was used to speaking to strangers all the time at her job. She had knocked on doors, cold-called people, challenged politicians, covered the most serious rape and murder trials, and held people to account who needed it. This felt different, almost a little personal, and April wasn't sure where this would go. Paul was wary of William Field, and now she was in a room with him – alone.

April reached into her bag and pulled out the USB and dossier, dropping it in front of William. Meeting his eyes, she told him candidly, "I'm April McCann, a freelance journalist, and I've been covering the Slaven trial. But I was a friend of Paul Shaw, who I'm sure you know."

The officer shifted in his seat, and his eyes glistened as they filled up.

She continued, "I know you know there was a problem with him and… Davie?" As she said his name, she lifted one of the still images of the man outside the dead officer's house from the table.

William looked impassive. "How did you—"

April pressed her lips and raised her eyebrows, making it clear that questions were not to be asked.

He sat back with his arms out, gesturing to her to continue explaining.

She cleared her throat. "Paul was threatened by this Davie on a number of occasions, he saved the messages and made copies. My guess is he was going to try and expose him over his involvement in Slaven's murder. He made it clear there was some problem. He actually thought you were involved," she said accusingly, leaning forward in her seat.

William shifted again, looking at documents before him, tears still swimming in his eyes.

April tapped the dossier sitting between them. "Davie repeatedly threatened Paul and was at his house the day before his attack after work, calling him a 'dead man'. You can't tell me he's not

209

MURDER CENTRAL

responsible. I know it's still fresh, but this suicide claim is a lot of shit. Who found him? His family?"

William dropped his head in his hands as the tears fell from his eyes, and he let out a wail.

April stopped talking, shocked by the sudden outburst from the police officer. She knew this was a sensitive subject and hadn't intended to upset him. Reaching over, she patted his shoulder. "I'm so sorry. I know this is all such an awful situation."

He shook his head furiously, muttering, "You don't understand, you have *no* idea."

April just about made out the words. Leaning across the table, she put her hands on his wrists. "What's wrong?"

Momentarily taking a break from his sobbing, he looked up with his bloodshot eyes and whispered, "Davie found him. He said Paul was late for his shift and he couldn't get hold of him, so he went to the house, and he found him. Seemingly, he was pretty upset..." The weeping officer barely finished his sentence when he broke down all over again.

It was definitely Davie on that footage, April thought.

After a few minutes of watching William sob in front of her, April thought there was nothing to lose now, and said, "I think your colleague Davie is behind Paul's death. And I think he was involved in Slaven's murder. And, I think you know something, too."

She didn't know whether to feel sorry for him or if she hated him for covering for Davie if he knew anything.

His face became distorted, and he transformed into a quivering mess like a terrified schoolboy cornered by the headmaster, not a police officer being quizzed by a journalist no older than him. It was as though fear slithered under the door, inched up the table, and rose over them, hanging in the room like a dark cloud.

"You need to tell me what you know. Confirm that it is Davie in the pictures, then go to your boss with this information and get to the bottom of this. He is responsible for Paul's death."

Silence fell between them and William slowly nodded. "I have something I need to do."

PART III

"If you don't, I will." She laid a finger on the evidence on the table between them.

April's phone vibrated. "Shit." She reached into her bag to check. "Verdict is in. I need to rush to court."

William moved to gather up the incriminating evidence like he'd won a round in poker but April stopped him with a hand that landed on top of his.

"Sorry, officer, you'll understand why I'm not trusting anyone just now. We'll report this to your boss together when you call me later."

Not giving him a chance to respond, she dropped a business card on the table and left the room, fixing all the vital evidence into a plastic folder and placing it carefully into a zipped section in her bag. She had a rush of emotion that no matter what the outcome of the case, one corrupt officer would be made to pay.

April broke sweat running across the Albert Bridge, sprinting to the High Court building, arriving in time to hear the verdict. The court was packed full, and not wanting to draw attention to herself or miss anything, she sat at the back nestled among eager eyes from all sides of the trial.

She took her seat in the crowded room. Looking round she counted police officers dotted around the courtroom, preparing for trouble she presumed, ready to pounce on anyone who so much as breathed too loudly.

"Can the jury spokesperson please stand?" the clerk asked once the judge had taken his seat and the jury looked on gingerly.

A nervous looking fifty-something year old woman stood.

"Has the jury reached a verdict?" the clerk asked.

The lady nodded and muttered that they had.

"What is the verdict, in respect of the accused, James Cain, on the charge of murder?"

"Guilty."

There were gasps and wails from one side of the court and an almighty "Yes!" from the other.

"Quiet," all six officers shouted at varying decibels but all at once.

"Is that unanimous or by majority?" the clerk continued, unfazed by the drama unfolding.

"Unanimous," the woman squeaked, clearly perturbed by the reactions.

April, as always, felt a mixture of tension and excitement at each verdict. All too aware that the outcome would devastate a family, but also recognised a sense of closure for those connected to any victims.

There was an element of closure for her, too, after following matters from the commission of the crime right through to the conclusion. Particularly in this case when she had such an emotional investment and was about to blow the whistle on police corruption that saw a well-respected, much-loved police officer die.

"What is the verdict in respect of the accused, Mark Deacon, on the charge of murder?"

"Guilty."

Despite the warnings, there was a roar of cries and cheering as the police desperately tried to control the public. They made so much noise that it was impossible to hear if it was unanimous or not.

"What is the verdict in respect of the accused, Barry Harris, on the charge of murder?"

"Guilty."

The court erupted.

On the judge's orders, each officer took hold of the closest person to them and removed them from the court.

April sat watching the spectacle in front of her. Grief-stricken friends and family of Josh Slaven weren't there for the gangland thug who tortured and maimed others. They were there to see justice for him because the three men standing in front of them took his life away.

Laura Slaven threw herself onto the ground, wailing like a banshee. Supporters rallied round her, leading her out of the courtroom as she howled.

Meanwhile, supporters of the men convicted screamed, "He's a good boy!"

PART III

"He's innocent."

"He can't go to prison," and similar phrases as they were dragged out of the court.

Racing against the clock to get her story out as soon as possible, April turned her attention to the more pressing issue and set up her laptop in a quiet corner of the court foyer again.

"GANGLAND SHOOTING: GUN THUGS CONVICTED OF THE MURDER OF JOSH SLAVEN."

April thrashed out her article as quickly as possible, now removing all mentions of "charged with", "alleged", and "claims". The verdict was in, and the jury had decided these men were cold-blooded murderers. The more April wrote, the more anger she felt. Paul wanted to expose his corrupt colleague. Davie was also a cold-blooded killer, and she was convinced of it.

But why? April still couldn't figure out why he wanted to silence Paul. If Davie found out Paul was speaking to the press, he would know it was about William Field, so why was he so precious? While she frantically typed, her phone rang. An unknown number.

"Hello?" she answered, trying not to be curt or sound frustrated.

"April, it's PC William Field. Can you meet me, please?"

She stopped mid-sentence to focus on the call. This was important. "Okay, somewhere that's not too quiet, so we can talk freely? Babbity Bowster off High Street. Meet me there in an hour."

She continued with the article, relaying the details of the public shooting.

Twenty minutes later, she read over for the third time, making sure all charges were correct: guilty of murder, possession of weapons, dangerous driving, and breach of the peace. April had to run back inside and check all the verdicts for each of the perpetrators with the clerk. There was so much drama and chaos at the time she hadn't waited around for all the details after hearing the murder verdicts.

April marched up Saltmarket towards the pub, striding with purpose. As she crossed the road, passing KK Snaps photography studio, she saw a young family come out with a newborn after one of

213

MURDER CENTRAL

their famous photoshoots. She felt a pang of sadness, thinking Paul would never have this; he'd never marry or have a family – Davie stole that from him.

She carried on past McChuills and thought about the night someone else answered Paul's phone. It had to have been Davie.

Why didn't I do more that night? She wiped away a stray tear that trickled down her cheek and took a deep breath.

April had failed him in life, so she'd do everything she could to expose the truth now and do right by him.

She opened the pub door and saw William waiting for her. He looked even worse than when she'd seen him earlier if that was possible. She got herself a drink and sat with him.

Skipping pleasantries, April asked, "So what are we doing about this? What do you know, and what does this all mean?"

PART III

CHAPTER 53

William took a gulp of his cider as April walked into the pub. She looked angry. He watched her stride to the bar, order herself a drink, then bring it over to her table. Although he had been dreading this after feeling ambushed by her earlier, a part of him was relieved that everything might come to an end.

Looking around to make sure no one could hear them, William took a deep breath. "Okay, off the record? You journalists are like priests, aren't you? Keep stuff to yourself if you need to?"

April nodded, and her face softened. "How about this, do you have Davie's number? Can we match it with this first, to be sure?"

William felt a shiver run up his spine. After everything hearing Davie's name was a trigger.

"Yes," he replied, pulling out his phone from his jacket.

He found the contact and held the screen so he and April could see it.

She held the printout of the messages for them to compare.

"Ah fuck," William muttered.

Why the hell did Davie use his own number? Was he that brazen?

As much as he hated Davie Donovan, he was hopeful he wasn't capable of murder and bitterly regretted ever getting involved with him.

April nodded, seeing from his reaction they were both on the same page. She pulled her laptop from her bag and slotted the USB stick in. Opening the files, she showed William the clips.

"Stop that there," he ordered, tapping at the screen. "There's someone at the edge of the screen." He pointed excitedly.

April stopped and started the footage another two times. He jumped as she suddenly said "Yes, you're right!" and paused it at the relevant point.

"There's definitely someone else. It looks like they walk from the back of the house up the driveway, at the very edge of the area covered by the camera." William leaned forward, squinting at the

215

MURDER CENTRAL

screen. "Who the fuck is that?"

"Whoever it is is connected to Davie, could it be someone else at your work?" April asked him.

Rubbing his temples with his thumb and middle finger William took a couple of deep breaths. His heart was beating fast. He felt overwhelmed by everything April showed him and the alcohol wasn't hitting the way he hoped it would yet.

"Right, are you coming with me to speak to your boss?" April asked, interrupting his thoughts. "This guy needs to be stopped in his tracks quickly. He is still out there. What's his deal with Slaven?"

"Genuinely no idea," William replied forcefully.

He shocked himself with how much he enforced this. With his recent history at the station and false connection with Slaven, he didn't want to be seen as trying to get his own back. He'd just returned to work and had even got back on track with Sarah.

"Why don't you just expose him in the newspaper?" he asked, draining the cider from the glass. "Another drink?"

Looking at her almost full glass, she said, "No, thanks. And I did consider it. It'd be the scoop of the year, but if this guy is a murderer linked to gangsters, he needs off the streets sooner rather than later. I've got the material for the story when he's behind bars."

William got himself another drink with a whisky on the side. As he sat, he started re-thinking his dealings with his colleague — the anger, the threats, the secrecy. *Some police officer.* He'd been so worried about himself he hadn't spotted a criminal in his rank, although he did recognise the irony in that too.

"April, you're right. It's Davie's number and him in that picture from Paul's house. Okay, you go get him; we might never know what Paul was keeping on him, but he's a dangerous man. I'll keep distanced from you just now but will keep an eye on things from the inside."

They said their goodbyes and he watched April make her way straight to the police station before she lost her nerve or something happened to the dossier. She looked like she was carrying a golden egg, clutching her bag closely.

216

PART III

William opened his phone to the BBC news app, where he saw the breaking news of the guilty verdicts. He couldn't get his head around how stupid he had been to think he could pull off working with an organised crime gang. No matter how big a favour he owed Phil.

He stayed in the pub for another two hours, sinking pints and questioning his life choices. Part of him felt lighter now that he had told Sarah, but the guilt he carried for how he had conducted himself as a police officer still ate away at him.

Without thinking too much about it, he pulled out the burner phone and turned it on to text Phil, trying to start distancing himself.

All guilty, they'll be behind bars for a long time.

Almost instantly, a message popped up.

Good riddance.

Then another.

We need to meet.

And another.

When are you free?

Nothing good could come of this. William mulled over his decision, but he knew there wasn't another option. He had put himself and Sarah through enough stress, and he didn't think his heart could take much more strain. He also knew saying no to someone like Phil carried its risks. Instead, he had to take himself out of the equation.

He texted Phil.

Tomorrow

William hit "send" and knew what he had to do.

MURDER CENTRAL

CHAPTER 54

April convinced herself it was just her imagination, but she felt like she had eyes on her as she walked the longest mile ever. With a sense of *déjà vu*, she walked back into the police station.

Immediately, she came face to face with the person she least wanted to see. Wearing plain clothes, Davie brushed past her and left the building. Had someone beaten her to it, or was he leaving before he was pushed?

She asked to see the sergeant and was taken in to see Arthur Black in his office.

"Miss McCann, to what do I owe the pleasure? Sit down, please," he said in a surprisingly welcoming manner.

"Thanks, Sir, I have…well, I have something sensitive I need to talk to you about. I need you not to ask too many questions, just to accept all evidence I present, then do your own research," she explained, flustered.

With his eyebrows furrowed, he clasped his hands and sat back in his chair.

April held up the dossier in the plastic folder then opened it to show the messages and pictures, watching for the sergeant's response. He looked at them with concern before rubbing his eyes fiercely. His gaze returned to her.

She slowly nodded, confirming his thoughts without exchanging any words.

The senior officer slammed his hands on the table and stood up quickly. "What do you want from this, Miss McCann?"

"For you to do something about *your* officer! He's murdered someone, and why? I think it's about Slaven—"

"That is quite the accusation, Miss McCann. Do you have any basis for such claims?" his anger was discernible.

April tried to remain calm and professional, but she took umbrage, believing the officer was accusing her of causing trouble.

She sighed. April wasn't going to get Paul into bother now he

218

PART III

was dead, so there was nothing to lose. "Sir, after Slaven's murder, PC Shaw contacted me. He told me he was concerned about PC Field. He didn't know what it was about, but he had overheard him speaking to Davie Donovan, told me he'd heard Donovan complaining about PC Field and that when he challenged his partner, he was dismissed by him. That's what he told me at that stage, before he was attacked and before he was, I believe, *killed*."

April took a breath and tightened her ponytail. Her eyes swam with tears. She swallowed hard.

"I was supposed to meet him the night before he was found dead, and when he didn't show, I called him, but another man answered. He said something about not being able to come out. I now believe that man was PC Donovan. And I have all of this." She tapped the various pieces of paper sitting between them. "I know that is PC Donovan's number matches the one used to text Paul *and* that he is the man in the images. He was caught on the ring doorbell camera! I believe PC Shaw was going to report all of this, and it is why he was building a case. But somehow, he was stopped in his tracks."

The sergeant paced the room listening, looking shocked at the claims but unable to refute them.

"Thank you, Miss McCann. We'll look into this at once," he assured her.

Confused and pointing in the direction of the entrance to the station, she asked, "I passed PC Donovan on my way in. Is he not working?"

The sergeant sighed loudly. "He is on compassionate leave after finding PC Shaw's body at his house."

April felt her jaw tighten.

How is this man playing everyone? And why? Three men had been convicted of Slaven's murder, and there was no mention of this bent copper.

"I trust you'll do the right thing, sir. I should make clear. I have made copies of this, so I, too, have the evidence." She smiled at him, adding, "For when it is needed, you understand."

MURDER CENTRAL

***

When April returned from speaking to the sergeant, John was still at work. The day's news took its toll on her, and she felt a lump rising in her throat.

Alone, she slumped on her couch and let the wave of emotion crash over her, taking hold. The lump grew bigger, and her eyes swam until she couldn't see clearly through the puddles that gathered. April eventually gave in and sobbed. Hard, loud sobs that once started were uncontrollable. Her body heaved, and she struggled for breath. April was sure the people on the street below would hear her cries. She howled from the pit of her stomach until she tired herself out.

The cushion below her was soaked with tears. When she looked at herself in the bathroom mirror, her cheeks and lips were blotchy and red, and her eyes bloodshot. Exhausted, she went to bed and curled into the foetal position, where she fell asleep.

April was awakened by the sound of a key in the lock, and John barged through the door. She heard the clanking of bottles; beer, she assumed, and within a couple of minutes, the sound of Twin Atlantic played through the Alexa speaker. It was Friday night; she had a hair appointment the next day, but she couldn't look forward to the pampering until she knew Davie Donovan was locked up.

She texted William.

Sgt Black has the dossier, if you hear anything let me know. Thanks for meeting today.

Realising she'd slept for two hours, she sloped into the kitchen to see her fiancé, needing a hug and some comfort from him.

His eyes lit up as she walked into the kitchen where he was sitting and drinking a Corona. He opened his arms up, inviting her over to him.

Turning the song up on the speaker made her smile. She hadn't spent much time with him, and if the past few days had reminded her anything, it was that life was short and precious.

We need to decide on a wedding date, she thought.

PART III

Memories of the night they met at the Garage nightclub five years earlier, the moment John proposed on a beach in Tenerife and the day they got the keys to their flat, flashed through April's mind.

She thought of the family outside KK Snaps. They looked so happy and would soon have a copy of the moment all three of them, Mum, Dad and the newborn were together and in love.

April walked to John, sat on his knee, and firmly planted a kiss on his lips. She could taste the cold lager.

She stayed there for a few seconds until she felt his hands round her waist, gripping her.

April pulled away momentarily then threw her arms round his neck, hugging him tightly. "Do you want to go into town tomorrow night after my appointment?"

Smiling back at her, he planted a quick kiss on her right cheek. "Sounds great. Let's show off your new hairdo."

CHAPTER 55

April's appointment began at 10 am at the salon Trend in Parkhead, where Chelsea was waiting on her with a smile. April's dark hair was starting to grey, far more than it should on her twenty-seven-year-old head. She sat in the chair and enjoyed the banter that went hand in hand with these trips.

"What stories have you been working on this week?" the cheery hairdresser asked, always taking an interest in April's work.

April laughed to herself as she sat, with her eyes closed, enjoying the relaxing atmosphere. "You wouldn't believe me if I told you!"

Ever the optimist, Chelsea stopped applying the hair foils and dye to ask, "Oh, how exciting. Is it a juicy court case?"

Using that as a springboard to give an answer that would make for a better conversation, April said, "Yes, the gangster who was murdered last year in the car park? It was that trial this week, three guys convicted and one still on the run."

"Wow." Chelsea looked shocked. "Your job is so interesting! I wonder where he went?"

"The chat is he's in Dubai, or at least was. Who knows, though!" April replied, still not opening her eyes.

This was the most relaxed she'd been in a while.

With everything going on and how mentally exhausted she was, April almost dozed as Chelsea washed her hair at the sink. She was convinced the hairdresser gave her an extra five minutes for her head massage.

April was mid blow-dry when her phone vibrated.

Pulling it out of her pocket she saw a message from William.

Been called in to speak to my gaffer, Davie Donovan being questioned too.

April almost let out a yelp of excitement but didn't want to get her hopes up.

"Everything okay?" The hairdresser shouted over the noise of the hairdryer.

PART III

April caught her own smiling expression in the mirror. "Yes, just work." Her smile widened as she made eye contact with Chelsea.

Next she moved to the beauty room at the back of the salon to get her nails manicured and round off the pampering. As her nails were buffered her mind wandered, picturing Davie Donovan in handcuffs.

April couldn't shake the image of him yelling outside Paul's house, calling his colleague a dead man. And someone else who looked like they walked past the camera from the back of the house.

Guilt hovered in her stomach, knowing William Field was roped into this, but the truth was the most important thing.

***

She and John walked into the city centre for their date night. They had cocktails at The Social at Royal Exchange Square, then crossed the courtyard to Glaschu for dinner. April loved the décor, and the food was always lovely. It felt nice to be dressed up and enjoying time with her partner.

As the night went on, the drinks flowed until April felt a warm glow and giddy from the alcohol. But in each quiet moment, her mind wandered to the dark points of her investigations and coverage of Slaven's public assassination. The family of Josh Slaven slammed the door in her face because they grieved for the man who meant the world to them.

She thought of the evidence from Helen McKenzie, probably mentally scarred by the shooting, and of her traumatised children. April also cast her mind to the jury members, most of whom had probably only seen court drama on TV but listened to gory details about a man not even thirty, shot at point-blank range.

Three men are now going to spend the next few decades behind bars because they were involved with a gang, she thought. *And now, the police officer has lost his life because he wanted the truth – about something – to be out.*

She stared at her fiancé as he spoke passionately about his work.

223

John spoke with one hand resting on hers, and the other was animated as he gestured. She felt a swelling of her heart and a rush of emotion.

They decided to call it a night at 10 pm and walk back to their flat. April put her jacket on and waited as John went to the toilet before they left. Glancing at her phone, she saw another message from William.

Davie arrested.

This is it, she thought. *It has to be.*

Until then, April had been feeling sleepy, but this gave her a renewed rush of energy.

John came back and held a hand out for her to take. She did and used it to pull him close for a kiss. After the week she had, he made her feel safe.

PART III

CHAPTER 56

April awoke with a start on Sunday, checking her phone, hopeful there would be more news. She had no doubt the three men in Barlinnie prison were responsible for the murder of Slaven, but she still couldn't shake that PC Donovan was also involved and that his colleague knew this.

She and John lay watching Netflix, April jumping every time her phone buzzed.

At noon, with the day getting on and still feeling the effects of the night before and unable to shake the lingering stench of wine, she went for a shower.

No sooner had she stepped in the steaming hot box of hot water when John put his head round the door. "April, your phone is ringing..."

"Answer it, now!" she screamed over the rainfall shower as she reached for the tap.

Reaching out to dry her hands and face on the towel hanging up, she heard, "Yes sir, hold on please I'll just get her."

Her chest was tight, and her stomach churned as she reached for the phone. "Hello, sir."

"Good afternoon, Miss McCann. Sorry to trouble you on the weekend," Sergeant Black said. "Thank you for the information you presented us with. PC Donovan's home was searched, and he has been questioned alongside his partner. He has been charged with PC Shaw's murder amongst other things."

There was silence as April felt her eyes burning again. Flooded with relief, she croaked, "Thank you, sir."

The Sergeant cleared his throat before saying, "He has also been charged with conspiring to murder Josh Slaven."

April was shocked. She did suspect he was in the know but conspiring to murder? "Oh shit, sorry, I mean, wow, thank you for letting me know."

"Now, I trust we are speaking off the record? And you aren't

225

recording this call," he asked with a slight laugh.

"Don't worry I'm off duty, sir, no recording equipment in sight." April laughed back.

"I feel you're owed an explanation." He sighed. "We searched Constable Davie Donovan's house and mobiles were recovered. There were several messages between him and a member of McColl's gang. He had information about Josh Slaven's whereabouts on the night he was shot, and he had tipped off the gang."

"Holy shit. What the hell?" April fidgeted with her towel. What she heard was unbelievable. This was a whole new level of police corruption.

"We believe, from voice messages on Donovan's phone from PC Shaw, that he must have known and threatened to report him for what he had done; he tried to urge him to do the right thing. You were right that Davie Donovan was at Paul Shaw's house the night before he was attacked, and phone records suggest he was with him the night before he was found. Davie claimed he found him dead and that there was a note, but all of this suggests otherwise. His girlfriend Melanie explained the full thing. She seemed happy to be able to report him, said he's up to his eyes in debt and was keeping in with McColl's gang. Seems he had threatened her if she did anything about his involvement. Poor woman is now free of him."

It all made sense to April, but the magnitude of what Davie had done was almost too much to comprehend.

She ended the call, shocked at the news. Paul knew about his partner's involvement and threatened to tell the truth.

April pulled on clothes and opened her laptop. This was the start of the latest update following the trial before his killers were sentenced.

Police officer charged with conspiracy to murder Josh Slaven.

She texted William to say she was in the loop and was sending an article about PC Donovan. Given the stage of the case, she couldn't name him yet, but she had the makings for the scoop when the time was right.

As soon as she hit send, her phone rang.

PART III

"Hi, April," William said before she even spoke. "I've not long heard myself. His missus shopped him and explained everything, throwing him right under the bus. I, eh, I should let you know I've not been squeaky clean in all of this. I have been a bad egg, but I've admitted everything and tendered my resignation. I'm not feeling it anymore and just wanted you to know. I had *no* idea Paul was going to go out, and I had no idea Donovan was behind the attacks."

It was a lot to take in at once, but she appreciated his honesty. "Thank you for letting me know. Maybe we'll sit down one day when you're ready to tell all?" She tested the waters.

"Aye, maybe, we'll see. I'll tell you all about it one day, just not sure we'll put it all in print." He sounded weary.

"Thanks for all your help and let's see what happens with Donovan."

Typing up her story, she added the word "Ends," marking the end of the article, but what would be the beginning of revealing this latest dramatic twist.

CHAPTER 57

William walked round his car, trying to keep himself calm. He took a deep breath, then another. He held his breath for a few seconds when he saw Phil's car pull into Strathclyde Park. The car drew up next to his and slowly came to a stop. Phil slammed the door as he got out of the driver's side.

"Billy. You wanted to see me in person." Phil cracked his knuckles and leaned back on his car, his arms crossed.

"Yes, thanks for coming. I'm done with everything."

"What does that mean?" Phil's brows narrowed.

"I've handed my cuffs in, so to speak." William looked at his feet then behind him to see who was near them. "I've quit. I can't do it anymore and I'm not cut out to be a cop. What I did all those years ago, I should never have been on the force. I can't keep putting my wife through this. It's not—"

"So, what are you telling me?" Phil took a step towards him, his fists clenched. William flinched.

"That I'm done with all of this. I'm not a copper anymore. I can't help with Daniel Tonner now. I'm sorry, but I need to put my wife first." To his surprise, Phil's demeanour changed. His hands relaxed and he rubbed his face.

"I'll need to deal with him another time, anyway. The boss wants him looked after, after everything. Fuck knows why, but I need to cool things off." Phil shook his head and looked up as though searching for something in the sky.

"Sorry it didn't go to plan, mate. I know I owed you and it didn't work, it's not how I wanted things to go. I can't say I'm sorry to be away from the stress, I've got too much to lose. I'll take this to the grave with me though." He held a hand out for Phil to shake.

Phil met William's gaze and took his hand.

"You got the sim from that burner, Billy? We can't fall at the last hurdle now."

"I'll destroy it and the phone. It's finished."

PART III

Phil nodded and shook William's hand firmly, "Don't make me regret leaving it with you." William felt a rush of relief as Phil got into his car and drove off. He hadn't confessed everything to April but he hoped the worst was over for him.

All of a sudden he felt lighter and that everything might actually be okay.

CHAPTER 58

Davie lay in his cell, staring at the ceiling. He'd been tricked into thinking the plan would be easy. They'd not get caught, he'd been assured. She offered him a good out to get rid of all his debts, but it had all gone to shit.

Spiralling debts don't go away when you start getting in with the big boys. Why did I listen to her?

He had trusted Mel, and she'd betrayed him.

***

A motorbike pulled up to Davie Donovan's house in Motherwell. Mel wandered to the top of the driveway. The biker took his helmet off.

She smiled at him.

"Chick, how's it going? Well, Davie's not getting out anytime soon. Everything was on his phone, so we're good. He thought he was Billy Big Baws, but he's the one who needed the cash, so blame falls to him."

"Well done, Mel. Using that Mancunian bloke as your alibi was genius. How did you manage to not get caught out being at that copper's house? Really thought that prick Shaw was going to spill when he caught wind."

She winked and laughed. "Aye, that was good fortune. I made sure I was 'off-screen'," she said, making the inverted comma gesture with her hands. "Those bastarding things catch everything! Hot head Davie was the main focus anyway, and he took care of Sexy Shaw. Bit of a shame it came to that, but he was the weak link. And I had Davie doing whatever I needed by then."

Chick laughed. "Davie did not know what he was getting into getting in tow with you, pal." He playfully punched the top of her arm, laughing. "So who's next on your hit list?"

Mel winked at him, smiling. "We'll see."

PART III

Ends

Printed in Great Britain
by Amazon